"I can see you are a daydreamer," the rider said in a low, deep voice. Cleona did not answer him. She had remembered that if she spoke he might realize she was not the farm girl she appeared to be. Then, before she could move, he had stepped near to her.

"You will never be of much use on a farm." Even as he spoke he tipped her face up to his, and, bending, kissed her on the lips. For a moment, Cleona could neither move, nor cry out, nor even fight against him.

"That farmer will be a very lucky man," he smiled.

THE COIN OF LOVE

Books by Barbara Cartland

- A SONG OF LOVE
- DESIRE OF THE HEART
- A HAZARD OF HEARTS
- THE COIN OF LOVE
- THE ENCHANTING EVIL
- LOVE IN HIDING
- CUPID RIDES PILLION
- THE UNPREDICTABLE BRIDE
- A DUEL OF HEARTS
- LOVE IS THE ENEMY
- THE HIDDEN HEART
- LOVE TO THE RESCUE
- LOVE HOLDS THE CARDS
- LOST LOVE
- LOVE IS CONTRABAND
- THE KNAVE OF HEARTS
- LOVE ME FOREVER
- THE SMUGGLED HEART
- THE CAPTIVE HEART
- SWEET ADVENTURE
- THE GOLDEN GONDOLA
- THE LITTLE PRETENDER
- STARS IN MY HEART (also published as STARS IN HER EYES)
- THE SECRET FEAR
- MESSENGER OF LOVE
- THE WINGS OF LOVE
- THE ENCHANTED WALTZ
- THE HIDDEN EVIL
- A VIRGIN IN PARIS
- A KISS OF SILK
- LOVE IS DANGEROUS
- THE KISS OF THE DEVIL
- THE RELUCTANT BRIDE
- THE UNKNOWN HEART
- ELIZABETHAN LOVER
- WE DANCED ALL NIGHT
- AGAIN THIS RAPTURE
- THE ENCHANTED MOMENT
- THE KISS OF PARIS
- THE PRETTY HORSE-BREAKERS
- OPEN WINGS
- LOVE UNDER FIRE
- NO HEART IS FREE
- STOLEN HALO
- THE MAGIC OF HONEY
- LOVE IS MINE
- THE AUDACIOUS ADVENTURESS
- WINGS ON MY HEART
- BARBARA CARTLAND'S BOOK OF BEAUTY & HEALTH
- A HALO FOR THE DEVIL
- LIGHTS OF LOVE
- SWEET PUNISHMENT
- A GHOST IN MONTE CARLO
- LOVE IS AN EAGLE
- LOVE ON THE RUN
- LOVE FORBIDDEN
- BLUE HEATHER
- A LIGHT TO THE HEART
- LOST ENCHANTMENT
- THE PRICE IS LOVE
- SWEET ENCHANTRESS
- OUT OF REACH
- THE IRRESISTIBLE BUCK
- THE COMPLACENT WIFE
- METTERNICH THE PASSIONATE DIPLOMAT
- JOSEPHINE EMPRESS OF FRANCE
- THE SCANDALOUS LIFE OF KING CAROL
- WOMAN THE ENIGMA
- ELIZABETH EMPRESS OF AUSTRIA
- THE ODIOUS DUKE
- PASSIONATE PILGRIM
- THE THIEF OF LOVE
- THE DREAM WITHIN
- ARMOUR AGAINST LOVE
- A HEART IS BROKEN
- THE RUNAWAY HEART
- THE LEAPING FLAME
- AGAINST THE STREAM
- THEFT OF A HEART
- WHERE IS LOVE?
- TOWARDS THE STARS
- A VIRGIN IN MAYFAIR
- DANCE ON MY HEART
- THE ADVENTURER
- A RAINBOW TO HEAVEN
- LOVE AND LINDA
- DESPERATE DEFIANCE
- LOVE AT FORTY
- THE BITTER WINDS OF LOVE
- BROKEN BARRIERS
- LOVE IN PITY
- THIS TIME IT'S LOVE
- ESCAPE FROM PASSION

BARBARA CARTLAND

4
THE COIN OF LOVE

A JOVE BOOK

Copyright © 1956 by BARBARA CARTLAND

All rights reserved. No part of this publication
may be reproduced or transmitted in any form or
by any means, electronic or mechanical, including
photocopy, recording, or any information storage
and retrieval system, without permission in
writing from the publisher.

Requests for permission to make copies of any part
of the work should be mailed to: Permissions,
Jove Publications, Inc., 200 Madison Avenue,
New York, NY 10016

Six previous printings
First Jove edition published December 1977
New Jove edition published August 1980

10 9 8 7 6 5 4 3 2 1

Printed in the United States of America

Jove books are published by Jove Publications, Inc.,
200 Madison Avenue, New York, NY 10016

1

'LUD, but I look a fright!' the Honourable Mrs. Wickham exclaimed, bending forward to peer into the gilt framed mirror on her dressing-table.

'How can Madam think that she can be anything but beautiful beyond compare!' the milliner exclaimed. 'See how the hat enhances the gold of Madam's hair and the peerless transparency of her complexion.'

Eloise Wickham pursed her lips, turning first this way and then the other until finally her red lips parted in a fleeting smile and she said:

'Very well, I will take them all. But don't think, woman, that you need come dunning me for the bill because Heaven alone knows when you will be paid.'

'Madam is most kind.'

The milliner was wreathed in smiles as she made a gesture to her assistant to pick up the empty boxes. It had been worth the long journey from London to get an order like this; and although she was well aware that her distinguished customer spoke the truth when she said it was no use dunning her for the bill, payment would be made eventually.

In the meantime there was the kudos of having provided the headgear of the acknowledged beauty of the moment. In fact, fashionable London gossiped of little else, for it was said that the Prince was definitely infatuated by the fair widow from Oxfordshire.

But Mrs. Wickham's thoughts, as she sat staring at her reflection in the mirror, were not occupied with the Prince of Wales—the First Gentleman of Europe—but with someone very different.

She had not moved among the *beau monde* of St. James's for the past three years without learning how ephemeral Royal favour could be. She had seen the Prince of Wales in love and she had seen him out of love, and she was well aware that, although at the moment he had vowed himself besotted of her, there was every possibility that tomorrow might bring a new face and a new infatuation to the very susceptible owner of Carlton House.

No, Eloise Wickham thought to herself, she was playing a deeper game than that.

She rose from the carved stool in front of her dressing-table and stood preening herself in the mirror. Her figure was perfect! There were not many women of her age who could wear the new fashionable high-waisted, almost Grecian gowns which the Napoleonic regime had introduced in Paris. Her figure was still like a young girl's, her waist tiny, her breasts tip-tilted, and her skin clear as if she habitually slept in the clean country air rather than amongst the smoke and fogs of London.

And yet she was thirty-seven! Every day Eloise Wickham remembered that she drew nearer to her fortieth birthday. The very thought of it terrified her. Every day she searched her face for the first signs of that tiny, spidery network of lines which would one day encircle her wide blue eyes.

At thirty-seven what had she got to look forward to? Only a fading beauty, old age and an ever-increasing avalanche of debts, unless—Eloise Wickham drew a deep breath—unless she found herself a husband!

She turned abruptly from the mirror and walked to the window. Outside the smooth, green lawns sloped down to a small stream winding its way through pleasant green pasture land. The chestnut trees were in bud; there was blossom on the cherry and apple trees; the daffodils were blowing in the long grass beyond the lawns.

Soon the lilacs would be in bloom and then the garden would be a miracle of loveliness with that fresh, surgent beauty that was so essentially English.

But Eloise Wickham saw only the empty landscape—trees which needed pruning and thinning; flower beds which needed at least half a dozen more men to work on them; a terrace with crumbling stone and moss covered flagstones. Petulantly she turned from the window. The garden was unkempt, the house shabby and unrepaired. Both were in need of money, money, money—and she had none of it!

'Faugh, how I hate the country!' She said the words out loud and had an instant impulse to order her carriage there and then to carry her back to London.

Then determinedly she fought against her own longing. To stay here was part of her plan—a deep-laid, long considered plan—and if it was to succeed she must not be impatient.

She walked across the room and rang the bell imperiously. A few minutes passed before it was answered by an elderly maid in a mob cap.

'There you are, Matthews,' Mrs. Wickham said disagreeably. 'I have been ringing the bell for nearly twenty minutes. I thought it must be out of order.'

'It is in perfect order, Ma'am,' Matthews answered. 'Indeed, it was clanging fit to deafen me.'

'Then why didn't you answer it?' Mrs. Wickham enquired.

'Because I was getting your chocolate ready, Ma'am. I've only got one pair of hands and we are short-staffed, as you well know.'

Matthews spoke with the familiar directness of an old servant, and Eloise Wickham bit back the words of anger which rose to her lips. She was well aware that Matthews, for all her irritating habit of taking her own time over everything, was an excellent servant and completely trustworthy.

'Very well. Put the chocolate down,' she said ungraciously. 'I only hope it is hot, now you have brought it.'

'It is hot enough,' Matthews said. 'Is that what you were ringing for?'

'No, no! Of course, I had forgotten. I rang to ask if there was a letter for me, or a message.'

There was no mistaking the eagerness in the question. Matthews answered with what appeared almost deliberate slowness.

'As I was leaving the kitchen, I did see a groom in livery turn into the yard,' she said. 'If the bell had not been ringing so loud, I could have waited and asked him who he was and what he wanted. But as you appeared to be in such a hurry, Ma'am, I thought it best to come upstairs without further delay.'

'A groom in livery! Oh, Matthews, he must be bringing a note. Hurry quickly; find out who he is. Hurry, Matthews!'

Eloise Wickham stamped her foot in her impatience and Matthews went from the room at her own pace. There was nothing that the beautiful Mrs. Wickham could do but walk restlessly across the threadbare carpet and pray that the groom was wearing the blue and buff livery that she had looked and hoped for every day since she had fled to the country.

She had a sudden glimpse of herself as she moved about the room. Pink and white, gold and blue. Those colours described her own Dresden china prettiness, and Lord Vigor had made it clear, not once but a dozen times, that that was what he admired in a woman.

But was admiration enough? Eloise Wickham asked herself agonizingly. Enough to ensure that he should wish to bestow his name and his fortune on the woman he had toasted as 'The Incomparable' at a dinner at Vauxhall?

For three months now he had danced attention on no one else. He was jealous of everyone. Yes, even of the Prince himself. But he had not come to the point of suggesting that their love affair should have a more permanent basis.

Eloise Wickham was not a fool. She knew perfectly well that the bets at White's Club were five to one against her inveigling Vigor into matrimony. And yet she went on hoping. It had been her own idea to run away. A wild, desperate effort to bring him to the point.

The door opened and she turned towards it, moving swiftly across the room like a kingfisher flighting over the water.

'Who is it, Matthews? What did the man say? Has he brought a note?'

The questions came swiftly; but before Matthews could speak Eloise Wickham had reached her side and taken the big white envelope from the silver salver on which it was resting.

One look at the writing was enough. She gave a little cry of triumph and held it against her breast. Then, with fingers that trembled, she tore the envelope open. She read a few lines and gave another cry which was one of sheer delight.

'He is here, Matthews! He has followed me. He is putting up at the inn at Woodstock, and he asks if he may call on me this afternoon. Oh, Matthews, Matthews! I have won! I swear it. I have won!'

'The groom is waiting for a reply, Ma'am.' Matthews' voice was flat and quite unemotional.

'Yes, of course he must take back an answer. What shall I say?' Eloise Wickham turned to look at the older woman, her eyes wide. 'He must come to dinner. The house looks its best by candlelight. The gardeners can fill the drawing-room with flowers and I will wear that new green gauze which I got from Paris. It will all be very spring-like, young and simple.'

'That will be one extra for dinner then, Ma'am?' Matthews enquired.

'No, no, of course not, you fool. Would I be so stupid as to have him alone and let him think that I have come here specially to trap him? No, it must be a party. Whom can we have? The Marlboroughs—I know they are at home.

The Barclays—they are sure to come if I ask them. And who else? We must be eight at least.'

There was a moment's pause and then Eloise Wickham held up her hand.

'But, of course! How stupid of me. Lady Beryl Knight is at the Castle. Cleona was saying yesterday that she had seen her out riding. Cleona!' Mrs. Wickham stopped suddenly and put her fingers up to her lips. 'I had forgotten Cleona,' she said in a very different voice.

'I thought perhaps you had, Ma'am,' Matthews said.

'But, of course, she is only a child. There is no question of her coming to dinner.'

'Miss Cleona was eighteen last month, Ma'am. You will remember that I wrote and reminded you of her birthday.'

'Yes, and I sent her a present,' Mrs. Wickham said defiantly.

'Not a very suitable one, Ma'am. The dress was much too small and too young in shape.'

'Well, how was I to know the child had grown so enormously?' Mrs. Wickham asked crossly. 'When I went away, she was only tiny, playing with her dolls, and now I come back to find a strapping young woman.'

'The same height as yourself, Ma'am, and very like you, if you will forgive me saying so.'

'Very like me!'

There was something like terror in Eloise Wickham's voice as she repeated the words, and then almost instinctively turned her head to look at herself in the mirror. Yes, Cleona was very like her! She had seen that the moment she had walked into the house, after nearly three years' absence, and seen her daughter waiting for her.

She had the same heart-shaped face, the same pale gold hair and blue eyes, the same delicate white skin with those soft, peachlike cheeks and full red cherry mouth. And she was young; young!

'Matthews, what am I to do with her?'

'She's your daughter, Ma'am, and she loves you.'

'I know that. But you must see, Matthews, that I can't proclaim to all the world that I have a daughter of eighteen.'

'It's unnatural for Miss Cleona to live here year after year seeing nobody, having no one to care for her but myself. I've done my best, Ma'am, but it is time she took her rightful place in Society.'

'Not now; not at this very moment,' Mrs. Wickham cried. 'And not tonight—not when Lord Vigor is coming.

You will keep her upstairs, Matthews; you will keep her away. Tell her anything you please, but keep her out of the way.'

'Keep who out of the way, Mamma?'

The question came from the open door and both Mrs. Wickham and Matthews turned, with the quick, uncomfortable start of those who feel guilty about what they have been saying.

There was no doubt at all that Cleona Wickham resembled her mother, but whereas every known artifice of coiffeur, cosmetic and fashionable *couturier* contributed to Mrs. Wickham's beauty, Cleona was as natural as the spring itself.

She wore an old out-moded cotton dress of pale blue, from which the colour had faded. Her sash was darned in a dozen places and the hem of the dress was several inches off the ground. It was too high, too skimpy, for her sweetly curving figure, with its promise of future maturity. And yet, somehow, it did not look absurd on her, but it seemed as if, in fact, the very shabbiness of her clothes enhanced the radiance of her loveliness.

'Whom is Matthews to keep away, Mamma?' she asked again. 'Do not say poor mad Polly has been here again. She was such a nuisance a fortnight ago that we really contemplated asking the magistrates if they could do something about her.'

'That is just what Matthews was telling me,' Mrs. Wickham said. 'And, as you know, I detest mad people. Now, listen, Cleona. I want your help. I have got a dinner party and I want Henry to ride over to Blenheim and ask the Marlboroughs to come and George to go to the Barclays. They live in opposite directions or one man could have done both, but that disposes of both the horses and so I wondered if you could walk across the park and ask Beryl to be my guest.'

'Yes, Mamma, of course. I would love to,' Cleona answered. 'She was looking so beautiful when I saw her on Wednesday. She had a riding habit of crimson velvet and a crimson feather in her hat. I wanted to speak to her, but I felt shy.'

'Well, you can leave the note at the door if you do not want to see her,' Mrs. Wickham suggested.

'I would like to speak with Beryl again,' Cleona answered. 'It is silly to feel shy of someone whom I have known all my life. Of course, she is older than I, but when we played together as children I always thought of us as being the same age. When I heard she had run away and got married at Gretna Green, I couldn't at first believe it.'

'It was a very stupid thing to do,' Mrs. Wickham said sharply, 'and, if you ask me, Beryl was a very lucky young woman that her husband got killed as soon as he did.'

'Oh, Mamma!'

'Indeed, it is no use mincing words about such matters,' Mrs. Wickham remarked. 'It was a disastrous marriage for the Earl of Forncett's daughter. An obscure Captain of Artillery—how did she ever meet such a man?'

'Out hunting, Mamma.'

'Well, there you are! I have always said that it is dangerous to bring up girls in the country. They are liable to meet all sorts of undesirable people, while in London, properly chaperoned, they meet only the most desirable *partis*.'

'Are you going to take me London, Mamma?'

Mrs. Wickham turned quickly towards the writing-desk.

'Really, Cleona,' she said pettishly, 'I can't think how you can be so selfish as to keep me here gossiping when you know I have so much to do. There are all the arrangements for tonight to be made and you had best help Matthews get out the fine linen tablecloths and lace-trimmed napkins. I hope they are not lost.'

'No, of course not, Mamma.'

'Lord Vigor's groom must not be kept waiting too long either,' Mrs. Wickham continued. 'I will write that lettter first, Matthews, and you can take it down to him. At the same time tell George and Henry to get ready to carry the other notes. And you, Cleona, can start across the park as soon as I have written to Beryl.'

'Very well, Mamma. It will not take me long and I can help Matthews when I come back.'

Cleona went towards the door and then, as she reached it, she stopped a moment.

'It was me, Mamma, that you wanted kept out of the way this evening, was it not?'

Mrs. Wickham looked up from the writing-table at which she was already seated. For a moment it seemed as if she would deny the accusation; and then, as she looked at her daughter, her eyes hardened. What if Lord Vigor should see her?

'Yes, Cleona, it was,' she answered, and her voice was sharp almost to brutality. 'You have no decent clothes to wear. I would not want my friends to be ashamed of you.'

'Do not worry, Mamma. I will keep away from them. I

do not mind about your friends, but I would not want you to be ashamed of me.'

Cleona ran from the room, but not before both Eloise Wickham and Matthews had seen the tears in her eyes.

'That was cruel, Ma'am,' Matthews said quietly.

'It cannot be helped,' Mrs. Wickham replied defiantly. 'This is my last chance, do you hear me? My last chance. Oh, I have had offers and I shall have others—but not from anyone who matters; not from anyone who can give me the position I want.'

'And supposing his lordship does offer for you?' Matthews asked. 'Are you never going to let him see the child? Are you going to keep her hidden for ever?'

'Lord, woman! Don't worry me with such senseless questions at this moment,' Mrs. Wickham said angrily. 'Sufficient unto the day. It is tonight that matters, get that into your head. Tonight! For Heaven's sake go and see to the dinner table or nothing will ever be ready. And tell the cook I want to see her now.'

'Very good, Ma'am.'

Matthews went from the room. At the top of the staircase she hesitated for a moment. She knew Cleona had gone to her own bedroom. Matthews guessed that she would be sitting on her bed fighting against her tears; fighting, too, against an inexpressible feeling of hurt that her mother's words would have caused her.

She was too young, too vulnerable for this sort of thing, the older woman thought. She would not understand it or know how to cope with it. And then, because Matthews, too, felt unable to cope with the situation, she walked slowly down the stairs towards the kitchen.

Half an hour later Cleona set off across the park. Her mother's letter was in her hand and two black spaniels, without whom she seldom stirred anywhere, were at her heels.

She crossed the rickety wooden bridge which joined their own park with that of Lord Forncett. Her father had never owned the old manor house in which she had been born and where she had lived the whole of her life. He had rented it from his distant cousin, the Earl of Forncett, and had forgotten to pay the rent for so many years that it had become accepted by him and by everyone else that he was, indeed, its natural owner.

Both Cleona and the Lady Beryl were only children, and being distant cousins, it had seemed a most sensible arrangement on both sides that they should spend as much time as possible together and even take their lessons from the same teachers. It was only when, at seventeen, Beryl had eloped that Cleona had been startled into the knowledge that her friend was far older and more experienced than herself.

Those two years' disparity in their ages had never seemed obvious until then. But now, Cleona thought, she was meeting not so much her childhood's companion, but a stranger.

Because she was suddenly overcome with shyness at the thought, just as she had been the other day when she had seen Beryl riding by and had not called out to her, a sudden panic made her turn from the gate which led through the herb garden to the Castle. She decided to take the longer way across the paddocks which adjoined the stables.

She had just reached one of the swing gates when she saw someone riding towards her. It was a man on horseback—a very large man; his excellently cut riding-coat showing off the breadth of his shoulders, his black polished boots shining with every movement of his horse.

She stood watching him approach. Thinking not of herself, but appraising the way he rode the spirited animal which, prancing and rearing, seemed ready to fight against the restrictions of the bridle. The rider was at the gate before Cleona realized that he would wish to pass through it. He looked down at her and said sharply:

'Come along, my girl, aren't you going to open the gate for me?'

For a moment Cleona's eyes widened in surprise, and then she realized that he must have mistaken her for one of the milk-maids whom Lord Forncett employed in the dairy. It was not surprising, she thought. Her dress was shabby enough, and although she had set off with a bonnet on her head, she had found the warmth of the sun so inviting that she had pulled it off and was carrying it now by its ribbons.

Half amused and half embarrassed she put out her hand towards the gate.

'I can see you are a day-dreamer,' the rider said, in a low, deep voice, his eyes watching her as she moved. 'That's not the way to get your work done, you know.'

Cleona did not answer him. She had remembered that if she spoke he might realize from her voice that she was not the farm girl she appeared to be. They all spoke with a soft, broad Oxfordshire accent. Although she hoped that

13

her voice was musical, she knew that at least it was cultured.

She struggled with the gate, but it would not open. She put all her strength to pulling and tugging at it, but it was too heavy for her. Finally, with a sound that was half exasperation and half amusement, the man watching her sprang from his horse and came to her assistance.

It seemed as if at the mere touch of his hand the gate swung open, and then they stood facing each other.

He was taller than she had imagined he would be, seeming, she thought, to tower above her. But she felt sure, by the elegance of his clothes, the jewelled fob hanging from his vest pocket and his gold-mounted riding whip, that he was someone of importance.

He was handsome, but there was an uncompromising severity about his dark straight eyebrows, and the hard line of his mouth was broken by a cynical twist at the corners of his lips. It was the face of a man who mocks at life because he has been disillusioned.

'I suppose I must reward you for your help,' he said, 'inadequate though it proved.'

He held out his hand towards Cleona and she saw that he held something that glittered between the fingers of his gloved hand. Hastily she backed away from him and spoke for the first time:

'No! No!'

Now he was smiling and his eyes were flickering over her face. They rested on the astonishment in her blue eyes, the dishevelment of her gold hair, blown by the wind about her cheeks, and the soft swell of her breasts beneath the tightness of the outgrown dress. And then, before she could move, he had stepped near to her.

'You will never be much use on a farm,' he said, with laughter in his voice. 'But doubtless you will make some young farmer very happy.'

Even as he spoke he tipped her face up to his and, bending, kissed her on the lips. His action was so unexpected, so unanticipated, that for a moment Cleona could neither move nor cry out, nor even fight against him. One moment she was free, the next moment his fingers were against her chin and his lips had found hers.

She felt them, hard, warm, possessive, and was frozen into immobility. She could only feel the very surprise of his action paralyse her voice and her limbs so that she might have been turned to stone. His lips held her captive, but a second later she was released.

14

'That farmer will be a very lucky man,' he smiled.

He put something into her hand and then, swinging himself on his horse's back, had cantered away before she could move or even cry out against him.

She stood staring after him and then, very slowly, raised the fingers of one hand to her lips. As if the touch restored to her a full consciousness of what had happened, she stared down into the palm of the other.

He had given her a guinea, a golden guinea, and he had left on her lips the first kiss she had ever known! She raised her arm and with all her strength flung the guinea as far as it would go and then she stared after the retreating horseman and, with a stamp of her foot, defied him.

'How dare you? How dare you?'

Her voice sounded weak and ineffectual even to herself. The dogs stared up at her and then drew nearer as if they thought she had called them.

'How dare you?' she repeated again. She took a handkerchief from her waist and rubbed vigorously at her lips, trying to rub away the touch of his mouth, to erase, at the same time, the sense of insult in her own mind.

Had she been mad, she asked herself, to stand there as if she were, indeed, some half-witted dairymaid? How could she have been so inane, so stupid? Bewitched because a man had mistaken her for a farm wench and commanded her to open the gate!

The unknown rider's kiss was still burning on her lips as she reached the door of the Castle. The old butler greeted her with respectful affection.

'Yes, her ladyship is in, Miss,' he said. 'And it's glad we are to see her home again. There has been great rejoicing here, I can tell you. And his lordship's like a young man again.'

He talked all the time he led Cleona down the passage to the drawing-room which looked out over the rose garden.

'I'll inform her ladyship that you are here, Miss,' he said.

He left Cleona alone and she moved across the room to look out of the window. What fun she and Beryl used to have chasing each other round the fountain and even splashing each other with the water from the marble basin!

Intent on her thoughts and reminiscences, she started when she heard the door open at the further side of the room, but when she turned she saw it was not Beryl who entered, but Rex, the big mastiff who was Lord Forncett's constant companion.

He came across the room to her side, thrusting his black nose into her hand while the spaniels pranced around him with wagging tails, delighted to see a friend they had missed sadly these past eighteen months since Beryl ran away.

Rex had left the door open which led, as Cleona knew well, into the library, and now she heard voices speaking on the other side of it.

'I tell you I will not allow you to make a fool of yourself with this man any longer. You need not think that because I am old I am out of touch with what is happening—not where you are concerned at any rate. You are making a cake of yourself, my girl, and well you know it.'

'Father, it is ridiculous to take up that sort of attitude. Surely, as a married woman, I can have what friends I like.'

'You're not a married woman, you're a widow—and thank the Lord for it! But you are still my daughter and if you think I am going to have you talked about, your name bandied by every young blade who hiccoughs in his cups, you are much mistaken. Mountavon is a married man, and you will see no more of him.'

'Are you sure you can prevent me?'

How well Cleona knew that provocative, almost too sweet voice of Beryl's, which she assumed when she was most angry!

'I have every intention of preventing it,' Lord Forncett said. 'In fact I have made arrangements to do so. You are engaged to Raven, and I do not intend this time to have you break your promise or mess up my plans for you.'

'Really, Father, you might be mediaeval in the way you go on. It is true I have agreed to marry Lord Raven, but that does not mean to say that I intend to be a prisoner in this house, and I do not believe he expects it of me.'

'No, indeed, he does not,' Lord Forncett agreed. 'For you are not staying in this house.'

'Not staying here! What do you mean?'

'I am sending you abroad at once. A grand tour, my child. It is time you improved your mind; and now that peace has been declared with those demmed Frenchmen, you can see a bit of the world and, let us hope, get a bit of sense knocked into your head.'

'So that is what you and Lord Raven were talking about last night,' Beryl said accusingly.

'Yes, that is what we were discussing. It is all arranged.'

'Perhaps you will be kind enough to inform me of your plans—for me.'

'You will leave for the Continent next Tuesday. You will have no time before that for saying good-bye to Mountavon, or any other mountebank. You will pack your trunks and travel to Rome to stay with Raven's mother. She wishes to see you and approve the match her son is making.'

'So Lord Raven is behind all this, is he?' Beryl asked. 'I thought he was determined not to lose the estates a second time. He does not want to marry me, Father; he wants to marry your fifteen thousand acres of good Worcestershire soil.'

'And why shouldn't he?' Lord Forncett enquired. 'Our lands have marched together for the last six generations. Raven's a sensible chap. He wants a wife who will be some use to him, and you want a husband, my girl—make no mistake about it. You will go out to Rome with Raven escorting you. You will meet his mother, and on your return you will be married from here, as I always intended you should.'

'La! that is certainly a very pretty plot to get your own way,' Beryl said. 'And does his lordship relish the idea of prancing over the Continent alone with me—a prisoner at the wheels of his carriage?'

'Alone! I'm not so raw as all that,' Lord Forncett ejaculated. 'You will be properly chaperoned, my dear, and no mistake about it. Your cousin, Hester, is going with you. If anyone can keep you in order, she will.'

'Cousin Hester? Now that is, indeed, the outside of enough,' Beryl ejaculated. 'If you think I am going anywhere with Cousin Hester, you are very much mistaken. I shall run away again—and this time I will not come back. I will marry the first man who wants me; I will pick up a beggar out of the ditch—but I won't go abroad with Cousin Hester, not if you beg me to do so from now until next Christmas.'

'Now, now; what is wrong with your cousin?' Lord Forncett asked, a little gruffly.

Beryl's passionate remonstrances had obviously surprised him.

'Everything is wrong with her,' Beryl said fiercely. 'It was she who drove me away in the first place, if you wish to know. It was she who made me so unhappy here that I jumped at the idea of marrying poor Arthur, without for one moment considering the consequences. Oh, yes, I admit

I made a mistake. There wasn't a chance of our being happy together, and if he had not been killed I do not know what I should have done. But it was Cousin Hester's fault that it all happened, I can promise you that, Father. And if you send me away with her now, Heaven knows what will happen—that is if I don't murder her long before we get to Dover, let alone anywhere else.'

There was a moment's silence and then Lord Forncett said more gently:

'I do not want to be hard on you, Beryl. It is to stop your making another mistake that I have taken you away from London. It will be good for you to go abroad. Your mother and I had always planned for you to visit Paris and Rome, but with the War we have all been cooped up in our back yards these past eleven years. But you know as well as I do that you cannot go unchaperoned. You cannot go without another woman. Raven will be escorting you, but that does not make it better; some female has got to travel with you—the question is, who?'

'Not Cousin Hester at any rate,' Beryl said firmly.

'Well then, who?' her father demanded.

'Father, shall I tell you a secret . . . ?' Beryl began.

It was then Cleona realized, as if for the first time, that she was eavesdropping. It had been bad enough to stand there listening, almost despite herself, but now the idea that she might hear a secret forced her to overcome her shyness and walk across the drawing-room and through the open door into the library.

Lady Beryl Knight and her father were standing in front of the fireplace as she entered. They both looked round as if surprised at being interrupted, before Beryl called out her name:

'Cleona, my dearest love!'

She ran towards her, her face alight with genuine pleasure, her hands outstretched. And then, as she reached Cleona, before she kissed her, she turned towards her father.

'Here is the answer to your question, Father,' she said. 'The perfect answer to who will take Cousin Hester's place. Cleona, of course—my own dear Cleona!'

2

'PRAY forgive me,' Cleona said shyly, 'but I overheard your conversation. I couldn't help it—Rex opened the door.'

'Then you know how irritating his lordship is being,' Beryl said laughingly. 'He is trying to force me to take Cousin Hester abroad with me, and you, my love, of all people are aware how detestable she has always been to me. I declare that I will not stir a foot out of this place if she accompanies me! But a fig for Cousin Hester—everything is settled; you will come in her place.'

'Hold hard! Hold hard!' Lord Forncett exclaimed. 'You are rushing your fences, Beryl. I haven't yet given my consent. Besides, I cannot allow you two feckless young creatures to gallivant about the Continent alone.'

'Have you forgotten I am a married woman, Papa?' Beryl asked. 'Besides, you can hardly call it alone, with milord Raven to escort us and at least six servants in our *entourage*.'

'Six!' Lord Forncett ejaculated with something like consternation.

'Yes, six,' his daughter repeated firmly. 'I can assure you, Sir, that all the best people travel *en prince!*'

'I still think that you and Cleona are too young,' Lord Forncett said, but it was obvious that he was weakening.

'*Ma foi,* Papa! As a sop we will take Captain Ernshaw as a courier. He is a dead bore, but you know as well as I do that he is trustworthy to the point of exasperation.'

'Oh, well; if Ernshaw will go,' Lord Forncett murmured, capitulating.

'Go? He will be in a-twitter at the opportunity,' Beryl smiled. 'All through the War we have listened to nothing but his eulogies about the ruins of Rome and the art galleries of Florence. Now he will be able to take us there, and it will serve him right if we do not find them half as romantic as he has made them out to be.'

'Very well, then. Have it your own way,' Lord Forncett said. 'I only hope the two of you don't get up to your old tricks.'

He smiled as he spoke, recalling the pranks they had

indulged in as children and the times he had been called upon by Cousin Hester to give them a lecture.

'Do you really mean it?' Cleona asked, her eyes alight with excitement as she looked at Beryl. 'Do you really mean to take me with you? Indeed I must be dreaming for I cannot believe it's true.'

'Of course it's true, you goose. And don't think that it's going to be as wonderful as all that. His lordship is sending me away as a punishment.'

'No, no! Not a punishment, but a safeguard!' Lord Forncett put his hand, as he spoke, on his daughter's shoulder and there was no mistaking the affection and pride in his face as he looked at her.

It was not surprising that he should love his only child, for Beryl was very attractive. She was taller than Cleona and above the fashionable height; nevertheless, she carried herself proudly. She had a small straight nose between dark eyes, which seemed always a-twinkle with mischief, and a red mouth which pouted adorably when she did not get her own way.

There was so much grace in the tilt of her curly head and in the movement of her white hands that it was not surprising that Lady Beryl Knight's arrival in London as a newly bereaved widow had sent the bucks of St. James's scurrying to Lord Forncett's house in Berkeley Square.

'We shall make good foils for each other,' Beryl said later to Cleona as they sat alone with so much to say to each other that it was difficult to know where to begin.

'Foils! What do you mean?' Cleona asked.

'Oh, don't be bird-witted, dearest. You know exactly what I mean. I am dark, you are fair; and we are both exceedingly attractive young women. If we don't cause a sensation in Italy, I, for one, will die of chagrin.'

'You will cause a sensation,' Cleona smiled. 'But you know full well that I shall be content to watch you and to stay in the background.'

Beryl laughed.

'Haven't you learned yet, dear love, that being unselfish and self-effacing never gets one anywhere?'

'But I don't know where I want to get,' Cleona replied.

'I can tell you what you want,' Beryl said. 'A nice rich, distinguished husband.'

'No, indeed, that is not true,' Cleona replied. 'Besides . . .'

She stopped suddenly and put her hand to her face in a gesture of horror. 'Beryl, I had forgotten Mamma's letter—

that is why I came here. She sent me with it and it is an invitation to dinner.'

'Your Mamma is at the Manor!' Beryl exclaimed. 'Good gracious, she is the last person I expected to hear had taken to the country.'

'She arrived two days ago quite unexpectedly,' Cleona replied. 'We were all very surprised to see her.'

'I should think so, indeed. Why, when I left London everyone was talking about . . .' Beryl stopped, then added: 'Perhaps I oughtn't to say such things to you, or do you know?'

'About the Prince of Wales being very attentive?' Cleona enquired. 'Oh yes indeed, Mamma told me all about it as soon as she arrived.'

'And about Lord Vigor? Has he come up to scratch?' Beryl asked. 'No, of course he hasn't—what a silly question. Your Mamma wouldn't be here if he had.'

'He is coming to dinner tonight.'

'Is he really?' Beryl's voice was eloquent of her surprise. 'Then he is really serious this time. The betting was heavily against it being anything but a passing phase.'

'What is he like?' Cleona asked.

'Personally I have no partiality for him,' Beryl answered. 'But he is rather a friend of my father's. In fact, now I come to think of it, perhaps that was who Papa was entertaining this afternoon. I was told there was a gentleman with him and as I had an idea it was someone very different, I slipped out into the orchard and hid in the oak tree where we used to hide when we were children—do you remember?'

'You think Lord Vigor was with your father,' Cleona said slowly.

'It might easily have been him if, as your mother says, he is staying at Woodstock. I expect really he was trying to get Papa to invite him to stay here. Oh, I pray that Papa avoided that snare. In some ways Lord Vigor is quite detestable.'

'What is his appearance?' Cleona enquired.

Beryl did not notice that her voice sounded strange.

'He is tall, dark, and in my opinion rather sinister.'

Almost instinctively Cleona's hand went up to her lips. So it had been Lord Vigor whom she had met at the end of the paddock! It was Lord Vigor who had asked her to open the gate and who had given her a guinea and kissed her because she had failed to do his bidding. She felt again that surge of anger which had shaken her whole body as

21

she had watched him ride away. How could he have dared to insult her in such a manner? And he was the man whom her mother wanted to marry!

Beryl's voice broke in on her thoughts.

'What are you thinking about, Cleona? You look so serious and yet, somehow, fierce. Has anything made you angry?'

'No, no, it is nothing,' Cleona said quickly. 'Tell me more about Lord Vigor.'

'Well, he is noted for his wealth and his *amours*. He has made love to every pretty woman who has ever set foot in St. James's. All the match-making mammas have been trying to catch him for years, but they have had no success. He is far too wily for them. Of course, your mother may succeed where everyone else has failed.'

'She talks as if it is the only thing which will make her happy,' Cleona said.

'I do not envy her, but of course he is very rich—nearly as rich as Sylvester.'

'Who is Sylvester?' Cleona asked curiously.

'Don't be provoking, Cleona. You know full well that Sylvester is the Earl of Raven, whom I am to marry.'

'Do you love him?'

Beryl looked at Cleona and pouted her pretty lips.

'What has love to do with marriage? Not sensible marriages at any rate. I have known Sylvester ever since we were in our cradles together. I am told that his father and mine agreed at my christening that we should be wed and the two estates joined as one. Last year when I returned to London a widow, Sylvester was the first person to call on me. I promised to marry him, but I am determined to be in no hurry about it this time.'

'But, Beryl, I could not help overhearing your father speaking of someone else—the Marquis of Mountavon!'

Beryl got suddenly to her feet and walked across the room. There was a great vase of hot-house flowers on the side table. She stood rearranging them and then abstractedly pulled a carnation to pieces.

'I would like you to meet Ian Mountavon,' she said at last in a low voice. 'He is so very . . . different from anyone I have ever known before . . . in the whole of my life.'

'And . . . and you love him?' Cleona asked, her voice hardly above a whisper.

'Yes, I love him.' The words seemed to burst from

Beryl's lips before she turned and walked back towards Cleona.

'But . . . but——' Cleona began, only to be interrupted.

'But what's the use?' Beryl asked in a voice which she made deliberately light. 'He is a married man and I am betrothed to milord Raven. As I have already told you, Cleona, love has nothing to do with marriage.'

'How can you say such a monstrous thing?' Cleona asked. 'It is not true.'

'But it is, I assure you. You forget that I married for love once, only to be exceedingly disillusioned within a week of our marriage at Gretna Green. Oh dear, how foolish one is when one is very young! I thought Arthur Knight entrancing until I was married to him, and then I found he was both a bore and a prig. My father was right when he said it was a lucky day for me when he was killed fighting Boney.'

'Beryl, how can you say such things?' Cleona asked in a shocked voice.

'But they are true.'

'I don't believe it,' Cleona cried. 'I have dreamed that one day I shall fall in love, that I shall find someone who will love me and whom I shall both respect and admire. I have no care if he is rich or important or if he is just a very ordinary person—as, indeed, I am sure he will be. If we love each other, nothing else will matter.'

Beryl stopped suddenly and kissed the earnest little face looking up into hers.

'Dearest Cleona! You haven't changed in the slightest!' she said. 'Do you remember how, when we were children, I used to call you my conscience, because you always made me remember that I must do the right thing and be good when I wanted to be bad? Dear, good little Cleona! What fun we will have in Rome! I had forgotten when I was in London how much nicer you are than all my smart new friends put together.'

'Oh, Beryl! How sweet of you to say so! I still cannot believe that you really intend to take me to Rome with you. It is not only wonderful for me, but Mamma will be so glad, too. She wants me out of the way.'

'I am not surprised,' Beryl retorted. 'Lord Vigor has a *penchant* for fair women with blue eyes, especially when they are young and unspoilt.'

'Indeed he mustn't see me whatever happens,' Cleona exclaimed, adding loyally: 'Not that he would look at me when Mamma is about. But I am of the opinion that

Mamma has not confessed to him that she has a daughter, especially one who is grown up.'

'You don't look very grown up,' Beryl laughed. 'Especially in that frock. I remember it well. The very first time you wore it you tried to climb the monkey-puzzle and Matthews was furious because you tore a hole in the skirt.'

'It is still there,' Cleona said, showing her a neat darn. She smoothed it with her fingers, then rose to her feet. 'I must return home. I had forgotten what a lot there is to do.'

'I hate to lose you,' Beryl said. 'There is so much to talk about and so much I want to tell you. We won't have any secrets from each other, will we, Cleona? Do you remember how we always swore, when we were children, that we would tell each other everything?'

'Yes, no secrets,' Cleona said, but she did not look at her friend as she spoke and there was a note of doubt in her soft voice.

She felt at that moment she could never bring herself to tell Beryl what had happened to her on her way to the Castle. She felt the shame of that incident at the paddock gate had burned itself into her soul so that she wanted only to forget it, to erase it utterly from her memory. Pray heaven that she would not encounter Lord Vigor again—not at any rate until he was safely married to her mother.

'I must go now,' she said quickly. 'Shall I tell Mamma that you will come to dinner?'

'Yes, tell her I shall be delighted to accept her kind invitation, and ask her to forgive my ill manners in not writing her a note.'

'She will be so pleased that you can come,' Cleona said. 'Do not forget that you must not speak of me.'

'Tell your Mamma that you are coming to Rome with me on Tuesday and that if I don't get a chance to talk of it with her alone tonight, I will come over and see her tomorrow,' Beryl said. She bent to kiss Cleona and added: 'It will be the wildest fun, dearest, won't it? Just you and I setting out alone to explore the Continent.'

Cleona drew back.

'Have you forgoten my Lord Raven?'

Beryl gave a little laugh.

'Indeed I had for the moment, and Sylvester's not a person one forgets easily. Most people are afraid of him, but I'm not—and he knows it. We needn't worry about him, and we will have Captain Ernshaw with us to cope with the abigails and the coachmen. They are sure to be troublesome when crossing the Channel.'

'I swear Tuesday will never come,' Cleona said simply, and Beryl laughed and kissed her again.

Returning home by the more direct route through the gardens, Cleona felt that her heart was dancing with all the excitements that had happened since she had left home only an hour previously. Then she had felt shy at the thought of seeing Beryl again, and now she was warmed by a friendship which had not been changed by two years' separation.

And yet, superseding in her thoughts even the delights of the journey ahead, was the picture of two dark, quizzical eyes looking down into hers, of a mouth that seemed to smile cynically, of lips which in their insistence had taken her very breath from her.

Why should she keep remembering that kiss? she asked herself. It had meant nothing to him; he would never think of her again. She was just a farm wench who had caught his fancy for the moment and to whom he had tossed a guinea in payment for the favour he had stolen.

'I hate him!'

She found herself saying the words aloud as she walked through the park and hurried over the wooden bridge which spanned the stream.

'I hate him!'

She said it aloud again as she looked up at the grey stone house, with its gables and its lattice windows, which was her home.

She had no sooner entered the hall than Mrs. Wickham came hurrying out of the drawing-room.

'There you are at last, Cleona,' she said sharply. 'You have been an unconscionable time. Is Beryl coming tonight?'

'Yes, Mamma! And she thanks you very much for the invitation. And, oh, Mamma! I have got something so very exciting to tell you. . . .'

'La, but you can't chatter now, Cleona. There is too much to be decided. As Beryl can come, that makes us a man short. I have got to think of someone, and George or Henry, whoever gets back first, can take a note. Is Major Ludlow at home?'

'No, Mamma—at least, I don't think so.'

'Faugh! Who else is there? Heavens above, was there ever a more benighted part of the country than this, where one has to scratch one's head to think of neighbours?'

Talking as she went, Mrs. Wickham led the way back to

25

the drawing-room. The gardeners had been working hard since Cleona had left and the room was a veritable bower of spring blossoms.

'How lovely!' Cleona exclaimed.

'I am glad you think so,' Mrs. Wickham said sarcastically. 'Look at the covers—faded, torn and none too clean; the carpet—threadbare; the curtains—obviously about to crumble to dust. Do you think any man, especially anyone as perceptive as Lord Vigor, will be impressed by this?'

There was such a note of despair in Eloise Wickham's voice that Cleona longed to comfort her.

'Do not fret, Mamma. His lordship will have eyes only for you. You will look exquisite and you will sound so gay that he won't notice the house or the dinner.'

'Lord, child, don't remind me of the dinner,' Mrs. Wickham cried with a little shudder. 'I am terrified to think what that woman will serve us up tonight. Whatever I suggested was beyond her comprehension. If there is a morsel on the menu worth eating I shall be astonished. Indeed I am reconciled into dying of mortification with every course!'

'It will not be as bad as that, Mamma,' Cleona said soothingly. 'Hannah may be old, but she is quite reliable when it comes to the point, and I will help her with the soup. She is rather inclined to forget to add the sherry.'

Mrs. Wickham looked at her daughter and smiled.

'You are a good child, Cleona,' she said. 'If only you hadn't grown so much while I have been away it would be easier.'

'Yes, I know that, Mamma. But I can't help growing up, can I? But if you can listen for a moment, I have got something to tell you.'

'Cleona, this is no time for confidences. You know I haven't yet thought of an extra man. Why, oh why, did I have a dinner party? Can you imagine anything being worse than Lord Vigor arriving here and finding me a man short? He has got to think that I am——' She broke off suddenly as Matthews came into the room. 'What is it, Matthews? Is George or Henry back yet?'

'No, Ma'am, not yet. But——'

'Then what do you want, Matthews? I am trying to think and you keep interrupting me.'

'A groom has arrived, Ma'am, with a note.'

'A groom with a note! Pray Heaven it's not from Lord Vigor to say he has changed his mind and that he will not come. Cleona, if it is that I swear that I shall swoon away.'

'It is not Lord Vigor's groom, Ma'am.'

'Well then, whose is it, woman? For the love of Jove don't stand there talking in riddles. Bring me the note.'

'I regret, Ma'am, that the groom's instructions are to give the note into your own hands. I think that he is a little in doubt as to whether you are actually here in person.'

'What is this all about?' Mrs. Wickham asked.

'I am afraid I cannot tell you, Ma'am,' Matthews replied, 'save that the groom is wearing the Royal livery.'

'The Royal livery!'

The words ended almost in a shriek.

'Why didn't you say so at first? It is the Prince! He has followed me. Gracious Heaven, this is the most wonderful thing that ever happened!'

Mrs. Wickham sprang to her feet and ran from the room into the hall. There she paused for a moment to see with her own eyes the groom, wearing the Prince of Wales' colours, standing in the courtyard holding his horse. She stood for a moment getting her breath and then sauntered very slowly through the front door and on to the steps. At the sight of her the groom came forward eagerly.

'I have a note from His Royal Highness, Ma'am.'

'From His Royal Highness!' Mrs. Wickham said, surprised. 'I had not expected to have news from London in this sylvan retreat.'

'His Royal Highness is not in London, Ma'am.'

'Not in London! Then where can he be?'

'At Woodstock, Ma'am.'

'Indeed! I had no idea that the Prince was acquainted with this part of the world.'

Mrs. Wickham took the note, read it with deliberate slowness, then said:

'You had best wait while I write an answer to His Royal Highness.'

'Very good, Ma'am.'

She retreated into the house; then, forgetting her pose of indifference, she ran with the letter in her hand into the drawing-room.

'Prinny is at Woodstock,' she told Cleona. 'Just think; he is playing into my hand. Lord Vigor is there, too. They will find that they are both staying in the same hotel; they will glare at each other; they will both know why the other is here. Oh, could anything be better? The Prince wishes to come over and see me at once. I shall tell him that I will be delighted to receive him for dinner. There is my extra man! Think of it, the Prince himself.'

'Oh, Mamma, I am so glad for you.'

'If this doesn't bring Lord Vigor to the point, nothing will,' Mrs. Wickham said firmly. She sat down at her desk and picked up her quill. 'I shall be very effusive,' she said, almost as if she was talking to herself. 'It will put the Prince in a good temper, and if he is in a good temper Lord Vigor will guess the reason for it. Oh, my luck's in.'

Mrs. Wickham would have started her writing, but her eyes were arrested. A stream of sunlight had come through the window to illuminate Cleona as she stood by the writing-desk. It turned her hair to living gold; it revealed the white transparency of her skin, the darkness of her long lashes as they curled back from the bird's-egg blue of her eyes. Eloise Wickham put down her quill.

'Faith, chit!' she exclaimed. 'If anyone tonight gets so much as a glimpse of you, my plans are ruined. Do you realize that?'

'Yes, Mamma. I will keep out of sight, I promise you. But, please, do listen to me for a moment. Beryl has asked me——'

'Now, Cleona, you know I am trying to write a letter. Tell me about Beryl later. You know I can only concentrate on one thing at a time.'

It was useless, Cleona thought, to try to arrest her mother's attention at such a moment.

The rest of the day seemed to pass in a flash, as she helped Matthews with the linen; assisted old Bennett, the butler, who was nearly blind, with the silver; fetched and carried for Hannah in the kitchen, and finally got out the dress and jewels that her mother was to wear that evening.

'How can I manage without a hairdresser?' Mrs. Wickham bewailed. But Cleona managed to arrange her hair in the latest shape, with the curls falling from a Grecian knot at the back and with a band of diamonds and emeralds set high above her white forehead.

'Mamma, I vow you look like a Queen!' Cleona breathed, as finally the dress of transparent gauze was tied beneath Mrs. Wickham's breasts with velvet ribbons and a band of emeralds and diamonds was clasped round her white neck.

'The gown is passable,' Mrs. Wickham admitted grudgingly. 'But the Lord knows it will never be paid for unless . . .'

There was no need for her to finish the sentence.

'But those jewels, Mamma!' Cleona exclaimed. 'Where did you get those wonderful jewels? I have never seen them before.'

'They are not really mine,' Mrs. Wickham replied honestly, 'for I have not paid for them and have no likelihood of being able to do so. The jeweller hopes that the Prince will present them to me, but I am determined they shall be my wedding present from Lord Vigor.'

Cleona turned away. Somehow she could not help a little shudder whenever Lord Vigor's name was mentioned.

'I had best go now, Mamma,' she said.

'Go where?' Mrs. Wickham enquired.

'I thought it was a mistake for me even to remain in the house,' Cleona answered. 'You know what a temptation it would be to peep over the banisters—or, indeed, Beryl might come in search of me—so I have arranged to go down to the village and see old Nanny Danvers. I have some soup to take her, anyway, as she is not well, and I will stay with her talking until your guests have gone.'

'I think that's quite a sensible idea,' Mrs. Wickham approved. 'And hurry, child, because Lord Vigor might be here at any moment.'

If anything had been needed to speed Cleona's footsteps, nothing could have succeeded better than that last sentence. She ran out of her mother's room, picked up a woollen cloak which was lying on the settle in the hall, and swinging it over her shoulders collected from the kitchen her basket in which she had already put the soup for her old nanny.

She left the house by the side door. The way to the village led through the shrubbery and then down the back drive which joined the main road before it passed through the village of Little Cokeham and came eventually to the main entrance to the Manor. That was the way the guests would come, Cleona knew, and as long as she kept clear of the front drive she was unlikely to encounter anyone of importance.

The sun was sinking in a blaze of gold and red as she moved through the shrubs and trees to join a narrow drive that was badly in need of repair. It turned and twisted through the park land where the cows grazed contentedly and the first spring lambs gambolled beside their mothers.

She was humming a little tune to herself as she left the shelter of the trees and overgrown rhododendron bushes, and then suddenly she practically collided with a large, rather stout gentleman who was standing under a tree contemplating the grazing sheep.

'I . . . I am sorry,' she stammered, only to stand transfixed as he exclaimed:

'Eloise! I was not expecting to find you . . .'

There was, for Cleona, no mistaking the rather protruding eyes that stared at her; the heavy features which still held some semblance of beauty; the hair, skilfully arranged in juvenile curls on either side of the temples; the fat fingers heavily bejewelled with rings. She sank down in a deep curtsy.

'I . . . I am not . . . Mrs. Wickham, Sire,' she stammered. 'She is awaiting you at the house.'

'No, I can see now, you are not Mrs. Wickham. But you are uncommonly like her!' the Prince exclaimed. 'Come, let me look at you.'

'Your Royal Highness must forgive me. I have an urgent and important message to deliver in the village.'

'It can wait; it can wait,' the Prince said testily. 'Let me look at you, I say. Gad, but you might be Eloise. The same hair, the same eyes, and damme if it isn't the same mouth.'

'I crave you, Sire . . .' Cleona began, trying to back away. But the Prince reached out his hand and took hold of her arm.

'The spitting image of Eloise herself. Here, Vigor must see this. He'll be as surprised as I am.'

'No, Sire, I beg of you,' Cleona said. 'Please, please.'

She struggled, but the Prince was holding her arm tightly. Beyond him she could see a coach drawn up in the drive and a groom attending to one of the leading horses.

'Vigor! Come here, Vigor!'

The Prince's voice boomed out, and in response a head appeared at the carriage window. But even as he shouted, Cleona with a sudden effort had shaken herself free of his restraining hand and was running away from him.

With her cloak flowing out behind her, the soup splashing over her basket, she sped with the swiftness of a young deer back into the shrubbery and behind the shelter of the rhododendrons. She heard the Prince's voice shouting after her; she heard him call for her to stop, and call again, but still she ran.

It was only when she had put a considerable distance between herself and her Royal pursuer that she paused for breath. Panting, she leant against the trunk of a tree and listened.

Far away in the distance she heard the sound of horses trotting and the rumble of wheels—the Prince had resumed his journey.

It was then, as she stood there, her cheeks burning, her dress and cloak covered in soup, her breath coming painfully between her parted lips, that Cleona realized that she had disobeyed the Royal command of the Prince of Wales and had run away because she dare not face again the man who that very morning had left a guinea in her hand and a kiss on her lips.

IN THE library of a house in Curzon Street Mr. George Canning rose to greet a visitor.

3

'It is exceedingly kind of you to call on me, my lord.'

'I regret that I was unable to do so sooner,' was the answer. 'Your note was brought to me in the country and I posted to London as soon as I had read it.'

The men were well contrasted. George Canning, theatrical, impulsive, and the most brilliant orator of Pitt's Government, punctuated every word he spoke and every movement he made with a gesture of his hands and a movement of his thin fingers. His guest, on the other hand, reserved and enigmatic, settled himself with the least expenditure of energy in the comfortable chair indicated to him and then seemed to wait without any indication of curiosity for an explanation.

'You may think it strange,' Mr. Canning began, 'that I should ask you to visit me, and also that in this enlightened age, in the year of grace 1802, it should be necessary to add secrecy to urgency. But I had my reasons.'

'I was sure of it,' was the quiet reply.

'As you know, at the moment I am of no consequence whatsoever in the House,' Mr. Canning said.

'I am well aware,' his visitor conceded, 'that when Mr. Pitt resigned last year the fact that you followed him was almost as great a loss to the country.'

'It is kind of you to say so, my lord. But although I am out of office, I am perhaps the only man who sees the terrible dangers which confront this nation. The fools who govern us think we are at peace, but I am convinced that all Bonaparte has asked for is a breathing space.'

'You really believe that?'

Mr. Canning brought his fist crashing down on the table beside him.

'Lord Raven, I would stake my life on it! But this wretched pusillanimous, toad-eating Administration led by that mass of conciliation and clemency—our Prime Minister, Henry Addington—believe only what they want to believe, and the First Consul is, I am determined, leading them by the nose.'

'What you are saying,' Lord Raven said, 'rather confirms my own quite unimportant opinion. Yet I fear, Mr. Canning, there is nothing we can do about it.'

George Canning rose to his feet and walked across the room.

'We disarmed at almost indecent speed; ten days after the signature of peace Addington's very first Budget abolished Pitt's income tax. With the national debt standing at double its pre-war figure, that meant drastic reductions in the armed forces. Do you know that last year we discharged forty thousand sailors and relegated hundreds of experienced officers to half pay? And at a time when the greatest military power the world has ever seen remains mobilized on the other side of the Channel.'

'You really think that Bonaparte intends to attack us?'

'I am sure of it,' Canning replied. 'He has made peace at this moment so that he can use the breathing space which we have given him to build ships of war. In my estimation he can produce twenty-five of these annually. In six or seven years, with two hundred sail-of-the-line, he will be as invincible on sea as on land.'

'Does Pitt know of this?'

'I am in constant touch with him. He remains at Walmer Castle concerning himself with his garden and apparently unmoved by the plight into which Britain is drifting. But the day will come, Lord Raven; the day will come—and it is not far off—when the nation will turn to him for salvation.'

'In the meantime, how can I help you, Sir?'

Canning's smile lit up his whole face.

'I was hoping you would ask that. The polite world—the *beau monde* with which we are both well acquainted—looks on you, my lord, as a seeker of pleasure. But I have heard you speak in the House of Lords and I have a very different estimation of both your character and your powers.'

'I am gratified.'

Lord Raven bowed, but there was a slightly sarcastic twist of his lips.

It was obvious that he found Mr. Canning's rather fulsome compliments slightly amusing. But as he leaned back in his chair, entirely at his ease, he was watching with the keen penetration of a hawk the statesman who had fought his way into prominence by a merciless wit, a wit which it had been said would fetch the hide off a rhinoceros.

'I have been told, I think from reliable sources,' Mr. Canning continued, 'that you are going to Italy.'

'Indeed!' Lord Raven's eyebrows were raised. 'Your informant must have brought you the news on wings for I only knew it myself but forty-eight hours ago.'

'My informant was Lord Forncett.'

'In that case the information was entirely correct. His lordship is in a position to know the truth.'

'So I gather,' Mr. Canning smiled. 'May I offer you my most fervent congratulations? I understand your engagement to Lady Beryl Knight is to be announced on your return.'

'That is our intention,' Lord Raven agreed. 'But I cannot believe, Sir, that you brought me here just to proffer me your good wishes.'

'No, indeed. I wanted to ask you to be of service, not to me but to your country.'

'While I am in Italy?'

'While you are in Italy.'

'In what way?'

Mr. Canning turned to his desk and picked up a pile of papers.

'I have here,' he said, 'letters from our agents telling me that Napoleon is breaking one after another of the terms of peace. To my mind his bloodless conquests in Europe are even more alarming than those made at the cannon's mouth.'

'I must admit,' Lord Raven said slowly, 'that the Government is being extremely feeble in the way they have dealt with Boney over the Forces he has despatched to the West Indies.'

'That is bad enough,' Mr. Canning agreed. 'But I have here evidence that his agents are swarming into every Italian capital, talking Treaties and Concessions, surveying ports, forts and harbours, and stirring up the Italians themselves.'

'Can this indeed be true?' Lord Raven enquired.

'I have no reason to doubt these letters,' Mr. Canning answered. 'Colonel Dyott, with whom you may be acquainted, has recently visited Boulogne and Turin. He tells me that he found the inns packed with French officers living free; the theatres full of filthy brawlers; the ballet an obscene, bawdy display of naked women; the convents destroyed; the palaces and gardens devastated; and everything Frenchified according to the true *bon patriot* system.'

'It sounds appalling!' Lord Raven exclaimed. 'Do you think I am wise in escorting Lady Beryl to Italy under such circumstances?'

'I think her ladyship will be safe enough,' Mr. Canning answered. 'As you know, the Duchess of Devonshire and Lady Elizabeth Foster have recently made the journey, and a large number of our friends seem to have found Paris very much to their taste. The only word of caution I would add is not to stay too long. I have no faith in the efficiency of this peace.'

'And if I reach Italy, what do you wish me to do?'

'I wish you to report to me the truth of what is actually happening there. Your mother is, I believe, living in Rome at the moment.'

'Yes. She went out last year. She longs for the sunshine and almost before the ink was dry on the Treaty she was *en route* for her beloved orange groves.'

'The Dowager Lady Raven knows, I think, everyone of importance. In her house you should meet the people who will be useful, the people who can tell you, directly or indirectly, exactly what Bonaparte is planning.'

'You think he knows that himself?' Lord Raven asked with a smile.

Again Mr. Canning's fist came down heavily on the table.

'I believe that he intends to conquer the world. He has behind him a nation of more than thirty million, drunk with military power and eager for new conquests. He has acclaimed himself the new Charlemagne and is erecting in the *Place de Vendôme* a pillar like the Column of Trajan to commemorate his victories. But don't think because of that he is satisfied. He wants more and yet more. And the only thing that has balked him to date is our stranglehold at sea.'

'I am sure you are right, Mr. Canning.'

'I only wish there were more people to think so. As I

have already said, there is only one man who can save us,' Canning cried dramatically, 'and that is Pitt.'

'Pray Heaven the country calls on him before it is too late,' Lord Raven said. 'In the meantime, Sir, I will do what I can. But I make no promises. Things may not be so easy as they sound here in the peace and quiet of this very charming room.'

'I felt sure I could rely on you, my lord. No one will suspect you of having any other reason for visiting Italy save that of wishing to present your betrothed to your mother.'

'There I hope you are right,' Lord Raven said. He rose to his feet and held out his hand. 'And equally I hope you are wrong in all you anticipate that lies ahead of us, although, demme, I have the secret suspicion events may prove your words.'

'I thank your lordship.'

Canning's bow would have graced the playhouse, and Lord Raven, his coat collar turned high to conceal his face, left the house and was driven away by a coach which had waited for him round the corner in Shepherds Market.

Although it was growing late, London had not gone to bed. Beneath the floating pall of congealed smoke that rose from the chimneys of one-hundred-and-sixty thousand houses and furnaces, the carriages of the aristocracy were moving through the narrow streets behind drays and coal wagons. The street organs and musicians were still making a noise for which they demanded alms from every passerby. The sellers of hot and cold food were crying their wares at the street corners.

Near the river fireworks and rockets were blazing up into the darkening sky amid a yelling crowd out for all the fun they could get. Amongst them the thieves moved, soft-footed and light-fingered, and there was no sign of the scarlet-waistcoated Bow Street Runners, who usually, at this time of night, thought discretion was the better part of valour.

The coach carrying Lord Raven drew up at White's in St. James's Street. His lordship on entering the Club found the usual crowd of members thronging the morning-room. He ordered himself a glass of brandy. Then as he paused to speak to an acquaintance reclining in the bow window in which only the more privileged might sit, he heard a guffaw of laughter at the far end of the room. A high-pitched, slightly intoxicated voice was protesting at something which had been said.

'Who is that?' he enquired.

'Joseph Coker,' was the reply.

'Never heard of him,' Lord Raven said briefly, as if that damned a man for ever.

'Oh yes, you have, Raven. He's known as Farmer Joe in the House of Commons. For ever complaining that the farmers are neglected and that growing corn is the first duty of a patriot.'

'If he says that, he is a wise man.'

'You wouldn't say so if you knew Farmer Joe. He may be a good farmer, but on his hind legs he's only a windbag. Listen to him now.'

The two men ceased their conversation and Sir Joseph Coker was heard saying querulously:

'I tell you, there is nothing more comely than an English dairymaid. I have several on my estates who would outshine the most fabulous beauty you can see at Carlton House.'

'Blasphemy!' somebody quirked, followed by several lewd remarks suggesting what Farmer Joe did with his dairymaids and what part they played on his farm.

There was no doubt that Sir Joseph Coker had dined well. Now, as he swilled down another glass of port, his red face took on an almost purple hue, both from heat and anger.

'Devil take ye!' he shouted. 'If you think I'm bamming, I'll show you that the dairymaids of Norfolk are finer wenches than can be found in any other part of the British Isles.'

'What'll you wager?' a member asked.

'One hundred guineas!' was the reply.

'Bring the betting book,' someone called. 'Who will take up Farmer Joe's challenge? What about you, Auckland? Or you, Campbell?'

Both men so addressed shook their heads.

'I haven't thought of a dairymaid as being a female for the past twenty years,' Lord Bathurst was heard to confide to a contemporary as old as himself.

'A hundred guineas,' Sir Joseph repeated. 'Will nobody take my bet? Zounds! It just shows how you landlords neglect your estates.'

Whether it was the second glass of brandy that he had just drunk almost absent-mindedly while listening to the altercation at the end of the room, or whether it was the memory of two surprisingly blue eyes, of golden hair blown enticingly in the wind, Lord Raven could not afterwards determine, but, somewhat to his own surprise, he heard himself say:

'I will accept that. I can produce a dairymaid who will challenge and defeat yours any day of the week.'

All the heads in the room were turned in Lord Raven's direction, and then one of the members began to laugh.

'Do you know a dairymaid when you see one, Raven? They don't sing like the nightingales in Berkeley Square, you know.'

'How do you know they don't when a Raven croaks at them?' a wit remarked.

'If Raven produces a dairymaid, then I vow I'll produce a goose-girl to look after the geese in the House of Commons,' someone said.

There was a burst of laughter at this, and Sir Joseph walked across the room to his lordship's side.

'A hundred guineas is what you will owe me, my lord.'

'That remains to be seen,' Lord Raven replied. 'Where's the contest to be held and who are to be the judges?'

This matter was settled in a few minutes. Lord Wellesley, Mr. Granville and Colonel Pellay offered to judge the respective merits of the contestants, and another member of the Club offered his house in St. James's Square as a convenient meeting ground.

'The only difficulty,' Lord Raven said, 'is that the contest must take place this week. I leave for the Continent on Tuesday.'

'Going to pay your respects to the Little Corporal?' Lord Wellesley asked.

'If you must know, my real objective is to drink a decent glass of brandy again,' Lord Raven replied.

'Well, what day will suit you?' Sir Joseph interposed, annoyed to find that the focus of attention was slipping away from him.

'Saturday or Sunday,' Lord Raven suggested.

'The sooner the better,' Sir Joseph replied. 'I am eager to collect your guineas.'

'I shall find yours a help towards my travelling expenses,' Lord Raven retorted; then, as if bored with the whole conversation, he left the assembled company and went upstairs to the card-room.

After three extremely successful hours at the whist table he came downstairs to find his travelling coach, as he had already commanded, waiting for him in the street. Drawn by six horses, it had been built for speed, and they were soon free of the city and out in the open countryside.

Lord Raven leant back comfortably in his seat and relaxed. He intended to sleep for an hour and then, as he was wont to do, he would take the reins from his coachman and drive himself. He trusted no one with his horses when the l nes grew narrow and twisty and they must fight not only the darkness but the badly kept roadways if they were to make good time to Raven Royal.

As he shut his eyes preparatory to falling into an almost childlike slumber, he smiled as he thought of Sir Joseph's discomfiture when he produced his contestant in St. James's Square on Saturday. She was not, of course, strictly his own dairymaid, but she would be by that time. There were none who could not be bribed to change their service if one paid them highly enough.

He wondered what she had bought with the guinea he had given her. Perhaps some ribbons or a bonnet to bewitch some gaping farm lad as he escorted her to church on Sunday. How young she had looked! How fresh, after the powdered and painted ladies of St. James's! And her lips had been soft as rose petals and he could almost swear there was the sweet scent of honeysuckle coming from her skin.

Perhaps Farmer Joe was right when he said there was only one place to live and that was the country! The scent of flowers and the lips of dairymaids! But doubtless one would grow monstrous tired of them both after a little while. Lord Raven was asleep!

He was, however, very much awake as he drove his coach at a spanking rate down the drive of Raven Royal just before noon the following day. His arrival was later than he had intended, and far later than was usual when he left London in the early hours of the morning. For although his own horses were stabled at every posting house between London and Oxford, he had, on this occasion, experienced a most irritating delay when his off-leader cast a shoe some distance out of High Wycombe and it had meant waking up a blacksmith to do the necessary repairs.

His lordship had breakfasted while the last change of horses was being made, and the six he was driving now had, by their very swiftness, eased some of his irritation at not being able to equal his usual time on the homeward journey.

The chestnuts, all perfectly matched, pulled up at the front door of Raven Royal, and the grooms came hurrying to their heads as Lord Raven flung down the reins and dismounted from the driving box.

'I am late, Bates,' he said to his butler, who was waiting to take his hat and driving cape.

'I know, Milord. We were anxious lest some accident should have befallen your lordship.'

There was another cape and hat lying in the hall and as Lord Raven's eyes rested upon them, his lips tightened.

'Who is here?' he enquired.

'A visitor, your lordship, arrived nearly an hour ago. I informed His Royal Highness that you were expected and he said he would wait.'

'Demme, but I wanted a bath,' Lord Raven said, half under his breath. But dutifully he turned towards the breakfast-room.

The Prince was seated at the table and had obviously just finished an extremely good meal. He was carefully, and perhaps over-ostentatiously, dressed for the country; but in the morning light he looked fifty instead of forty and, despite his elegant curls, pearl-powdered cheeks and his careful corset, his far too solid flesh weighed heavily upon him. He was, however, in excellent spirits.

'Good morning, Raven! You did not expect to see me here.'

'No, indeed, Sire! But I hope my poor house has accorded you a fitting welcome in my absence.'

'I have had everything I want, thank you,' the Prince replied, waving his hand over the vast collation of dishes upon the table and the half empty bottle of brandy.

'Can I guess the reason Your Royal Highness honours this somewhat obscure part of the country?' Lord Raven asked.

The Prince chuckled.

'You may not. Did everyone in London wonder where I was?'

'Everyone was entirely mystified,' Lord Raven lied. 'May I join Your Royal Highness at breakfast?'

'Of course! Of course!' the Prince said. 'Let me recommend the pâté. Your chef has excelled himself.'

'That is praise indeed,' Lord Raven replied. 'I shall have to raise his wages.'

'Perhaps you would like to spare him to me; I need a new chef at Carlton House.'

'I, myself, am always at your service, Sire, but that does not include the use of my chef.'

The Prince laughed and filled up his glass.

'To "The Incomparable"!' he said. 'Although, devil take it, that was Vigor's description of her.'

'Is Vigor here, too?' Lord Raven asked.

'He is indeed,' the Prince replied, his face darkening. 'Lord, how I detest that man, and as we are both at the same inn I can't avoid him. He has been trying to steal a march on me this past month, but I spiked his guns last night. He was going to sneak off alone to see her before I was ready but I commanded him to accompany me in my own coach. He was white with anger, but what could he do but obey?'

'I commend you, Sire,' Lord Raven smiled. 'It is always wise to keep your opponent in sight.'

'That is exactly what I thought myself,' the Prince said delightedly. 'But do you know, Raven, the most extraordinary thing happened. We had trouble with a stone in one of the horses' hoofs. It was just after we had lost our way; I think, actually, we were on the wrong drive. Anyway, the carriage had to stop. Because I was so bored by Vigor's company, I got out to stretch my legs. I was walking along, thinking, if the truth were told, of Mrs. Wickham, when suddenly round the corner a girl almost bumps into me. And, would you believe it, Raven, she was the very spitting image of Eloise herself!'

'Indeed!' Lord Raven said, helping himself to boar's head.

'You wouldn't believe me if you hadn't seen her,' the Prince went on. 'She had that same heart-shaped face, the same blue eyes and dark lashes, the same gold hair. Of course, it wasn't arranged fashionably as Mrs. Wickham arranges hers; it was just falling around her cheeks—as pure gold as the spring daffodils themselves. By the way, that's not bad, is it? Really quite poetical.'

He was gratified to see that Lord Raven had set down his knife and fork and was staring at him with what appeared almost rapt attention.

'Who was this girl?' he asked at length. 'And where did you meet her?'

'My dear Raven, I have just been telling you; on the drive going up to Mrs. Wickham's house. For a moment I thought it was Eloise; and when I tried to call Vigor to look at her, she escaped me and ran away into the wood. The most extraordinary thing is that, when I told Eloise about it, she denied the story. She told me I was dreaming and there was no-one who could possibly look like her anywhere in the neighbourhood. At the same time, I had a feeling that she knew more than she would say. If you ask me, her father must have been a gay spark in his youth.

The girl was obviously a blood relation but, I have a suspicion, on the wrong side of the blanket—love children are always beauties.'

'You interest me strangely, Sire. I should like to see this girl.'

'Well, thank goodness that you, at least, credit me with speaking the truth!' the Prince said. 'Eloise said I must have been either dreaming or drinking. That fool Vigor, of course, agreed with her; declared that from the glimpse he had of the chit she was nothing like our hostess. But I assure you I was not mistaken. You do believe me?'

'I believe you implicitly, Sire.'

'You are a good fellow, Raven; that's what you are,' the Prince said. 'Now I will be leaving you. I came here for breakfast because I didn't think I could stand seeing Vigor's face so early in the morning. I am off to call on "The Incomparable". Think she will be pleased to see me?'

'I have no doubt of it,' Lord Raven said.

'Well, thank you for your hospitality,' the Prince said, rising heavily from his chair.

Despite the careful cut of his coat and the corsets which made him hold his breath when he was laced into them, there was no disguising his paunch. He was getting fatter, Lord Raven thought. The fabulous good looks of the First Gentleman of Europe would be lost if he didn't do something to check the obesity which increased year by year.

Lord Raven bowed respectfully over the Prince's hand, escorted him to the door and saw him into his coach. Then, as the horses clattered away with their postilions and outriders, he walked purposely up the steps into the hall.

'Get my bath ready, Bates,' he said. 'And mind the water's hot or there will be hell to pay.'

It was late that afternoon before Lord Raven, reining in his horse, admitted himself defeated. He had visited every farm within a radius of ten miles. He had called on Mrs. Wickham, who had laughed in his face and told him that he was as demented as the Prince himself.

'It must be the local ghost,' she said, 'that you all keep seeing, although I have never been told before that she resembled me. My husband's family always swore it was a nun who walked across the churchyard wailing and wringing her hands.'

He kissed her hand and rode away. It was useless, he thought, with a sudden surge of irritation, not so much at the idea of losing one hundred guineas but of Sir Joseph Coker's smug satisfaction at being declared the winner.

Well, he had made a fool of himself enough for one day. He would abandon the search and go and see Lady Beryl. He would tell her what had occurred. It would make her laugh. It was the type of situation which would appeal to her somewhat puckish sense of humour.

He turned his horse's head towards the Castle. But instead of going to the front door Lord Raven rode straight to the stables. If there was one thing in the world he cared for, above all else, it was his horses, and he had experienced before the rather lazy ministrations of Lord Forncett's grooms, who were not sufficiently interested in horseflesh to avoid neglect or slap-dash methods in rubbing down.

He gave his instructions to the head groom, in the tone of one who intends to be obeyed, and then walked from the stables through the gardens towards the side door of the house.

It was growing late in the afternoon and Lord Raven was conscious that he was tired. So little sleep last night and the frustrations of the afternoon had taken their toll even of his iron physique. And then, suddenly, he was alert and alive as a foxhound who suddenly sees his prey ahead of him.

Along the paved path down which he was walking, coming straight towards him, there appeared a girl carrying in her arms a huge bunch of daffodils which she must have been gathering from where they grew in thick profusion at the far side of the lawn.

She was humming a little tune to herself and did not see Lord Raven until they were almost upon one another. Then she stopped suddenly, her lips parted to emit a sudden exclamation, a note which seemed to him to hold both surprise and terror. Her blue eyes were wide as she looked up at him.

'So here you are!' he exclaimed. 'I have found you at last. Where have you been hiding yourself? Do you know that I have searched half the countryside for you?'

'You have been searching for me!'

Her voice was low and surprisingly cultured; but now, as he looked at her, the blood which had receded from her face when she first saw him came flooding back, the lovely rosy colour staining the paleness of her skin.

'Yes, indeed!' Lord Raven said. 'Now, who are you? Tell me your name?'

'I . . .'

It seemed as if her voice had died in her throat; and

because he felt he had frightened her, he added more kindly:

'You haven't forgotten me, I hope. Have you spent the guinea that I gave you yesterday? What did you buy? I thought perhaps you would choose some ribbons or a new bonnet with which to fascinate the young farmer, who, as I have told you already, is a very lucky fellow.'

His eyes were on her lips as he spoke, remembering the softness of them like the petal of a rose. Then suddenly, before he could stop her, she had turned and fled.

'Stop! Look here! Don't go! Hi!' he shouted after her.

But it was too late. He saw only her flying figure speeding helter skelter towards the Castle, while at his feet there lay a bunch of golden daffodils, their heads bruised against the flagstones.

4

CLEONA had spent a miserable night after her encounter with the Prince. She had not gone to see her old nanny after all, thinking it would be difficult to explain her soup-soaked dress. Instead she had sat in the wood until the cold and darkness had driven her home. There she had crept secretively up the back stairs and into her own bedroom.

Below she could hear the sound of laughter and knew from the frequency and noise of it that her mother's party was going well. She was not hungry although she had had nothing to eat since midday, but she did feel an empty melancholy creep over her.

She did not light the candles in her bedroom, and as she sat on the hearth-rug in front of the small fire and stared into its embers, she found herself thinking, as she had done so often before, about her father.

When he had been there, the Manor had seemed a place of enchantment. There was always someone to run to in trouble or joy; someone who was interested in what she had to say; someone who loved her and someone to whom she gave her whole heart in return.

When he was alive, she had accepted him unquestionably, as all children accept their parents. Now that he was dead she missed him at every turn, knowing how greatly his presence could have enriched and intensified her enjoyment in growing older.

As she sat in front of the fire she found her whole being yearning for him. If only she could tell him of her troubles and her difficulties. It would not have been hard to confide in him and speak of that kiss by the gate, which had both insulted her and held her spellbound.

Had it been Lord Vigor? And if so how could she bear the thought of his becoming her stepfather? She hated him, she told the dying fire, and yet, even as she said it, her cheeks burned at the memory of his kiss. And she thought she would never forget those dark, quizzical eyes which had looked down into hers; that square chin with the little cleft in it; those full, almost brutal lips which had seemed to curve in a cynical smile.

If that was the man her mother was to marry, how could she face a future in which she must be in close proximity with him? She gave a little sob and laid her head against the seat of the chair.

'Oh, Papa,' she whispered. 'Why aren't you here to help me, to tell me what I should do?'

She must have fallen asleep for she awoke with a start to hear the door open. There was a light blinding her eyes; then, as she grew used to it, she saw it was only a candle held in her mother's hand.

Mrs. Wickham set it down on the dressing-table and turned to look at her daughter. The fire was nothing more than a glowing ember and Cleona shivered as she thrust her hair back from her forehead and looked up apprehensively. The shadows in the room gave her a curious fragility, so that with her tiny pointed face and wide, rather frightened eyes, she looked like some very young angel who had fallen from Heaven into an uncertain and perhaps menacing world. Possibly it was this which made Mrs. Wickham's voice particularly harsh as she said:

'You tiresome girl! How could you have put me into such a pucker? I declare, I have never been through such an uncomfortable quarter-of-an-hour as when the Prince arrived to say he had met you on the way.'

'I am indeed sorry, Mamma,' Cleona replied. 'I could not imagine that His Royal Highness would be walking about the back drive. I was struck with horror when I almost bumped into him.'

'If you hadn't been bird-witted, you would have seen him before he saw you,' Mrs. Wickham said. 'It is so like you, Cleona, to go mooning about and getting yourself, and me, into a tangle which might have proved absolutely ruinous to all my hopes if I had not kept my wits about me.'

'Oh, Mamma, what did you say?'

Angry though she was, Mrs. Wickham could not miss the chance of relating her own cleverness.

'I told the Prince he must have been dreaming and there was no-one on this estate who looked in the least like me. "Are you really inferring, Sire," I said, "that you cannot tell the difference between me and some fat-fisted country wench? At least three-quarters of the females in this kingdom have fair hair and blue eyes, but I cannot credit, Sire, that we all look alike." Of course he began to doubt his own senses, and then I inferred, very subtly, that because he was thinking of me every woman seemed to wear my face.'

'That was clever of you, Mamma.'

'I needed every ounce of cleverness to extricate myself from the trap you had sprung on me,' Mrs. Wickham said sharply. 'But unfortunately Lord Vigor was only too anxious to disagree with the Prince. He said that in his opinion there was no resemblance whatsoever.'

'He couldn't have seen much of me,' Cleona protested, 'because when he looked out of the window of the coach I was already running away into the wood.'

'Faugh! What an scape, you provoking girl!' Mrs. Wickham exclaimed. 'But, at least, his lordship is not suspicious. Fortunately he and the Prince arrived early, so I was able to ask them not to say anything in front of my other guests. "Indeed, Sire, with your acute sensibility, I wouldn't be surprised if you have seen a ghost," I said to the Prince. "And the Duchess of Marlborough is terrified of ghosts. In fact she swears if there is any more talk of them she will remove to the family house in London and never set foot in the country again." Pretending a fondness for that tiresome creature, I made both His Royal Highness and Lord Vigor promise not to mention their strange encounter in the drive while the Marlboroughs and Barclays were with us.'

'Did Lord Vigor offer for you, Mamma?'

Mrs. Wickham gave a little laugh.

'I was never alone with him for a moment the whole evening. I was far too clever for that. When he and the Prince took their leave together, I divided my favours between them impartially. I took a rose from my breast and

45

gave it into the Prince's hand. "I pray its fragrance will bring you happy dreams, Sire," I whispered. Then with a little start I looked up at Lord Vigor. "And I would not wish your dreams, my lord, to be anything but sweet," I said softly and gave him its twin. They glared at each other and departed. I wouldn't mind wagering that their conversation, as they drive back to Woodstock, will be in surly monosyllables.'

Cleona clapped her hands.

'How subtle you are, Mamma! And to think that tomorrow . . .'

Mrs. Wickham smiled, and then suddenly her eyes narrowed and her lips were a hard line.

'If Lord Vigor doesn't call tomorrow—and alone,' she said harshly, 'I shall know that I have failed.'

'And the Prince?'

'I can console His Royal Highness after I am married.' Mrs. Wickham gave a little yawn. 'I must to bed . . . La! But I was forgetting! What I really came to say to you, child, was that you must be away from here. The risk of discovery is too great. If Lord Vigor finds out now that I have a daughter, I am convinced that it will destroy my chances of becoming his wife. No one wants to saddle himself with another man's offspring—and least of all his lordship, who has evaded marriage for so long.'

'He will have to know some time,' Cleona said practically.

'We can cross that bridge when we come to it,' Mrs. Wickham replied complacently. 'In the meantime, chit, you must be gone.'

'But where, Mamma? As I told you this evening, I am to start for Rome on Tuesday, but I doubt if you paid any heed.'

'Indeed I did,' Mrs. Wickham answered. 'And I am delighted to hear of your proposed journey. It will be a most instructive experience for you. I spoke to Beryl about it this very evening.'

'You did?'

'Yes, I went upstairs with her while she took off her cloak and warned her to say nothing in front of the others. She was very sensible.'

'Oh! That reminds me, Mamma. I must have some new gowns; you know that I have nothing to wear.'

'New gowns!' Mrs. Wickham's voice was suddenly sharp.

'Why, yes, Mamma. I haven't had anything new since

you went away. I am afraid I have outgrown everything
I possess.'

'But, Cleona, I am pledged to the very limit. One of the
reasons I was glad to leave London was that the duns were
for ever at the door. It would be difficult to spare you a
pound or two, let alone to find you a trousseau.'

'Not a trousseau, Mamma. Just a travelling gown and
one to wear in the evenings.'

'It is impossible,' Mrs. Wickham began, and then
stopped. 'Wait, I have thought of something. Come to my
bedchamber.'

She picked up the candle and led the way, Cleona
following. In the bedroom, with its carved four-poster bed,
there was a blaze of light from at least a dozen candles.
Mrs. Wickham stopped for a moment to look at her reflection in the mirror.

'These emeralds are certainly becoming,' she said. 'I
should hate to give them back—even though I believe the
Vigor family jewels are worth a fortune.'

She moved her neck so that the light flashed on the
gems, and then, with a little sigh, half of satisfaction and
half of anxiety, she crossed the room to her wardrobe.
When she opened the door, the rows of elegant gowns
hanging inside fluttered as if a breath of life passed through
them.

'It is impossible for me to dispense with any of these,'
Mrs. Wickham said positively. 'But there is that travelling
gown and pelisse of mine that I bought before I went to
London. I noticed when I returned home that Matthews
had preserved them carefully.'

As she spoke, she pulled the dress from the corner of
the wardrobe, and Cleona's heart sank. She knew it only
too well. Her mother had bought it in a hurry on her last
visit to London before her husband's death. She had chosen
the material by candle-light from a small pattern, and it
turned out very different, both in the piece and in daylight.
What should have been a soft, deep blue had turned out
to be a hard, cold grey, extremely unbecoming to Eloise
Wickham's fragile prettiness.

'This will do you for the journey,' Mrs. Wickham said.
'And now you want something for the evening.' She looked
through her dresses again. 'I really can't part with any of
these,' she murmured. 'I was wearing that blue the night
the Prince fell in love with me. I haven't even dared to
look at the bill for that white satin from Paris or for that
silver gauze. It was Lord Vigor who said that I looked

like a moonbeam in it. I really don't know what to give you. Oh, what about this?'

She pulled out a white dress which was modelled in the very latest fashion; a little Grecian in its conception with soft draperies falling away from a high waist. Cleona was just about to give an exclamation of delight when she saw that on the front of the dress was a large ugly patch.

'That happened at Devonshire House,' Mrs. Wickham said, following the direction of her eyes. "I was talking to Beau Brummell himself, and somebody jogged his elbow. He was in a terrible rage about it and absolutely annihilated the man who bumped into him, but that didn't prevent my gown from being utterly ruined.'

'What a tragedy, Mamma! But how can I wear it like that?'

'Ask Matthews if she can do anything about it. Oh, but I forgot—Matthews won't have time to do anything for you if you are to leave tomorrow morning.'

'But, Mamma, where am I to go?'

'Don't be so thick-headed, child. To Beryl, of course. If she is having you on Tuesday, what does it signify if you arrive a few days early? You have always spent most of your time at the Castle anyway.'

'I hardly like to ask them, when they have already been so hospitable,' Cleona said shyly.

'Oh, pray don't make any more difficulties. My head aches with all this arranging and rearranging,' Mrs. Wickham complained. 'It is your own fault. If you hadn't been such a nitwit as to run into the Prince, you could have stayed here and no-one would have been any the wiser.'

'Very well, Mamma, I will ask Beryl if she will have me,' Cleona said meekly.

'That's a good child, and now go to bed. No, wait—you can help me out of my gown and put away my jewellery.'

It was nearly an hour later before Cleona had finished maiding her mother. She blew out the lights, one by one, and tip-toed away to her own bedroom. She carried her new gowns with her, and yet, as she laid them down on a chair, she could hardly forbear a little shudder at the thought of her appearance in Rome.

'But it won't matter,' she told herself sensibly. 'Everyone will be looking at Beryl and they will only think I am a kind of companion to her—which, indeed, I am.'

It was hard not to feel a little bitter when she thought of the rows of beautiful, elegant gowns in her mother's wardrobe; of the dozen trunks which she had brought down with her from London, containing jewels, scarves and feathers; of the bonnets, which seemed almost to fill the empty dressing-room next door; and the shoes, gloves and elegant sunshades which had taken Matthews nearly a day to unpack.

'Perhaps she will feel kinder in the morning,' Cleona thought optimistically before she fell asleep. But in the morning Mrs. Wickham had a headache and it was hard to persuade her that Cleona could not go to Rome either bareheaded or unshod.

Fortunately her mother's things fitted her, although her waist was a fraction smaller, a point which annoyed Mrs. Wickham so much that it was only on Matthews' insistence that she dispensed with a few very necessary articles of underwear and several pairs of gloves, which in fact she would never have worn again because they had already been darned.

It was Matthews who found the bonnet which matched the travelling dress and added a scarf to the white dress, and who finally persuaded Mrs. Wickham to give Cleona five pounds for the journey.

'You will be able to spend some of it on muslin,' Matthews told Cleona when they were out of her mother's room and packing in her own. 'Lady Beryl's maid's a decent-hearted woman. I know her well. She'll run up some pretty, fresh gowns for you, and I have included with your things two silk sashes which your mother will never be missing—not at least until you are too far away for her to ask you to return them.'

'Oh, Matthews, ought I to take them?'

Matthews said nothing; her lips only tightened and Cleona, knowing that the old maid had a very poor opinion of her mistress, forbore to say more.

It was only when she was unpacking at the Castle, after Lady Beryl had welcomed her with open arms, that she found included in her luggage all sorts of small things which Matthews must have taken without permission. It was too late now to do anything about them, Cleona thought, and although her conscience pricked her a little, she could not help wishing, a little wistfully, that her mother had been more generous and there had been no need to take what hadn't been offered.

Lady Beryl's maid, however, was kinder than Cleona had dared to hope. A gaunt woman of unprepossessing appearance with the inappropriate name of Swallow, she was nevertheless as kindly as Matthews had promised.

'It is, indeed, a nasty mark, Miss,' she said, as Cleona showed her the wine-stained evening gown. 'I wish we had some more of the material, but I can tell by the texture that it came from Paris and there will be no matching it this side of the Channel.'

'But what can I do, Swallow?' Cleona asked miserably.

'Just leave it to me, Miss,' Swallow said comfortingly.

She was not as old as Matthews, but she had the same comfortable, reassuring authority about her, and Cleona was only too happy to leave the problem in her competent hands.

'Thank you so much,' she said softly.

'And don't you worrit, Miss, about buying any muslin either,' Swallow said. 'Miss Matthews sent me a note to say that that's what you intend to do, but her ladyship's got rolls of it here. I will run you up a couple of dresses in no time.'

'Oh, Swallow, how kind you are,' Cleona said. 'I really do not know how to thank you.'

'That's all right, Miss,' Swallow said a little gruffly. 'It's a pity you can't wear her ladyship's frocks, but there, they would be far too big for you.'

'I mustn't impose on her ladyship,' Cleona said. 'She has been so kind to me already. I can never say how grateful I am.'

'It's her ladyship who is grateful, if you ask me,' Swallow retorted. 'If she had to go abroad with her cousin, Lady Hester, they would have torn themselves to pieces like a couple of tigers.'

'I am indeed gratified that I can save her ladyship from that,' Cleona said with warm sincerity, but with a hint of laughter in her voice.

'So am I, Miss,' Swallow replied. She spoke dryly, but Cleona felt she had found a friend and ally in Beryl's maid.

She was thinking how lucky she was and how kind everyone was to her as she walked back to the Castle with the big bunch of daffodils she had picked in the long grass beyond the lawns.

'Can I do anything to help you?' she had said to Beryl as they sat talking in the Red *Salon* which overlooked the rose garden.

'If you could pick me some flowers for father's writing-table I would be vastly obliged,' Beryl answered. 'I always arrange the vase myself, but as it happens I have a letter to write.'

She spoke a little coyly and Cleona said at once:

'Can I guess whom it is to?'

'No, because you would guess right,' Beryl answered, and suddenly her expression changed and her mouth drooped at the corners as she added, 'I am going to say good-bye.'

'Does he know you are going abroad?'

'No, of course not. When father brought me away from London after he had heard the gossip which was connecting our names, I only had a few seconds in which to scribble Ian a line. I sent a footman round with it to Mountavon House, but he had gone to the races at Newmarket.'

'Have you heard from him?'

'Yes, I received a letter this morning. He said that he loves me and that he will always love me.' Beryl gave a little sigh and then turned towards her writing-desk. 'But we have got to forget each other, I can see that. Only it is not going to be easy.'

'Poor Beryl.' Cleona's voice was soft, and because she knew there was nothing she could say and nothing she could do, she went out into the garden to pick the flowers.

Twenty minutes later she burst into the *Salon* then slammed the door behind her, to stand with her back to it, panting.

'What on earth is the matter?' Beryl asked, looking up from the writing-desk, then jumping up and going towards her. 'What has happened to you, dearest? Why have you been running?'

Cleona put her hand to her heart as if to check the tumult there. Then, as she attempted to find her voice, she put out her other hand and drew Beryl towards the window.

'Is . . . is that Lord Vigor?' she asked, pointing to a tall figure walking slowly through the rose garden, a bunch of daffodils in his hand.

'Lord Vigor?' Beryl questioned in surprise. 'But of course it isn't. That is Sylvester—Lord Raven. I thought you knew him.'

'Lord Raven!' Cleona's hands flew in consternation to her flushed cheeks. 'Goodness gracious, I had no idea that it might be him! Oh, Beryl!'

'What has he done to you? Why do you look like that?'

It was then that Cleona realized it would be impossible to tell Beryl of her betrothed's behaviour the first time she had met him. How could she possibly relate what had happened when he had mistaken her for a farm girl and commanded her to open the gate? Desperately she racked her brains for a plausible excuse and fell back on a half truth.

'I . . . I thought he was . . . Lord Vigor,' she stammered. 'And you know, as I have already told you, that Mamma did not wish him to see me.'

'Yes, yes, of course; I understand,' Beryl smiled. 'But I can't comprehend how you could mistake Sylvester, who is at least a handsome man, for that tiresome, rat-faced Vigor.'

'That . . . that was why I ran away,' Cleona said, a little desperately.

Beryl laughed.

'He will think it odd of you, but never mind. Quickly, tidy yourself, Cleona. I want him to like you. After all, you will spend a lot of time in his company, and Sylvester's a person of very strong likes and dislikes.'

'I cannot . . . meet him,' Cleona cried, in a sudden panic.

'But that is nonsensical,' Beryl replied. 'You have got to be introduced sooner or later. Tidy your hair, dear love. See, I have a comb here in my reticule. And slip my scarf over your shoulders.'

Fortunately it took Lord Raven several minutes to walk through the gardens to the front door. There was a further delay before the butler escorted him to the Red *Salon* and announced him. As he entered the room he saw Beryl standing waiting for him. He raised her hand to his lips.

'You must forgive my tardy appearance so late in the day,' he said courteously. 'But I have had many things to occupy my mind since I returned from London.'

'I wonder what can be more important than seeing me?' Beryl questioned a little mockingly. 'But now you are here I am delighted to see you, my lord. Have you brought me a bouquet?'

She looked with raised eyebrows at the daffodils he held in his hand. Lord Raven laughed.

'They are your own flowers and therefore no gift from me,' he replied. 'But I have brought them because they are, in effect, a clue.'

'A clue?' Beryl questioned.

'To the identity of the person who picked them,' he answered. 'It is a puzzle that I thought you would be able to untangle for me, for the person in question, having flung the flowers at my feet, fled away from me like Daphne pursued by Apollo and disappeared into the Castle.'

'Well, you are fortunate in that she did not turn into a tree,' said Beryl, who had read her mythology. 'Daphne is here, but actually her name is Cleona.'

She turned as she spoke and indicated a figure sitting demurely in a secluded corner of the room, an embroidery frame in her hands.

Cleona found it hard to look up with what she hoped was the ordinary calm civility of a young woman about to be introduced. But Lord Raven, after one quick start of irrepressible astonishment, was admirably controlled.

'Cleona dearest, may I present the Earl of Raven?' Beryl said. 'Sylvester, this is my dear friend, Cleona Wickham, who is coming with us to Rome.'

'Your servant, Ma'am.'

Lord Raven bowed with grace. Cleona swept him a deep curtsy and then, because she dared not look up into his face, kept her eyes downcast, her long dark lashes touching cheeks that were still rosy after her flight from the garden.

'I fear that I must have startled you, Miss Wickham,' Lord Raven said.

One fleeting glance was enough to show Cleona that he was smiling—that horrible, cynical smile which twisted the corners of his lips and which made her feel small and gauche and somehow utterly unprotected.

'I must apologize, my lord, for my stupidity in mistaking you for someone else,' she said quickly.

'Someone else?' Lord Raven queried.

'A gentleman I am most anxious to avoid,' Cleona answered.

She knew by his expression that he thought she was referring to himself, and she had the satisfaction of hoping that she had made him, in some way, uncomfortable. And then she saw his eyes flicker over her shabby cotton gown; her golden hair, which despite Beryl's ministrations still lay tangled at the base of her neck; at the quick rise and fall of her breasts. And she hated him anew.

He had the power to disturb her. Because no man had ever made her feel like this before, she loathed him with an intensity which frightened even herself.

'You are looking forward to our journey to Rome, Miss Wickham?'

'Very much, my lord.'

Simple, conventional words, yet Cleona felt they hid a wealth of things unsaid. And then Beryl pulled at Lord Raven's arm and took him away to show him a map on which her father had traced the route for them to take once they arrived in France.

They stood, with their backs to Cleona, at the writing-desk, so that she could abandon her pretence at working on Beryl's embroidery frame and look unperceived at the man she had imagined, so foolishly, was about to become her stepfather. How could she have been so stupid as not to guess from the very beginning that the rider who had asked her to open a gate might be Lord Raven? And yet, even if she had, what could she have done about it when his action had taken her so completely by surprise?

She found herself remembering how his lips had captured hers and how his fingers had cupped her chin, tipping back her head so that he could find her mouth. If only she could have her revenge; if only there was something she could do to insult him, as he had insulted her.

And yet she was powerless! And when they had started for Rome she would be beholden to him for his protection, even as she would be beholden to the woman he was about to marry for her food and lodging and for the very coach that would carry her as their companion on the journey.

It was an almost intolerable situation, Cleona thought. But there was nothing she could do about it. She could not even go home, for her mother did not want her.

Lord Raven turned from the writing-desk towards Cleona. She had not expected the movement and she found herself looking straight into his eyes. Her head was silhouetted against the window. Behind her the sunlight was on her hair; the blue scarf which Beryl had draped round her shoulders echoed the blue of her eyes, as the sky is reflected in a lake beneath it.

'And does Miss Wickham approve of our plans?' Lord Raven asked.

He was mocking her, Cleona thought. Pretending to give her an importance to which, she was well aware, she was not entitled.

'Cleona is enchanted by everything,' Beryl answered for her. 'She has never been abroad before.'

'Let us hope Miss Wickham will not be disappointed,' Lord Raven said drily.

'I am not afraid that places will ever disappoint me,' Cleona said slowly, 'only people.'

It was not a very brilliant remark, but she felt as if she might count it as a point in her favour. Then Lord Raven laughed.

'I hope that I shall not be one of the people to disappoint

you, Miss Wickham!' he said, and Cleona knew that he challenged her.

'I do not believe that my present estimation of your lordship could be changed easily,' she replied, and this time she met his eyes boldly.

However insensitive he might be to the feelings of others, she thought, he must be aware that she hated him.

5

CLEONA was wondering how she could slip away and leave Beryl and Lord Raven alone when a footman entered with a note on a silver salver. He presented it to Lady Beryl, who opened the envelope and then began to laugh.

'Lud! Was there ever such a coil?' she exclaimed.

'About what?' Lord Raven enquired.

'This letter is from Mrs. Wickham,' she explained. 'She says that the Prince has signified his desire to dine here tonight and to bring her with him. She begs me to invite Lord Vigor to accompany them and to hide away Cleona so effectively that there is no possible chance of her being seen.'

Beryl laughed again and holding out her hand to Cleona cried:

'I vow, my dearest love, that your mother sets me an almost impossible task, for you have a *penchant* for running into trouble.'

'You must lock me in my bedchamber and take away the key,' Cleona said. 'Oh dear, how difficult everything seems to be! Does my mother's letter sound as if everything were going well?'

'It is hard to tell,' Beryl answered. 'She seems in a flutter at the idea of the Prince coming here—but His Royal Highness might upset anyone.'

'He might indeed!' Lord Raven exclaimed. 'Why can't Prinny go back to St. James's? 'Tis a cursed nuisance having him dropping in on us when we least expect him, although I am at a loss to understand why Miss Wickham shouldn't be here when he calls.'

Beryl looked at him in consternation.

'Faith, but now we will have to explain it all!' she said. 'I thought you of all people, my lord, would find it easy to guess why Mrs. Wickham has deserted St. James's; why Lord Vigor and the Prince have followed her; and why Cleona, with a countenance such as hers, is very much in the way.'

Cleona blushed as Lord Raven turned to inspect her as if, she thought, he was seeing her for the first time.

'I am beginning to understand the more subtle points of Miss Wickham's predicament,' he said slowly and she winced at the hint of sarcasm behind his words.

'You would be more bird-witted than I give you credit for, if you couldn't,' Beryl said tartly. 'What are we to do, that is the question?'

'We?' Lord Raven raised his eyebrows.

'Yes, to be sure! You couldn't be so mean, Sylvester, as not to help us out of this hideous dilemma. First, of course, we must not mention Cleona's existence to anyone who dines here. I will make it clear to Papa that his lips are sealed. I am afraid that he was never very susceptible to Mrs. Wickham's charms, so he is unlikely to be over-conversational this evening. The next thing we have to decide is where we can hide Cleona.'

She looked at Lord Raven meaningly as she spoke, and before Cleona could cry out in protest he had said politely:

'Of course, Raven Royal is entirely at your disposal.'

Beryl clapped her hands together.

'Splendid! I knew I could rely on you! Cleona can ride over with you now. When you have dined, she can come back here—but not too early, I beg of you.'

'No, no,' Cleona interposed. 'Let me stay upstairs in my room. If I promise not to cross the threshold, it will be impossible for me to bump into the Prince or anyone else.'

'I dare not trust you,' Beryl said. 'You are the type of person, Cleona, who attracts adventures. Lord Vigor would burst into the room by mistake, or the ceiling would give way and you would suddenly drop in upon us in the dining-room. No! We must not risk jeopardizing your Mamma's very carefully laid plans. Besides, Sylvester will be delighted to entertain you.'

'You take the very words from my mouth,' Lord Raven remarked.

Cleona was uneasily conscious that his eyes were watching her, mocking her, so it seemed, because a situation had developed which was bound to cause her acute embarrassment.

'It is most gracious of your lordship,' she murmured at length. 'But I feel that for me to dine at Raven Royal might cause local gossip which——'

'Local gossip be damned!' Lord Raven exclaimed. 'People have talked so long and so loud about the goings on at Raven Royal that there can be little left for them to say. Besides, I can assure you, Miss Wickham, that the conventions will be fully safeguarded. I have staying with me at this moment my maternal grandmother, the Duchess of Wantage. She will, I am convinced, be delighted to act as your chaperon.'

'Then that is decided!' Beryl said. 'Now hurry, Cleona, and change into your riding-habit. The sooner you leave here the better I shall be pleased. In the meantime I had best order a good dinner for His Royal Highness. We must at all costs keep him in a good humour.'

'What time shall I bring Miss Wickham home?' Lord Raven asked.

'I cannot believe that the Prince will stay very late,' Beryl answered. 'Oh dear, I wish that you could be here to help me.'

Cleona, who was about to leave the room, turned from the doorway.

'Please let Lord Raven dine with you, Beryl,' she pleaded. 'I am very sensible of your kindness and of his lordship's generosity in suggesting that I should go to Raven Royal, but I shall be safe enough here, I promise you. It would be far less trouble for me to have a bowl of soup in my room than to put Lord Raven to the necessity of taking me to his home.'

'Sylvester is only too delighted to have you,' Beryl declared positively, and again Cleona saw the detestable twinkle in his lordship's eye as he said:

'I will reiterate my delight if it pleases you.'

There was nothing more Cleona could say. Lord Raven was playing with her and making the situation far more uncomfortable than was necessary. There was a decided flounce in the manner in which she turned on her heel and went from the room, shutting the door decidedly behind her.

Upstairs in her room she found Swallow waiting to fit the muslin dress which was practically finished.

'Swallow, what am I to do?' Cleona cried. 'I have to ride over to Raven Royal for dinner and my habit is in a lamentable state. I know that when she packed it Matthews apologized that she had not had time to clean it since I last went riding.'

'I noticed that, Miss,' Swallow replied, 'but the habit is so old there is little I can do to it. You can't wear it to Raven Royal, that's as sure as eggs is eggs.'

'But I must,' Cleona protested. 'I have nothing else to wear and her ladyship has arranged for me to leave immediately.'

'It's a shame that you should be going out, Miss, when I hear that His Royal Highness is honouring us this evening.'

'How do you know that?' Cleona asked curiously.

'The groom who brought the note from your home told the footman to whom he gave it that the Prince was coming here—the chef is in a rare taking at having such short notice.'

'What else did the groom say?' Cleona enquired.

'If you will forgive me mentioning it, Miss, he did say as how your lady mother was in a rare pucker in case anyone should know that you were a-staying here. He said there was to be no chattering to His Royal Highness's servants.'

Cleona sighed. There seemed to be a whole army of people who must be let into the secret of her flight from home and of her flight from the Castle to Raven Royal.

'My mother is ... er ... anxious for me not to meet the Prince ... or Lord Vigor at present,' she said hesitatingly. 'You will appreciate, Swallow, that I have not yet made my début.'

It was the only excuse she could think of on the spur of the moment, and Swallow was far too polite to show that she knew there were other and far more vital reasons for Mrs. Wickham to hide her daughter.

'Well, Miss, you can't go to Raven Royal in that old habit,' she said, 'that's a fact.'

'And I certainly cannot ride a horse in my new muslin dress,' Cleona said with a smile, 'lovely though it may be.'

'Now let me cogitate,' Swallow said—a bony hand to her forehead. 'Her ladyship had a habit in blue velvet that was put away nigh on two year ago. I think I can lay my hand on it.'

'Her ladyship's habit would be much too big for me,' Cleona smiled. 'I would look ridicuolus.'

'You would indeed, Miss, but this was a habit her ladyship wore before she was fully grown. Drat my memory! If I can find it, I'm certain sure it will be the very thing!'

Swallow hurried from the room and Cleona walked across to the bed on which lay the nearly completed muslin gown. She touched its crisp fragility with a little thrill of pleasure. A new dress! What it would mean after years of shabbiness!

How kind Beryl was to her, but then everyone was so kind—everyone except one particular person!

She felt herself tremble as she remembered the smile on Lord Raven's lips, the glint in his eyes as he had looked across the room at her and she had defied him, only to find a little later that she was forced into the position of being his unwilling guest. She felt a sense of panic at the thought that they must ride alone to Raven Royal. What could she say to him? What could they talk about?

The door opened and Swallow came hurrying in.

'Here it is, Miss. And unless I am very much mistaken it should fit you like a glove.'

Swallow was not mistaken. The riding-habit, of sapphire blue velvet, which had been made by a Bond Street tailor for the fifteen-year-old Lady Beryl, fitted Cleona to perfection. It was cut by a master hand and when Cleona had got into it and stood staring at herself in the mirror she could hardly forbear to cry out in delight at her own appearance.

It accentuated her tiny waist which might have been spanned by a man's two hands. The colour framed the clear transparency of her skin, and the lace jabot at her neck was provocatively feminine in contrast to the sculptured severity of the habit itself. There was a little *tricorn* hat of the same velvet with a shaded feather which curved over the brim and coquettishly touched the side of one cheek.

'Odds-bods, Miss, it might have been made for you!' Swallow cried, standing back to admire the effect.

'It might indeed!' Cleona agreed. 'I only hope her ladyship won't mind my wearing it.'

'Mind?' Swallow questioned. 'Why, her ladyship thought I had thrown it away a long while ago. It was no more use to her, as you can well see, and it is only because I am what my old mother used to call a born hoarder, that I have kept a large number of things that I was told to dispose of, just in case they should come in.'

'This has certainly come in as far as I am concerned,' Cleona smiled, 'and at exactly the right moment! Thank you, Swallow. I do not feel so frightened of going to Raven Royal when I am dressed like this.'

'Now, don't you go being afraid of his lordship,' Swallow admonished. 'You can take it from me, Miss, he isn't as bad as he is painted. Oh, I know there's been a bag of tittle-tattle about him and plenty of folk ready to wag their tongues and shake their heads! But what can you expect when a nobleman's rich and powerful with a countenance that handsome he turns the head of every foolish wench as looks at him?'

'I only hope her ladyship will be happy,' Cleona said stiffly.

'We are all praying for that, Miss. But one can never tell with her ladyship. She's that self-willed. Always been the same she has ever since she was a tot, but, if you ask me, she's met her match this time.'

Cleona hesitated a moment and then she asked a question which she could not help being uppermost in her mind.

'Do you think that his lordship will love Lady Beryl to the exclusion of everyone else?' she asked in a low voice.

'Lor love us, Miss, what a question!' Swallow exclaimed. 'It's what we anticipates, as you might say, for every bride and groom! But up in London we looks at things in a somewhat different way to what you does in the country. Ladies and gentlemen in Society have their flirtations here and there, but often they mean nothing more than what a handshake is to more simple folk. It's just a way of passing the time, so to speak. His lordship's been a very gay blade, from all I hear, but there's no reason why he shouldn't settle down. Her ladyship's enjoyed herself, too, if it comes to that.'

'I am afraid I have no comprehension of such things, Swallow,' Cleona said. 'I thought if people fell in love and got married they were content with each other for ever.'

'And a very nice sentiment, too, Miss,' Swallow said approvingly. 'It's what we're all after hoping for, high or low, but sometimes it doesn't work out that way.'

'No, of course it does not,' Cleona said slowly, remembering Beryl's first marriage.

'Now don't you go worriting your head about such things,' Swallow said kindly, seeing the perplexity on her small face. 'You will be finding yourself a nice husband one of these fine days—someone who'll love and cherish you to the very end of your days. That's what'll happen, Miss, you mark my words.'

'I do hope so,' Cleona murmured.

She felt, even as she spoke, that it would never happen to her. Yet she knew too, in that moment, that she would never be satisfied with half measures, with a marriage which meant flirtations on the side and a craving for something gayer and more amusing that the companionship of the man one had married.

'I want love—real love!' she told her reflection in the mirror silently. 'And to give in return my whole heart.'

She saw her own eyes grow soft and misty at the thought of it, and then deliberately she turned from the mirror and smiled at Swallow.

'Thank you so much,' she said sweetly. But in reality she was thanking the maid not for the beautifully cut riding-habit, but for clearing her thoughts and establishing an ideal within herself which never before had she formulated into words.

Slowly she went downstairs, and a little shyly because she was so conscious of her new appearance she opened the door of the *Salon*. Beryl and Lord Raven were standing by the fireplace. Beryl had her hand on his lordship's arm and was looking up into his face. There was something possessive in her attitude and for a moment Cleona felt as if she were an intruder. Then they turned, saw her and Beryl cried:

'How quick you have been, my dearest love, and how entrancing you look!'

It was, as Cleona well knew, the fashionable way of talking, on the model set by the ladies of Devonshire House, but she could not help but be warmed by it, insincere though she fancied it might be. It was, however, difficult to detect anything but the utmost sincerity in Beryl's expression and voice as she took Cleona's hands in hers and said:

'La, you are lovely! That colour becomes you better than anything I have ever seen you in. Don't you agree with me, Sylvester? And wait until you see Cleona on a horse—she rides like an angel.'

'An angel on horseback!' Lord Raven said.

Beryl gave a little scream of laughter, while Cleona looked bewildered. She was not to know that a new delicacy of an oyster wrapped in bacon had recently been proffered for the Prince's delectation and described on the menu as—'Angels on horseback'.

'Faith, Sylvester, you are exceeding witty,' Beryl flattered; but Cleona only hated him because, inadvertently or by intent, he had once again made her feel foolish.

'And now you must go,' Beryl said. 'I have only got a bare hour in which to change and be ready to receive the Prince.' She bent to kiss Cleona. 'Enjoy yourself, dearest; tomorrow you can tell me what you think of Raven Royal. You have never been there, if I remember rightly.'

'I hope Miss Wickham will give me her impressions tonight,' Lord Raven said, and once again Cleona felt that he was mocking her.

Because she was afraid he would see the anger in her eyes, she hurriedly bade Beryl good-bye and led the way across the hall and through the front door to where the horses were waiting.

They trotted a short way down the drive, then turned to cross the parkland. They cantered for some distance, not speaking until they were forced to rein in their horses to ride through a small wood which lay on the boundary of the two estates. It was then that Lord Raven, drawing in his horse close beside Cleona's, said:

'Have you forgiven me?'

'For what?' she enquired innocently, and then felt the blood rush to her cheeks as she saw by the look in his eyes to what he referred.

'For mistaking you for a farm wench.'

She was silent for a moment, trying to school herself to say the right thing; but because she could not help but express the fundamental honesty of her emotions, her answer eventually burst from her lips.

'It was unforgivable!'

'As bad as that?'

She knew that he had raised his eyebrows, as if finding her answer a little ill bred, a little unrestrained.

'Yes, quite as bad as that,' she said hotly.

'It was not intended as an insult.'

'I was not thinking of myself,' she retorted scornfully, 'but of Beryl. You are affianced to her, and yet, because you see someone who . . . who . . .'

She was at a loss for words, and instantly he supplied them.

'Who was lovely beyond compare,' he said. 'So lovely, in fact, that the memory of her has cost me one hundred guineas.'

'Cost you one hundred guineas!'

It was impossible for Cleona to prevent her curiosity by inviting an explanation.

'Yes, indeed!' Lord Raven said. 'I went to White's yesterday evening, and one of the members, a man called

Sir Joseph Coker, challenged anyone to produce a prettier dairymaid than one he employed. The wager was one hundred guineas and I took it.'

'Thinking to produce me?' Cleona asked.

'Exactly! I searched for you everywhere possible. I even called on your mother to ask if she knew who you might be.'

'And her answer?'

'She disclaimed all knowledge of any female answering such a description.'

Although she had expected such an answer, the pain of it made Cleona silent for a moment.

'What will you do now that you cannot produce your answer to Sir Joseph's challenge?' she asked at length.

'I must forfeit a hundred guineas, of course,' Lord Raven replied. 'It is galling because he is a bumptious, tiresome fellow, but there is nothing else I can do about it.'

'There are many dairymaids in these parts.'

'They don't look like you.'

'No, and I am glad in a way that you should forfeit your money.'

'Glad?'

'Yes! As I have already told you, your behaviour was inexcusable.'

'If you are still looking at it from the point of view of Beryl's sensibilities, I doubt if my behaviour would cast her into a despondency. I behaved as she would expect of me—or any other full-blooded man who saw a girl as pretty as you wandering about unattended. Incidentally, have you told her?'

'No, of course not.'

'So vehement! Why?'

Cleona was silent, and watching her face Lord Raven said:

'Was it perhaps because you were too shy to confess that I had kissed you?'

His words made Cleona flame into revolt.

'Shy is not the right word,' she said angrily. 'I was ashamed, disgusted, horrified, anything else you like to suggest.'

'Then you have never been kissed before?'

'It is not for you to ask me such questions, my lord. We will talk of something else or—not talk at all.'

They were through the wood by this time and Cleona touched her horse sharply with the whip. It bounded forward and suddenly she was spurring him on, urging him into a headlong gallop, conscious all the time that Lord Raven, without any seeming effort, was keeping level with her.

On, on she galloped until the roofs and outbuildings of Raven Royal were in sight. Only then did she almost involuntarily slacken her pace, to find him still at her side and hear him laugh lightly.

'You won't escape me this time,' he said, and she turned her head to see the smile she most hated on his lips.

'We will not speak of this again, my lord,' she said, but her flushed cheeks somehow belied the coldness of her voice.

'As you wish, Miss Wickham,' he replied.

'We will behave as if we met today for the first time,' Cleona insisted. 'I love Beryl; she is my dearest friend. I would not do anything or speak of anything which might hurt or offend her in any way.'

'Most admirable sentiments,' Lord Raven agreed. 'But are you sure it is Beryl of whom you are thinking?'

Cleona did not deign to answer him. She turned her head away, holding her chin high, her back very straight and disapproving.

And so in silence they came in sight of Raven Royal just as the sunset was crimson against the sky and the dying fire of it was reflected on a hundred windows, so that it seemed as if a light burned in every one of them, while the lake which stood on one side of the house was a bowl of burning gold.

Angry though Cleona was, incensed to a point when it was hard to think clearly, the beauty of Raven Royal seemed, for a moment, to sweep every other thought from her head. She could only stare at the great Elizabethan building which looked as if it had been built with fairy hands, so delicate and so beautiful was it and so glorious in its setting and in its position. High above grey stone terraces which encircled it like a necklace, it was protected to the north by green woods that cosseted it as if it were a precious jewel. So it had stood for almost four centuries, from the time that Sir Humphrey Raven had entertained his Queen and it had been christened, in her honour, Raven Royal.

How long Cleona looked at the house without speaking she did not know, but suddenly she heard Lord Raven's voice saying, in a very different tone from the one he had used when he teased her:

'Well, what do you think of my home?'

'It is so wonderul that I fancy I am but dreaming of its perfection,' she answered, and there was no mistaking the awe and admiration in her voice.

'That is what I feel every time I return,' Lord Raven said quietly.

'If you love it so much, why do you go away?' Cleona enquired. Her eyes were on the light-filled windows which seemed to radiate a welcome.

'Perhaps one day I will answer that question,' he replied. 'For the moment let me ask you one. Would you respect a man who, having great wealth, great power and an enquiring mind, made no further use of such things than to stay at home and grow potatoes?'

'We do other things besides that in the country,' Cleona answered stiffly. 'While you in London . . .' She stopped.

'Yes? What do we do in London?' Lord Raven prompted.

She turned on him then.

'You are only asking me to proclaim my ignorance,' she said. 'But I have heard talk of the gambling hells where noblemen throw away a fortune, and often their very homes, on the turn of a card; of wild parties where men drink too much and women forget they are virtuous; of affairs of the heart which do not merit to be called by the sacred name of love. Oh, you think I am only being foolish and you are laughing because I am so simple and unversed in the ways of Society, but I cannot let you sneer at country folk and country ways and think yourself so vastly superior.'

She turned away from him then because the very passion of her words had brought her near to tears. She spurred her horse forward and to her surprise he made no attempt to catch her again but followed behind until she reached the front door of the house. There, grooms ran to the horses' heads; but when one would have helped Cleona dismount, Lord Raven was before him.

She would have liked to refuse his ministrations, but before she could speak he had reached up and putting his hands on her waist had lifted her from the saddle. She had a moment of confusion as she felt herself close in his arms, as his face was near to hers, and then her feet were on the ground.

'At least you have courage,' he said quietly, as he set her free, and for once she realized that he was not sneering.

6

CROSSING to France took five hours and the sea was exceedingly rough. Beryl retired immediately to her cabin, moaning that she was a bad sailor; but Cleona, wrapped in a warm cloak, stayed up on deck to have her last glimpse of the white cliffs of Dover and her first of the coast of France.

She felt excited and at the same time a little apprehensive. There was something almost awe-inspiring in the idea that she was leaving her own country and going abroad. She had heard such terrible tales of what might be discovered in the new France. She had in the past years seen the bloodstained horror of Gilray's cartoons; she had heard repeated the terrible stories that the *émigrés* had recounted after they had escaped with their lives, but with little else, to the sanctuary of Great Britain.

Now she was to find out the truth for herself and she suddenly felt very young and inexperienced and somehow completely inadequate to take in all that was happening and not miss so much of the wonder and excitement of it all.

She had tried to express her feelings to Beryl as they journeyed towards Dover in big, luxurious chaise which Lord Raven had put at their disposal for the journey.

'You are feeling the very consternation that I experienced when I first went to London,' Beryl smiled. 'I vow that I thought I would never get used to the gaiety and the elegance of the *beau monde*, but it soon became quite commonplace. In fact, within a few months I was declaring that I would swoon of *ennui*, complaining that the food at the great banquets I attended was not up to snuff and the wine unpalatable.'

Cleona laughed.

'And did you mean it?'

'Indeed no! 'Twas the fashionable thing to do and one must be in the fashion or die.'

'I am sure I shall never be fashionable,' Cleona said, 'even if I get the chance—which is not likely.'

'Gammon! You have the chance now,' Beryl insisted. 'When you appear with me in Rome, my dearest love, I swear that you will be all the rage.'

'Now it is you who is talking fustian,' Cleona said. 'No-one will notice me. After all, I am only coming as your companion.'

Beryl stretched out and took Cleona's hand in hers.

'You are coming as my closest friend, my sister and my guardian angel,' she said.

She was exaggerating as usual, but there was no doubting the warmth in her voice or the affection in her eyes. Cleona bent forward to kiss her.

'You are so kind to me that I feel like crying,' she said, then added more seriously: 'I would do anything for you, anything, Beryl, that would bring you happiness.'

'You give me that just by being with me,' Beryl replied; but although it was a pretty speech Cleona knew it was not true.

Beryl was not really happy. She looked entrancing, with her dark curls peeping from beneath her bonnet of chip straw, which was trimmed with ruby-red feathers. Her travelling cloak was also of ruby red, while the huge muff she carried in the fashionable manner was of rich brown sable.

Cleona felt that no man could help but adore Beryl at the very first sight of her, and she was not surprised when Lord Raven, raising her hand to his lips, had remarked that very morning:

'Your ladyship is in amazing good looks!'

He spoke in his usual cynical manner, but Cleona could not help but believe it had become so habitual with him that even when he was most sincere it was hard for any outsider to be aware of it.

Lord Raven elected to ride most of the way on horseback rather than travel in the chaise, comfortable though it was.

'I could not have borne to go abroad in Father's old berlin!' Beryl exclaimed. 'It is badly sprung and so heavy that one needs elephants rather than horses to drag it.'

Lord Raven's chaise was the very latest up-to-date type designed for travelling and the six horses which drew it made light work even over the worst roads and up the highest hills. Another coach, not so elaborate but equally well constructed, came behind carrying Swallow and Ellen, Beryl's abigails, his lordship's valet, Mister Truelove—the *Major-domo* and the luggage. There were two coachmen and three postilions to each coach, and Captain Ernshaw sat on the box of the first one so that he could direct the coachman on the right route.

They stayed several nights with friends of Beryl's until they reached Dover. It was Cleona's first insight into the gay social circle in which her friend was an uncrowned queen. She only wished these smart people, who all talked alike, expressed the same sentiments and laughed at the same jokes, were not so incomprehensible to her.

She had a feeling they were all acting a part. None of them dared be truly themselves or express their real sentiments about anything or anybody. They were the *bon ton*, and they must all think as the others thought and were secretly, Cleona was convinced, afraid of being left out of some particular magic circle which existed only in their own imagination.

'Are you enjoying yourself, my love?' Beryl asked more than once.

'I am entranced with everything,' Cleona assured her; and indeed she was thrilled with the big country mansions, the lavish hospitality, the new and unknown delicacies which were served at every table, the panorama of servants, possessions and wealth which was unrolled before her eyes at every place they visited.

Yet she felt that it was all a scene at the Playhouse and she alone was in the audience. Perhaps Lord Raven instinctively guessed what she was feeling, because one evening he strolled over to her where she sat a little apart in a great *Salon* which was filled with a laughing, chattering throng, and said quietly:

' "All the world's a stage".'

She smiled at the quotation.

'I am afraid there is no role for me, my lord.'

'Are you convinced of that or are you but pretending to be modest?'

'I never pretend,' Cleona replied simply.

'I believe that to be truth, incredible though it appears,' he remarked.

His eyes met hers for a moment and then he turned away and with his usual look of cynical indifference joined a table of faro at the far end of the room. They were the first words that Cleona had spoken alone with him since the night she had dined with him at Raven Royal and afterwards they had ridden home alone in the moonlight.

That night they had not been able to travel fast despite the light from the moon, because the ground was treacherous for their horses and led, at one point, through the dark purple shadows of a wood. At first they proceeded in silence; then, because Cleona felt she was being rude in not expressing her gratitude for what had been a far less frightening experience that she had anticipated, she said shyly:

'It is gracious of you, my lord, to accompany me to the Castle when it means that you must return this way again to reach your own home.'

'Are you suggesting I should abandon you to the mercy of any highwayman who might be lurking in the woods?'

Cleona laughed.

'Indeed, there are no highwaymen round here,' she said. 'The last one heard of was at Aylesbury over twenty miles away. The gentlemen of the road appear to have little interest in us. Perhaps it is because we have nothing worthy of their attention.'

'Are you speaking for yourself?' Lord Raven asked.

'Indeed I was,' Cleona answered. 'My brains are to let, for I forgot that you are wealthy and so is Lord Forncett. You have treasures that any robber would wish to acquire had he the opportunity. I have nothing, so I am safe.'

She raised her face as she spoke towards the sky, and the moonlight fell on her wide eyes and parted lips. There was a grace and delicacy about her movement which had an almost indescribable beauty, but Lord Raven only remarked dryly:

'Your innocence is refreshing!'

'My innocence?' Cleona asked, bewildered. 'I do not think I understand.'

'A beautiful woman who says she has nothing of which a man might rob her is either innocent or a *poseuse*.'

For a moment Cleona pondered his words and then the blood flew into her cheeks.

'I perceive your meaning, my lord,' she said in a low voice. 'My remark was a foolish one. I must try and think before I speak.'

'No!' Lord Raven said commandingly. 'It will spoil you. People who are truthful are rare—so rare that I can hardly remember when I last encountered one. Go on saying what you think.'

'So that it may amuse you, my lord?' Cleona asked with a sudden air of defiance.

She wondered why she must always feel so awkward and ill at ease with Lord Raven. It was true that all her life she had never pretended or tried to be anything that she was not. Now it seemed to her that this was a fault rather than a virtue, and all because the man who rode beside her was a cynic.

They said little else to each other until they reached the drive of the Castle. There were lights only in the upper windows, and Cleona, looking anxiously for any sign of coaches, said at length:

'I think the guests must have departed. We are safe.'

'Do you regret that you were unable to be present at the dinner party?' Lord Raven asked. 'Think what it means to have the chance of meeting the Prince of Wales—the future King of England.'

Cleona gave a little shudder.

'I have no wish to meet His Royal Highness,' she said. Then added quickly: 'I would not have you think that I am not a loyal subject of King George or that I do not revere the Prince for his great position. It is merely that I have no ambition to meet him at dinner or on any other social occasion.'

'Is that really true?'

She heard the amazement in Lord Raven's voice and turned to look at him.

'Why should it not be?' she asked.

'Because most young women in your position,' he said, 'spend their whole life scheming, fighting and intriguing to get themselves invited to Carlton House. It is their goal; their El Dorado; the Utopia of which so many dream and which so few attain.'

Cleona's laugh rang out.

'Well, at least I shall not add to their numbers,' she said, 'or take part in the competition for the Royal favour.'

'I wonder if you will say that in a year's time,' Lord Raven pondered.

'I am convinced that I shall think exactly the same as I do now,' Cleona answered. She hesitated, glanced up at him, and added: 'No, that is a nonsensical thing to say. In a year's time I shall have grown older and, I hope, wiser. Yet I cannot credit I shall ever find there is any wisdom or pleasure in running after people just because they are more important than one is oneself.'

They had reached the Castle by this time and from the shadows the grooms hurried to their horses' heads. Lord Raven dismounted but on this occasion Cleona was swifter than he was and had reached the ground before he could assist her.

'Thank you for your hospitality, my lord,' she said formally. 'Good night!'

He took her hand in his.

'Good night! And if you pray—which I have a fancy you still do—pray to remain as you are.'

She had no time to answer him before he had remounted his horse and without looking back had ridden away into the night. She stood watching him until he was out of sight and then she turned to go in through the front door.

What a strange man he was, she thought. She was afraid of him; she hated him; and yet at the same time she could not help being interested in him. He was different from anyone she had ever known before. And she was to think the same thing, not once but a thousand times, after they had started on their journey towards the Continent.

But once they had arrived in France Cleona had eyes for little but the countryside and the people who belonged to it. They need not have been anxious about their reception, because from the moment they came down the landing ladders it was obvious that the French citizens were ready to tumble over themselves to be friendly to the rich English milords.

Cleona was entranced by the appearance of the French men in cocked hats, tricolour cockades and gold ear-rings. The majority of them had long black whiskers and invariably carried a muff on their arms. The women, in their red camlet jackets and high aprons, with the long flying ribbons to their caps and wooden *sabots* with scarlet tufts, which made an incessant clatter on the cobbles, smiled at the visitors and proffered them gaily painted eggs in the market place or brought them coffee and long crisp rolls, which were more delicious than any bread that Cleona had ever tasted before.

The horrors with which Britain had been regaled were certainly untrue as regards Calais. There was no savagery, no villainous *sansculottes* and no unrelieved diet of frogs!

The peasants, and especially the children, looked well fed. But as they journeyed further inland, they came in sight of churches which were boarded up, the tombs desecrated and the windows smashed. There were, too, *chateaux*, houses and convents which all showed signs of revolutionary destruction.

It was strange for Cleona to find how little Beryl took account of what was passing the windows of the chaise

'Travelling is a dead bore,' she said more than once. 'It is the arriving that matters. Oh, how I long to be in Rome!

I am told that at the moment it is the gayest city in Europe.'

She slept a great deal of the time, or at least closed her eyes and gave the semblance of being unconscious of her surroundings. Looking at her face in repose, Cleona was struck more than once by the wistful droop of her lips, the look of sadness which was very obvious when she was not smiling animatedly.

She wondered more than once what the Marquis of Mountavon was like. Did Beryl really love him, or was it just a passing infatuation such as she had felt for her unfortunate husband? It was a question that Cleona could not answer.

They reached the hotel at Lausanne at which they had arranged to stay about five in the evening. It was a warm, clear night and the great Lake of Geneva rippled out blue and silver to where, in the distance, the snow-peaked Alps raised their heads against the sky.

It was so lovely that Cleona stood on the balcony of their sitting-room lost in the wonder and beauty of it and quite oblivious of anything that was happening around her.

Then, as she stood there divorced from reality and almost from herself, Beryl was suddenly beside her.

'Quick, come to my bedchamber. I must speak with you,' she whispered softly.

Brought back to reality, Cleona started, then walked from the balcony back into the sitting-room. Lord Raven was standing at a table pouring himself a glass of wine.

'I have asked Ernshaw to speak with me in here when he has finished superintending the stabling of the horses,' he said. 'I hope your ladyship has no objection.'

'No, no, of course not,' Beryl said. 'But at the moment I have need of my smelling salts, which Swallow, the tiresome woman, swears are lost. Come, Cleona, and see if you can find them for me.'

'Yes, of course,' Cleona answered, at the same time feeling shy at what was quite obviously a falsehood on Beryl's part.

She followed her from the room without looking at Lord Raven. Beryl closed the communicating door which led into her bedroom, and Cleona saw, to her surprise, that the languid young woman of the last few days had completely vanished. This was a Beryl with sparkling eyes, naturally pink cheeks and curls that bobbed excitedly against her white skin as she said:

'Oh, Cleona, something so exciting has occurred!'

'What is it?' Cleona asked.

'He is here—here in Lausanne. See, I have a letter from him.'

She drew a sheet of paper from between her breasts.

'Who is here and who is the letter from?' Cleona asked. 'I do not understand.'

'Don't be so blunt-witted, my love,' Beryl replied. 'Why, Ian, of course—my Lord Mountavon.'

'Here!' Cleona exclaimed. 'But, Beryl, I thought . . .'

'That I was sent away to be rid of him,' Beryl finished. 'I was! That is why I have been so unhappy, so miserable. I declare 'tis surprising my heart did not break. But now he has come here especially to see me. He must have ridden night and day to get ahead of us because he crossed the channel the day after we left England.'

'But, Beryl, you must not see him!' Cleona exclaimed. 'What would Lord Raven say?'

'A fig for Sylvester!' Beryl answered, then added more cautiously: 'He is, of course, not to know! Ian is at the hotel next to this. The gardens adjoin and he has begged me to meet him when dinner is over. You must help me, Cleona, for Swallow must not know what we are about. She is devoted to me but she wishes to see me wed to his lordship. An embroidered coronet is Swallow's ideal of happiness.'

'Oh, Beryl, are you wise?' Cleona asked. 'After all, he is . . . a married man.'

'I would not care if he had one hundred wives or as many concubines!' Beryl cried. 'I love him! Oh, Cleona, you are so young; you have never known love. You know not what it is to want a man; to ache for him; to lie awake at night whispering his name over and over again; to be assured that the only Heaven one is ever likely to reach is to be found within his arms.'

'Beryl! Beryl! What can I say? Think if you should be discovered.'

'I have thought of that,' Beryl answered more soberly, 'and I cannot run any risk of Sylvester coming upon us. That is why you must help me, Cleona. I have already thought of a plan.'

'What is it?' Cleona enquired.

'When dinner is over I shall say that I wish to retire. There is nothing strange in that—after all, we have had a long day. I shall then suggest that you and his lordship play piquet together.'

'Oh, no!' Cleona cried involuntarily.

'But, of course you must. It is of great import,' Beryl insisted. 'You see, Swallow must not think I am ready for bed or she will want to undress me. She knows perfectly well I would not undress myself—I never have. So I shall go into my chamber and tell her that we intend to sit late and that I will ring when I need her. She often waits in her own room when we are in London and I am out at a ball or an assembly, so she will not think it at all strange. Then I shall slip out into the garden and meet Ian. You must keep Sylvester amused until I return. When I get back I will whistle—the first few notes of a nightingale's song.'

'But . . . supposing you are gone a long time?'

'If it is an eternity, you must still hold him! Indeed it will not be hard to entertain Sylvester. He has been more pleasant and more amenable on this journey than I have ever known him.'

'Oh, but it will be exceedingly hard,' Cleona contradicted. 'I have no conception of what I can say to his lordship. He will be yawning after a quarter-of-an-hour of my company and be wishing for his bed.'

'That is the one thing that must be avoided,' Beryl said insistently. 'If Sylvester retires, his valet will be fetched from the stewards' room and Swallow will come in search of me. Please, Cleona, help me. You are the only person to whom I can turn.'

The pleading in her voice made Cleona respond to it instantly.

'I will help you in every possible way I can,' she said. 'But, oh, Beryl, I wish you wouldn't do this dangerous act.'

'Not see Ian when he has come all this way just for the sight of me! You must be crazed if you think I would hurt him by being so unkind—or, indeed, be so unkind to myself,' Beryl replied. 'Try and comprehend, Cleona, that I am happy—wildly. ecstatically happy. And it is exciting, is it not? An assignation in the darkness of the garden. What shall I wear? My loveliest gown—the gauze with pink ribbons—and that scarf edged with ermine which you thought so pretty when you tried it on last night.'

It was difficult not to be as stimulated at the prospect of the intrigue as Beryl was herself. Cleona found herself almost looking forward to the thrill of it all, until she remembered that her part was to be alone with Lord Raven and to keep him amused.

She dressed with unusual care, although she had nothing to wear but her only evening gown, which Swallow had made wearable by embroidering a design of *fleurs-de-lis* in silver thread over the stain on the skirt. Swallow was skilful with her fingers, but Cleona could not pretend that the dress did not look patched or that it could be compared with Beryl's exquisite new creations of which she had an inexhaustible collection.

She consoled herself, however, with the reflection that no one would notice her, and it was only when dinner was over and Beryl, who had been sparkling, laughing and irrepressibly gay all through the meal, suddenly sank back in her chair and half closed her eyes that Cleona felt herself grow cold and begin to tremble at the part she had to play.

'Lud, but I feel exhausted!' Beryl exclaimed. 'I wish our journey was at an end and that we had reached Rome.'

'I had hoped that the springing of my new chaise would not make it so tedious for you as might be expected,' Lord Raven said.

'It is certainly more comfortable than any vehicle that has carried me on previous occasions,' Beryl conceded. 'But all journeying is vastly fatiguing, and I long for a good night's slumber.' She stifled a little yawn.

'But I am not going to drag poor Cleona with me,' she continued. 'You must give her a game of piquet, my lord.'

'I shall be honoured if Miss Wickham will be my opponent,' Lord Raven said formally.

Cleona bit back the protest which rose to her lips. She longed to say that she, too, wished to retire. But because of her promise to Beryl she forced a smile to her lips and murmured that she would be delighted to play with his lordship, although she was afraid her skill was in no way equal to his.

'That is famous!' Beryl said, as the flunkeys cleared the remains of their meal from the sitting-room and set out the card table in its place.

'You are quite sure you do not wish to join us?' Lord Raven asked, and Cleona fancied there was something insistent in his voice.

'I crave your indulgence,' Beryl answered prettily. 'Morpheus awaits me!'

'In which case I must naturally waive my claim to your company,' Lord Raven replied courteously.

'Good night, my love!' Beryl said to Cleona, dropping a light kiss on her cheek, at the same time giving her hand a little warning squeeze.

'Good night, Beryl!' Cleona replied. 'Would you like me to come with you to your room?'

'No, indeed! Swallow will attend to me,' Beryl answered. 'Good night, my lord!'

She held out her hand to Lord Raven, who raised it perfunctorily to his lips.

'I am desolated that you must desert us,' he said. But his tone robbed his words of any emotion.

'If I stayed, I should only disgrace myself by falling asleep over the card table,' Beryl replied lightly.

As if conscious of the part she was playing she raised her fingers to her lips to stifle a yawn. Cleona felt that she was over-acting the part and to distract attention from her walked towards the card table.

'I hope you will find me an adequate antagonist, my lord,' she said as Lord Raven closed the door. 'My father taught me when I was small and we used to play together nearly every evening as I grew older.'

'We will begin with a trial game,' Lord Raven said, 'and then we will decide what the stakes might be.'

'Stakes?' Cleona questioned.

She went a little pale as she remembered how little money she had with her. Already she had parted with one of her precious sovereigns to Swallow—half as a present for making her the muslin dress which she wore every day and half for some ribbons Swallow had bought to trim a straw bonnet which Beryl had given her, having no further use for it.

'It is usual to gamble at piquet,' Lord Raven said.

'Yes, yes, of course!' Cleona agreed. 'I was only wondering what stakes your lordship would choose.'

'We will play our trial game first,' was the reply.

They played and Cleona, to her delight, found that she had won.

'I held good cards,' she said generously. 'My father always said that however skilled a player might be, the element of luck was needed to make one a winner.'

'Your father was undoubtedly a wise man,' Lord Raven replied. 'Now, shall we play for . . .'

He named a sum, but Cleona did not hear what it was. She thought for one moment that she heard a movement next door. Supposing, she thought anxiously, Swallow should come into the room to enquire what time her mistress wished to be called in the morning? Suppose she looked in the wardrobe, found that the fur-edged scarf had gone, thought that it had been stolen and came in search of Beryl to ask if by any chance she, herself, had taken it? Suppose . . . oh, Heavens! There were a hundred reasons why Swallow should discover that her mistress was not in the hotel and come hurrying to express her fears to Lord Raven!

Anxiety must have made her pale, for after a moment Lord Raven said:

'Are you feeling quite well?'

There was no further sound from Beryl's bedroom. Cleona drew a deep breath.

'Yes, indeed, my lord. Is it my turn?'

She played a card haphazardly and Lord Raven, looking at her across the table, said suddenly:

'I wonder what you are thinking about?'

'Why should you ask that?'

'I know not. But I have the impression that you are often thinking of different things from the average woman whose head is full of hats, gowns and gossip.'

'Seeing that I know so little of those three things it is not surprising that I do not think of them,' Cleona said.

Lord Raven's lips twisted.

'I stand rebuked,' he said.

'I apologize. I did not mean to be rude,' Cleona said hastily in a blushing confusion.

'You have still not answered my question.'

'Are you really asking me, my lord, what I think about?' Cleona enquired.

'I am! But I am also wondering if you will proffer me the truth.'

'If you sincerely desire the truth,' Cleona replied, 'I am thinking, at this moment, that it is surprising that you, my lord, should have noticed me enough to ask such a question.'

'That sort of answer is unworthy of you,' Lord Raven said sharply 'I am not thinking of this precise moment, but of your thoughts during the day. I noticed you at the carriage window this afternoon. We were passing through a dull part of the country without much to recommend it, and yet your eyes were alert and interested. You looked as if you were seeking something.'

'I suppose in a way that was what I was doing,' Cleona said. 'I am seeking experience, understanding, knowledge— of places, things . . . and people.'

'Myself, for instance?'

'No, no, of course not!' she exclaimed. 'I should never

attempt to understand you, my lord, or any of the people like you.'

'So truculent!' he said, raising his eyebrows. 'I wonder why? Is it pride or fear which makes you decide we are not worthy of your notice?'

'Neither—of course it is nothing like that,' Cleona said hotly. 'Why do you try to make me appear a prude and a prig? I only said I would not try to understand you, my lord, or your friends, because you are so much apart from the world I have always known and the things I have always loved and understood. I am not criticizing you. It would be unsuitable in the extreme, and I would not presume to do so. I only know that my place is not amongst those people whom you and Beryl call your friends.'

'Then whom are you trying to understand?' Lord Raven enquired.

Cleona drew a deep breath.

'I want to know and understand the ordinary people in the world,' she replied. 'Our own countrymen and those in other countries. The people in France for instance who have suffered both because of the Revolution and because of the war and are now trying to build up a new country on the ashes and desolation of the old.'

'And you think such knowledge and understanding will bring you happiness.'

'What is happiness?' Cleona asked. 'It means one thing to one person and something quite different to another.'

When she spoke she thought of her mother, wanting only Lord Vigor's title and position; of Beryl, risking her good name, her reputation, and future security to meet in the shadows of a foreign garden a man who was already married.

'What is happiness?' she asked again.

'I am inviting you to tell me that,' Lord Raven said.

Cleona stiffened. There was something in his voice which made her think that he was mocking her, leading her on to talk so that he could sneer and laugh at what he called her innocence, but which she believed was only her stupidity.

She was very conscious of the elegance of him, lying back in the high-backed velvet chair, his coat fitting his broad shoulders with an almost exquisite precision, his cravat falling in faultless folds over his white shirt, the diamonds on his fob glistening in the candlelight.

'My idea of happiness would have little in common

with your lordship's,' she said. 'Shall we return to our game?'

'If that be your pleasure!'

They played in silence and quite suddenly Cleona was consumed by a desire to beat him. She had a feeling that she must gain supremacy of the cards if of nothing else.

Concentrating, she forgot everything—the reason why she must hold her opponent's attention; Beryl, outside in the garden; Swallow, who might be moving in the bedroom; the clock, ticking its way slowly on the mantelpiece.

She thought only of the game and of how, by her wits, she might defeat and thus defy this man who disturbed her by his very presence. Game after game was dealt, played with a grim determination, discarded and another begun.

At last Cleona realized, with a sense of dismay which was out of all proportion to the circumstances, that Lord Raven was undoubtedly her superior. Try as she would, invariably he was more skilled and, at times, more lucky than she was.

Slowly, relentlessly, he drew ahead. And then suddenly, to her astonishment and delight, the situation changed. He made a mistake—only a small one, but it was enough for her to pounce on it. Again and again, it seemed to her that by a miscalculation or an error of judgment his lordship lost the trick.

The clock struck three o'clock, and almost at the same moment Cleona heard the sweet thrilling note of a nightingale. Lord Raven threw down his cards.

'You are too good for me,' he said, and Cleona's eyes were bright with triumph.

'I have won!' she cried a little breathlessly.

'Yes, indeed!' he replied. He made some brief calculations on the writing-block beside him. 'I am in your debt to the tune of twenty-one guineas.'

'Twenty-one guineas!' Cleona could hardly believe her ears.

'That is the sum—you might wish to check my conclusions, but you recall that you agreed the figure at which we were to play.'

'Twenty-one guineas!'

Cleona picked up the writing-block and stared at it. She had always been quick at accounts, having helped her father when he was alive with the moneys of the estate.

'My lord, I see at one moment during the game I owed you eighteen pounds,' she said at length.

'I dare say. That was before my luck changed.'

His voice was deliberately casual. But Cleona had risen to her feet.

'Do you realize that if we had stopped then I could not have paid you?'

'What does that signify? We did not stop and now I am the loser and you the winner.'

There was a moment's silence. Cleona was standing at the table. His lordship was still sitting, leaning back nonchalantly, one hand, ornamented with its plain emerald signet ring, resting on the arm of the chair. He appeared utterly at his ease and yet Cleona was aware that he was watching her.

There was something in his face, or was there some tension that she sensed beneath his assumption of ease, that made her suspicious? She stared at the writing-block, trying to recollect the moment when she began to win; recalling the cards he had played. A second later her eyes were blazing in her small face.

'You did it on purpose!' she cried. 'You let me win. You are far too expert to make the mistakes that you made unintentionally. I see it now, see exactly how it happened. And I thought I was being clever!'

'You are entirely mistaken, Miss Wickham,' Lord Raven said coolly. 'You won, and card debts, as you know, are a debt of honour. I must ask you to accept my losses.'

He drew his purse from his pocket and emptied it on the table. There was a clink of gold coins and then, from his breast pocket, Lord Raven drew out three five-pound notes and laid them beside the sovereigns.

'Do you really think I would accept your money?' Cleona asked, her voice low and passionate.

'You have got little choice in the matter,' Lord Raven said. 'As I have already informed you, I am in the habit of paying my debts. You won from me, and that is the end of the matter.'

'I won because you cheated,' Cleona said. 'Yes, I know that word shocks you,' she added, as his eyebrows were raised. 'Whatever your motive, it was still a cheat to lose deliberately when you knew you could win. Perhaps you meant to be kind; perhaps you were just ashamed of my shabby appearance and you thought that you would find an easy way to give me the money to buy better clothes.'

'Aren't you imagining a great deal?' Lord Raven asked coolly. 'You have accused me of cheating. I have not yet admitted the verity of that insult.'

'If I insult you, have you not insulted me?' Cleona

asked. 'It was a game to pass away the time; a game with which we might amuse ourselves; and you have made it an opportunity of foistering your charity upon me.'

'I think it was you who made it a battle of wits,' Lord Raven said quietly.

There was no gainsaying the truth of this and Cleona flushed, but she was too angry to be distracted by a side issue.

'I would rather die than take your money,' she declared.

'And I cannot keep what is not mine,' Lord Raven retorted. 'The money is yours—you have gained it.'

'Then I shall do with it what I did with the last guinea you foistered upon me,' Cleona stormed.

'What did you do with it, as a matter of interest?' Lord Raven enquired.

'I threw it after you,' Cleona answered. She saw the smile on his lips and hated him the more. 'It is easy to laugh. I should not have come on this journey with you. It was a mistake, but there was nothing else I could do. I had nowhere . . . to go. . . .'

She stopped, feeling the words choke in her throat and finding, to her horror, she was perilously near to tears. Lord Raven rose suddenly to his feet. He picked up the money, placed it in his handkerchief and tied it in a knot.

'We will, with your permission, give this much contested sum to the first convent we meet with on our journey where they tend the sick.'

His capitulation was so surprising Cleona could only stare at him with wide eyes.

'Does that meet with your satisfaction?' he enquired. And then, as she still did not answer, he smiled and said in a voice which was unexpectedly kind: ' 'Tis all right, you foolish child. You have won the battle.'

IT GREW warmer as they drove further south. And, indeed, the first heat of Italy was very welcome after the bitter cold, the snow and the biting winds of the Pass over the Alps.

At times Cleona felt that the horses would never reach

their destination as they strained up the twisting narrow paths with a sheer precipice on one side and the mountains peaking high above them on the other.

She and Beryl huddled beneath the fur-lined rugs, their hands thrust deep into their muffs, their feet on the footwarmers which were refilled with hot water at every stop. But even so their teeth chattered and their pretty faces were blue with cold by the time they reached an inn.

After they had entered Italy the journey became a trifle monotonous because at Beryl's insistence they were pushing on to Rome. Cleona regretted the haste because they stayed for such a short time in the various places through which they passed that she did not have time to view the sights.

They arrived at a town often late at night and left early in the morning; and one day came to seem very like another to Cleona as she sat beside Beryl, being rocked and bumped over the unkept roads, the clouds of dust rising so as almost to obscure her view from the window of the coach.

They saw little of Lord Raven. He preferred to ride whatever the weather and only occasionally could he be persuaded into handing over his horse to a postilion and sitting with them in the chaise to play cards or gossip.

In many ways Cleona could not help thinking that it was a good thing that he gave them so little of his attention, because Beryl had been depressed and unhappy ever since they left Lausanne and Lord Mountavon behind. She had taken no interest in anything, sitting wrapped in her thoughts or her memories and often being silent for hours on end or answering Cleona only in monosyllables.

'I know I am a dead bore, my love,' she said once apologetically. 'But to think that I am going further and further away from Ian plunges me into the very depths of despondency.'

'Have you no feeling of warmth for Lord Raven?' Cleona asked after a pause.

'Sylvester? Why, I am devoted to him,' Beryl answered. 'He is hard and ruthless, determined and obstinate—all things for which I have a partiality in a man. Don't fret, Cleona. I shall make my lord a good wife, even though he will not be able to ride roughshod over me as he does over everyone else.'

'Do you think it is fair on him . . . that you have an affection for someone else?' Cleona asked.

She hated his lordship and yet she felt that Beryl was

serving him a shabby trick in marrying him when her heart was given elsewhere.

'Fair on Sylvester!' Beryl's laughter rang out. 'My dearest, you have been reading too many of Miss Burney's novels. Sylvester does not expect me to love him wholeheartedly any more than he loves me.'

'Do you really mean that?' Cleona asked in astonishment.

'But, of a surety. His lordship lost his heart many years ago to the lovely Lady Jersey. You know she is one of the patronesses of Almack's, and I hope one day to take you there. Her beauty is unchallenged, and Sylvester, when he first came to London, was as crazed about her as if he were the merest country bumpkin—which I suppose in some ways he was.'

'What happened?' Cleona asked.

Beryl shrugged her shoulders.

'Lady Jersey grew tired of him—at least, that is the *on dit* of those who know all the gossip. I dare not speak of it to my lord himself. They say she favoured him for a little while and then cast him away and made fun of him, so that Sylvester turned cynic overnight. It must have been highly discomposing to his dignity.'

'That would account for the poor opinion he apparently has of our sex,' Cleona said slowly.

'How do you know that?' Beryl enquired.

'It is . . . it is what . . . I have sensed,' Cleona replied. 'But, oh, Beryl! How can you bear to marry him knowing that he loves someone else?'

'He doesn't,' Beryl answered. 'Raven loves no-one but himself. But he will make me a tolerable husband, just as I will make him a tolerable wife. And, dearest, he is so rich!'

Cleona felt there was nothing more she could say. There was the eagerness in Beryl's voice which was not unlike the tone in her mother's when she spoke of Lord Vigor. Why, she wondered a little bitterly to herself, did she not feel as these other women did? But she knew she could never care for money or position so that it decided whom she should wed.

'It is because I am greedy,' she told herself. 'I want so much more than gold and coronets. I want something so priceless that perhaps it is completely unobtainable—a man's heart.'

When they reached Milan, Beryl's spirits began to rise a little and she went with Cleona to see the Gothic Cathedral of white polished marble, and was appropriately impressed by the dark sanctity of the interior and the crowds of Capuchin monks with their shaven heads and long beards.

Soon they were on the road again, passing through Parma and Medina until they arrived at Bologna, where they stayed at a small and not particularly comfortable hotel, but which nevertheless was the best in the place.

The next day the sky was grey and clouded. It was thundery with almost torrential rain at times, and as they began to ascend the Apennines their carriage was tossed about like a ship in a storm. Beryl complained of a headache, and Cleona felt the heavy oppression of the atmosphere was enough to make everyone ache in some way or another.

They stayed that night at a small inn which did little to cheer them up. There were hard mattresses and there was little to eat except *pasta*—a sort of macaroni which Beryl had protested made her feel ill at the sight of it.

Cleona and Beryl shared a bedroom and when she came to undress them Swallow was shaking with fright, her face pallid with fear.

'Lud! What ails you, Swallow?' Beryl enquired. 'You look as if you had seen a ghost.'

'Not a ghost, milady. I would be less feared of something from the other world than what we are likely to find in this. 'Tis fortunate we'll be if we're not murdered in our beds this very evening.'

'Murdered in our beds!' Beryl exclaimed. 'What makes you afraid of that?'

'One of the postilions can speak this outlandish tongue, milady! And he has been telling us of the assassins who lurk in these mountains. Sometimes twenty or thirty of them are banded together to sally forth upon unfortunate travellers. Armed with stilettos they are, and afeared of no man—not even when he carries a loaded pistol!'

'You shouldn't listen to such tales, Swallow,' Beryl smiled. 'They are usually a hum! The postilion has been trying to make your flesh creep and from the colour of your countenance he has succeeded.'

Swallow's fears however were not assuaged and Cleona felt there was some justification for alarm as the previous day they had passed on the road nine men in chains who Captain Ernshaw explained were being taken to Milan to be charged with robbery and murder.

None of them slept very much, but the terrors of the

night were dissipated the following morning when the sun shone with an almost blinding brilliance and the low slopes of the mountains, which had seemed so bare and desolate the day before, were shown to be covered with wild flowers.

They had, however, unfortunately to spend another night in the Apennines, and once again it meant staying at a small obscure inn which was not much better than the one at which they had drawn up the previous evening. Captain Ernshaw had, however, been wise enough not to rely on the hospitality of such a place and had purchased chickens and eggs during the journey and also fresh vegetables and fruit.

His manservant was an excellent cook and when dinner was ready Beryl, who had developed a good appetite during the drive, declared that they would not have dined better in Carlton House. Because the evening was fine, the rough tables with their coarse linen cloths, the hard chairs and the carpetless floor seemed amusing and made their meal a picnic instead of a penance.

Beryl changed from her dusty travelling gown into a robe of pale pink satin which made the inn-keeper's wife and pretty Italian girl who waited on them stare at her wide-eyed and open-mouthed. Cleona had only an inevitable white muslin, but at least it was clean and fresh; and when she had drunk a glass of the light golden wine which Lord Raven poured out for her she forgot her appearance and joined in the general talk and laughter.

During dinner Beryl flirted with him in a gay, inconsequential manner which seemed to keep him amused and which made Cleona watch her with undisguised admiration. There was no one more fascinating when she pleased, and Beryl, glancing up at his lordship with her long dark eyelashes flickering over her bright eyes and her red mouth pouting provocatively at something he had said, made Cleona realize suddenly that they were a betrothed couple and she an outsider.

Because she felt they wished to be alone, she made an excuse when dinner was finished and walked out into the garden of the inn.

They had dined early and the evening air was warm while the sun was sinking in a blaze of crimson glory. Cleona felt suddenly very happy. This was a new world and she was here to explore it. There was so much for her to see, so much for her to learn, and she felt for a moment as if the very secrets of the universe were awaiting her discovery of them.

She wandered out through the little garden and on to the mountainside. Even the trees were strange and different from those with which she was familiar in England. She stooped to gather some flowers and they were of a variety she had never seen before, their colours so vivid and beautiful that she stared at them with delight.

She wandered on, content with her thoughts, thrilled with everything she saw, the beauty of a dark cypress silhouetted against the sky making her draw in her breath in rapture at the poetry of it.

It was then as she turned from contemplation of the tree that she saw a man standing watching her and felt suddenly alarmed. She had come too far from the inn. His clothes were stained and torn; round his waist he wore a broad sash in which was stuck a number of lethal weapons. A wide-brimmed hat was pulled low over his forehead and his gold ear-rings glistened in the setting sun as he moved towards her.

She looked back over her shoulder in the direction of the inn and as she did so saw that another man was approaching from behind her and yet another from either side. In a sudden panic she realized her danger!

It was too late! She would have run away, but the men closed in upon her. As two of them seized her arms she screamed, but almost instantly a heavy hand, coarse and brutal, was laid across her mouth.

'Come quietly, *Signorina*, and we will not hurt you,' one of the men said.

Cleona could speak Italian and although the dialect was strange and the voice uneducated, she managed to understand him. Twisting her mouth free of his hand, she asked:

'Where are you taking me?'

'That you must not see,' came the answer. 'But do not call for help, *Signorina*, or we must hurt you to make sure of your silence.'

It was no use screaming, Cleona thought. It was unlikely that Beryl or Lord Raven, intent on their conversation in the sitting-room of the inn, would hear her, while the servants would be in the kitchen where any noise from outside would be drowned by the clatter of saucepans and the shrill voices of the landlord and his wife.

'I will not call out,' she said quietly.

'That is wise,' one of the men said. 'It would be bad fortune to have to silence so pretty a *Signorina*.'

He looked at her with a lustful glint in his eye which filled Cleona with a terror such as she had never known before, and then from behind someone put a handkerchief over her face and tied it behind her head.

'Now you come with us,' a man said. 'And keep your mouth closed or we will gag you as well.'

He lifted her off her feet as he spoke and it was with a tremendous effort that Cleona forbore to cry out. She was carried a little way, then set on the back of some animal. She guessed by its gait that it was a mule, and she could only cling blindly with both hands to the saddle and be thankful that the men were on foot so that they proceeded no faster than a walking pace.

She knew that they were following a twisting and turning path, and she had the impression they were moving between and under overhanging trees. There was a rustle of dried leaves beneath the mule's feet, the creaking of a broken bough, a sudden whisper amongst the leaves as a soft wind rose.

Cleona wondered how long it would be before she was missed. Beryl and Lord Raven were talking, it might be hours before they enquired after her and then they could suppose she had gone to bed. The only blessing was that she and Beryl were sleeping together so that when the latter went upstairs she was bound to see that the room was empty, the bed unslept in.

What would they do then? Cleona asked. What ransom would these men ask? She was well aware she had been captured for ransom. It was an easy way to extort money from travellers and she had heard of it happening before. She supposed Lord Raven would pay the sum whatever was asked. It appeared, she thought bitterly, as if the question of money must always arise between them—starting with that golden guinea that he had pressed into her hand and which she had flung after him in her rage.

On, on, the mule carried her. They must have ccme from the shelter of the trees, for suddenly the wind was bitterly cold and Cleona shivered in her thin dress, with so little beneath it to keep her warm.

She was just wondering how long she could go on without protesting to her captors when the mule was jerked to a standstill and someone lifted her down from its back.

With her feet on the ground, she stood uncertainly, afraid to move because her eyes were blinded, but once again a man picked her up in his arms. He smelt of sweat, garlic and rank tobacco, so that, sickened, she turned her face away from him. And then after a few seconds she was on her feet again and now the bandage was taken from her eyes.

Surprisingly, because she had expected a cave, she found herself in a room. It was unfurnished save for a table, but there was a fire burning brightly on the hearth and a number of men standing around. The light, except for what seeped through the dirty, broken windows, came from three candles stuck in the necks of bottles.

For a moment after wearing a bandage it was difficult to see clearly; then as her vision cleared she perceived that the men who faced her were villainous desperadoes, of the type Cleona could well believe who made their livelihood by murdering and robbing unfortunate travellers.

There was one man who seemed to her to look even worse than the rest. He was taller and more swarthy in appearance, he wore a greater profusion of weapons in his waistband and his ear-rings were richer and of better quality than those worn by the others. It was obvious by his attitude and by the attention given him by those who stood near him that he was their leader.

'Why have you brought me here?' Cleona asked, breaking the silence which somehow seemed oppressive and feeling that her own voice was thin and ineffectual as it echoed round the empty room.

'You are beautiful, *Signorina*, and rich,' came the answer. 'Your friends will pay generously for your safe return. And if they will not—it would be sad for so charming a *Signorina* to die. We all have to die some time, but what a waste when one is so young and has had so little time to enjoy life!'

There was something in his voice which told Cleona this was no idle threat. She wanted to cry out in horror, even to beg for mercy, but pride kept her silent, her chin held high.

'You will write a note,' he added.

'A note?' Cleona asked.

'*Si*. To the friends with whom you are travelling. The English milord—is he your sweetheart?'

'No, he is not,' retorted Cleona. 'I am but a companion and of no import. If you ask too much, the English lord will not think I am worth such a ransom. They will drive away and leave me here, and then you will get nothing. A dead body is not very saleable, even in Italy.'

She could see that her words had some effect on the men standing around her even though they found it hard to follow her more cultured Italian and the phrases she used. Several of them began to murmur amongst themselves, but the leader said:

'You are no servant. The servants travel in another carriage. You are a friend of the lady and the milord. They will not abandon you; it is not the English way to desert their friends.'

Cleona felt there was nothing more she could say. Obediently she turned towards the table. A piece of dirty writing-paper was set down in front of her; a quill pen and an ink bottle containing some rather pale, watery ink was also provided.

'What do you wish me to say?' she asked.

'Tell the milord you are a prisoner. Tell him that unless a ransom of five hundred scudi is paid immediately to the man who brings the note, your life will be forfeit. Make it clear; do you understand?'

The bandit's eyes met Cleona's. She stared at him for a second and then began to write. She wondered what Lord Raven would think of her letter.

My Lord,

I have been Captured by some Horrible, Dirty and Brutal Bandits. There are sixteen of them in the Room as I write. We are in a House, but I cannot describe where for I was Blindfolded while I was brought here. They demand Five Hundred Scudi as a Ransom and threaten me with Death if it is not given to the Man who brings this.

It is with the Deepest Regret, my Lord, that I must write this letter because they Force me to do so. I can only Promise that if your Lordship is Gracious enough to Rescue me from these Assassins, I will do everything in my power to return to you any Moneys you expend on my Behalf.

I remain, your Lordship's most Obedient Servant,
Cleona Wickham.

She signed her name with a little flourish; then, as one of the bandits brought her some sand, she looked towards their chief.

'The letter is written.'

'Read it to me.'

'No!' Cleona replied. 'It is a private letter for the eyes of my friend. I have obeyed your instructions. I have asked him to give the man who carried this five hundred scudi.'

To her surprise he did not insist on her reading the letter.

'Very well,' he said. He took the letter from the table, shook the sand from it and folded it. 'The name of the milord,' he said, pointing to the folded letter.

Cleona inscribed, *The Right Honourable The Earl of Raven*, in her small, rather neat handwriting; and then, as the letter was taken from the table, the head bandit gave an order.

'Tie her up,' he said.

Before Cleona could move, her hands were bent behind her back and her wrists tied together with a rope. Someone made some other suggestion in a low voice. She did not understand what he said, but the head bandit replied angrily as if he were incensed at the idea:

'No! No! She is our prisoner. We have no use for foreign women.'

He gave a further command and Cleona found herself being half led, half hustled out of the room and up a rickety staircase to the floor above. She could see now that the house was derelict. It must once have belonged to some noble or well-to-do land-owner, but it had been abandoned, perhaps because its isolated position in the mountains made life too hard and too lonely. And yet once the house had possessed a certain dignity, and an architectural beauty. Now it was only a shambling wreck of what it had once been and the hiding place of robbers.

Cleona was pushed into a room on the first floor. It was covered in dust and the floor could not have been swept for months. There was a heavy wooden bedstead in one corner, but nothing else.

The men who had taken her up the stairs left her in the centre of the room, when one went to the window, from which the panes of glass had long since broken away, and slammed to the wooden shutters. The other set down on the mantelshelf the candle he carried and then kindled a fire in the grate on the ashes of one long since spent.

'You will be warm enough now, *Signorina*,' the man who had shut the window said. He smiled at her as he spoke and instinctively she backed away from him. 'Give us a kiss for our pains,' he said ingratiatingly.

'If you touch me I shall scream,' Cleona threatened. 'I will scream for your leader. He knows that you should treat a prisoner with decency.'

She was so virulent in her protest that the man stepped back and looked apprehensively over his shoulder as if he thought his leader might be watching from the doorway.

'Keep your tongue still, hell-cat! I was only trying to be friendly,' he said surlily, and he and the other man went from the room.

They locked the door behind them, also putting a heavy bolt across it. Cleona smiled wanly at the sound of the great piece of wood falling into the socket. They must think her very strong if they imagined she could escape from such a prison single-handed with her hands tied behind her back!

She tried to work the rope loose and after a time succeeded in loosening one strand. Her wrists were chafed and the skin broken and bleeding before finally she managed to free herself. She threw the rope down on the floor and went towards the fire. She was very cold and now at last the full terror of what she was experiencing made her feel weak and faint. She held out her hands towards the flames.

How long she crouched there she did not know. Down below she could hear the brigands laughing and talking. She wondered how long the man who carried the letter would take to get to the inn and return with the money. Would Lord Raven be angry when he received her note? She was being both a nuisance and an embarrassment to him, and yet what else could she do?

She felt very weak and helpless, and because the ignominy of her position was almost too intense to be borne she rose to her feet and walked across the room to the shuttered window. If she looked out, she wondered, would she see the man returning in triumph carrying the spoils?

A sudden thought struck her. Supposing Lord Raven gave him the money and even then they refused to let her go? Perhaps he would come with the man, and if that happened might not he step into the same sort of trap as had resulted in her being captured?

She must warn him! Cleona began to unfasten the shutters. They were old and dilapidated and creaked noisily as she pulled them open. She held her breath and listened, but the rough voices below had drowned the sound.

She looked out. Dusk had fallen and for a moment her eyes could see nothing. Then, as she grew accustomed to the twilight, she could see the trees silhouetted against a pale, translucent sky, the first evening star shining, a pinprick of shimmering gold over a distant mountain peak.

It was at that moment she heard a low whistle. Very low, no louder than an indrawn breath, and yet she heard it. She looked down. She could see nothing below her window but shadows, and then the sound came again and she saw the outline of a man. She would have drawn back, thinking she was being watched by one of the brigands, but she heard her name, hardly above a whisper and yet undoubtedly her name: 'Cleona!'

She bent forward. There was no mistaking who stood there. She could see his shoulders, square on each side of his white cravat; she could see his face turned up to hers. And then, almost before she could realize her gladness because he had come, he had started to climb.

It seemed to her like a miracle that anyone so big and so habitually staid and dignified in his movements could scale up the side of a house; and yet in the crumbling brickwork and where the plaster had fallen away he somehow found a foothold.

She could watch his head coming up towards her, and then, as she held her breath in suspense, his hands had reached the window-sill. A moment later he had pulled himself up and while she backed away, staring at him with eyes which seemed to fill her whole face, he climbed into the room.

His coat was dusty; there was a tear in the tight-fitting neatness of his breeches; but otherwise he appeared his usual imperturbable self and there was even that cynical twist at the corners of his lips.

'You have come! I cannot believe you have come!'

Cleona reached out towards him with trembling hands, and only when he took them in his own could she be sure that he was really there.

'Yes, I have come,' he answered. 'Did you expect me to abandon you to the tender mercies of your kidnappers?'

'Have you brought the money?'

'What money?' he enquired.

'The ransom, of course!'

'So they have asked for it already, have they? It is what I expected.'

'But, I do not understand.'

'Does it signify?' he enquired. 'Come, we had best be out of here.'

'But how?' She glanced towards the locked door. 'There are at least sixteen of them below.'

'I thought there might be something of the sort. They are

too cowardly except to hunt in numbers. Perhaps it would be best if we did not disturb the gentlemen.'

'Then how . . . ?' Cleona began.

But Lord Raven had already turned again to the window. He gave a low whistle; something came whizzing out from below. He caught it deftly and dragged it into the room. It was a thick rope. Cleona watched him wide-eyed as he attached it to the heavy bedpost, then linked it round the iron catch of the shutters and tested his strength against it.

'It will hold us,' he said. 'But perhaps it would be best if we descend one at a time. Hold tightly on to the rope. Ernshaw is waiting below to catch you.'

Cleona looked out of the window. It was not a very big drop and yet she knew she could not face it. Instinctively she turned towards Lord Raven.

'I cannot,' she whispered. 'I am afraid.'

He smiled as if at a child.

'Afraid?' he questioned. 'Yet you can be so fierce at times—so brave when it comes to words.'

'I know,' Cleona said miserably. 'And yet I am afraid to climb down that rope alone.'

She was ashamed even as she said it. She, who would ride a horse, however fresh, however spirited, who would go about alone in the dark, who would defy Lord Raven himself, was now trembling because she must step on a window-sill and trust her safety to a rope. Perhaps it was because she had been through so much already, perhaps because she was unnerved to the point when she was prepared to rely entirely and absolutely on the man who had come to her rescue.

'Hold on to me,' Lord Raven said, 'and we must trust it will hold us both.'

For one moment she did not understand what he intended to do. She gave a little gasp as his arms enfolded her, and then she was clinging on to him with all her strength, her eyes hidden against his shoulder, as, with one arm encircling her so that both hands could reach the rope, he moved cautiously over the window-sill and then slithered down hand over hand slowly but surely to the ground below.

Captain Ernshaw was waiting for them. Directly Lord Raven reached the ground and Cleona stood on her own feet, he hurried her away quietly and in silence into the shadows of the trees, Lord Raven following a few paces behind and covering their retreat. Picking up her skirts, Cleona scrambled over the rough ground, struggling to keep pace with Captain Ernshaw's quick strides, conscious that her heart was pounding, that her head felt curiously light.

'The horses should be here any moment, my lord,' she heard Captain Ernshaw say as she tumbled over a rough stone.

She felt a pain shoot through her foot and then, as if it was the last straw which must break her, she heard herself moan and knew that she could go no further. There was darkness creeping up from the ground into her mind, a darkness closing down upon her from above. She felt herself falling and then, at that very moment, was saved from the fall itself.

Someone picked her up in his arms. It was the same strong arms that had carried her to safety. She felt there was no need to struggle any longer. She was safe! She knew that, even as the darkness swallowed her up and she lost her last coherent thought in unconsciousness.

8

CLEONA felt as if she came to the surface from the depths of the sea. Slowly and painfully the mists cleared from her mind and a little gasp came from between her lips as she opened her eyes. She was being carried by two strong arms.

''Tis all right,' a voice said, surprisingly kindly. 'You are safe.'

'I . . . I was . . . afraid,' she stammered. And then, after a moment, as consciousness and memory returned more clearly still, she added: 'I . . . I can walk. It might be quicker.'

'The horses are just ahead of us.'

She felt too weak to protest further, and there was, indeed, something curiously comforting in being held so closely and so securely by someone who, even though she hated him, she could still respect.

She had never understood before how weak and helpless a woman could be when confronted by violence. She realized now what an effort it had been to control her terror and her sense of panic when she had faced the brigands and known herself utterly defenseless.

She knew, too, there were worse things in the world than dying. She had seen the looks the men gave her. She was not so innocent that she could not sense the lewd thoughts behind the bold staring of their dark eyes, the movement of their thick sensual lips. Here, in the arms of the man she had defied and battled against, was security.

The horses and their grooms were waiting near a clump of olive trees. Lord Raven set Cleona on the saddle and then, to her surprise, sprang up behind her. She would have protested, but he said quietly:

'It is only a short way and we have to hurry.'

She felt from the tone of his voice that she was nothing more to him than an inconvenient obstacle to their progress; and so, abashed, she was silent, letting herself lean back in the shelter of his arms and, when his horse gathered speed, putting one hand on his shoulder to hold herself even more securely.

She still felt a little dazed and when finally they reached the lighted parlour of the inn it was an effort to answer Beryl, who ran towards her with cries, both of relief and curiosity.

'Dearest love, what has happened to you? I have been in a tremble ever since Sylvester left,' she declared, helping Cleona to a chair.

'Give her a glass of brandy,' Lord Raven commanded.

'Cleona is as pale as if she had seen the Devil himself!' Beryl exclaimed. 'My poor love, what did they do to you?'

Cleona made no effort to answer until she had taken the glass of brandy which Lord Raven poured out for her and lifted it to her lips. She sipped it and then, as the fiery spirit made her choke, she would have set it down had he not crossed to her side and said commandingly:

'Drink more than that—'tis what you need.'

'No, I . . .' she began, only to meet his eyes and find it too tiring to fight with him on such a small matter. Instead she obeyed, finished the brandy and after a few seconds felt immeasurably better because she had done so.

'Now, tell us what occurred,' Beryl begged.

'One moment,' Lord Raven interrupted. 'I have ordered the coaches to be brought round and the maids to repack everything as speedily as possible.'

'We are leaving!' Beryl exclaimed in surprise. 'You mean

that you think ... the robbers might attack us, here in the inn?'

'I am taking no chances,' Lord Raven replied. He walked towards the door, then turned and smiled at Cleona. 'We have defeated them once. I have a fancy not to tempt fate too far.'

'I must possess my soul in patience then!' Beryl sighed, speaking to Cleona. 'Although, I declare, I shall die of curiosity. You sit quietly, my dearest, while I tell Swallow to bring down our cloaks and bonnets.'

Cleona was glad to obey. For a moment she let her head rest wearily against the back of the chair. It seemed to her as if she could still feel the movement of the horse beneath her, the strength of Lord Raven's arms round her slight body. Then, with a start, she looked up to find he had come back into the room.

'The horses are being harnessed,' he said in answer to her look of enquiry. 'And we have a prisoner who will accompany us.'

'The man who came with the note?' Cleona questioned.

'The same,' he replied. 'We will take him to Florence and hand him over to the military. I shall insist that they send troops to deal adequately with that particular nest of assassins.'

Cleona said nothing for a moment and then, after a pause, she forced the words to her lips.

'I must thank you, my lord,' she said at length in a low voice, 'for coming to my rescue.'

'It was fortunate that Beryl and I saw you abducted.'

'You saw!' Cleona exclaimed.

'Yes, indeed! We came into the garden and had a sight of you walking on the hillside; Beryl suggested that we join you. We are unfortunately still a long way behind when we saw the men converging on you. I realized what was happening and taking Beryl back to the safety of the inn I collected Captain Ernshaw and we followed you as swiftly as we could after giving instructions that the horses and grooms should meet us a certain spot which we considered the most likely direction in which you had been taken.'

'I am indeed thankful you came when you did, my lord,' Cleona said. 'I am deeply in your debt. But ... supposing you had not seen me taken prisoner ... what then?'

He smiled at that.

'Were you afraid that the price of ransom would seem too high,' he asked, 'even though you offered to repay it?'

Cleona blushed.

'So you have read my note?'

'I have it in my pocket,' he answered. 'I consider the robbers under-estimated your worth.'

'I do not doubt you are laughing at me!' Cleona exclaimed. 'Yet is was not very funny at the time.'

'I am devilish sure of it,' he said in a different tone. 'And if you must thank me, may I congratulate you on being exceeding brave?'

'There was nothing I could do but obey the robbers' commands,' Cleona said simply. 'But I was not brave. In truth, I am ashamed to remember how fearful and cowardly I felt inside myself.'

'Isn't that the meaning of true bravery?' Lord Raven asked. 'To feel afraid but not to show it?'

'I do not think I have ever been so glad to see anybody as I was to see . . . you standing below in the darkness,' Cleona said and there was a little tremble in her voice.

' "A familiar enemy is often better than a strange one",' he said, quoting an old proverb, and Cleona dropped her eyes before his, feeling embarrassed at the meaning behind his words.

He would have said something more but at that moment Beryl came into the room.

'Everything is ready,' she announced. 'Although Swallow is determined that we are to be murdered on the road and her body left in a ditch.'

'I see very little difference from Swallow being murdered in her bed,' Lord Raven retorted. 'Let us waste no more time.'

Beryl put Cleona's cloak around her shoulders and she fastened it at the neck, but she did not put on her bonnet. Instead she carried it by the ribbons and followed Beryl across the yard to the coach. The horses were tired, but they had been fed and had a short rest, so they set off at a good pace.

Cleona could not help but feel frightened as they drew away from the lights of the inn and out on to the darkness of the road. The lanterns gave very little light and the moon had not yet risen in the sky. Supposing, she thought to herself, the robbers were now lying in ambush for them? By this time they would have discovered her escape and perhaps realized what had happened to the man who had carried the note. The way was narrow and twisting, rising sharply at one moment merely to descend equally sharply a few minutes later.

'Pray tell me all about it,' Beryl begged.

She settled herself comfortably in the coach. Cleona obliged, but at the same time her thoughts were continually distracted by what was happening outside. She had heard Lord Raven say that he would ride ahead to guide the way, and now she wondered if this were wise. What if he were killed? Suppose a shot from one of the robbers knocked him from his horse before they attacked the coachmen and the postilions? It would be easy in that way to capture both coaches. What would happen to Beryl and herself if that happened?

It was hard to listen to Beryl's exclamations and excitement over her imprisonment. That had been bad enough, but there might be worse horrors ahead! And then, as the first quarter-of-an-hour passed and then another, and finally an hour had ticked by since they had left the inn, Cleona began to relax. If the robbers had the intelligence to organize an ambush, they would have run into it by now.

She felt relief seeping over her. She found at last that she could concentrate on what Beryl was saying. She found that her breath no longer felt constricted in her breast and she could lie back against the soft cushions of the carriage and remember the pain of her chafed wrists.

She must have slept a little later, because she awoke to find dawn streaming palely through the windows and the carriage moving very slowly behind the tired horses. When they stopped, it was to find themselves in a lovely valley where there was a monastery shaded by tall, dark cypress trees and cowled monks wandering along an avenue of majestic cedars. Beside it was a hostel where travellers could be accommodated, and here they found accommodation and a shelter and rest for their horses.

They had no more adventures before they reached Rome. Florence was lovelier than Cleona had ever dreamed, with its wide river, its bridges besprinkled with tiny shops, its high towers and twisting mediaeval streets.

But Lord Raven wished to push on and although Cleona was anxious to see more of the town and longed to spend days visiting the picture galleries and churches, they were once more on the road. Finally, as the sun was sinking, touching with a saffron light the hills known to the Caesars, they came to Rome.

There were the arches, domes, towers and palaces with their memories of the splendour and genius of Popes, Emperors and scholars; the narrow streets which had echoed with the tread of human feet for more than two thousand years; and a people whose history held passion, cruelty, folly and everlasting renown.

Afterwards Cleona tried to remember her first impressions of the Eternal City. She could recall most vividly a picture of slender cypresses dark against the sky, terraces of silvery olives, the sound of falling fountains and nightingales singing under the stars. It had a beauty that was almost beyond being captured by the senses, she decided. One must feel it rather than see it.

Beryl's spirits revived enormously when once they had arrived at the villa and found that their coming had been anticipated by the nobility of Rome. There were hundreds of bouquets and baskets of roses and orange blossom, carnations and mignonette, with cards of welcome attached. There was also a large pile of visiting cards which were added to day by day until they formed quite formidable proportions.

Their hostess, the Dowager Lady Raven, was quite different from anything Cleona had expected. Exceedingly beautiful, with almost white hair, a clear complexion and a slim, willowy figure, Lady Raven was exceptionally artistic, bored by Society and even less interested in sport.

'I feel at home here,' she told Cleona as she and Beryl exclaimed over the beauties of the villa and its exquisite contents.

Set high above the town, it had a garden of surpassing beauty, with a lake, a long avenue of dark ilex leading to vistas of temples and arcades with tall cypresses and parasol pines. There were flowers which left one almost intoxicated with their fragrance; there were blossoms which vied in beauty the statues which decorated the terraces.

Inside the villa was as lovely as its surroundings. Damask and painted walls adorned it and high ceilings decorated with rubicund gods, goddesses, and small, fat, winged cupids. To enter Lady Raven's home was to step out of the present into the classical past, and in her draped gowns and with her graceful movements she seemed to belong, as surely as her surroundings, to the days of Rome's greatness.

She greeted her son as if he were a friend whom she had not seen for so long that she had almost forgotten his very existence. She kissed Beryl and then turned to Cleona and held out her hand.

'Who is this exquisite creature?' she asked. 'She might have been the model for one of my statues. Indeed, she is very like the one of Aphrodite which stands in the library.'

Cleona felt embarrassed, but Lord Raven laughed.

'That is the sort of compliment I have never known you pay another woman, Mamma,' he said. 'Are you being influenced by the extravagances of the Italians?'

Lady Raven smiled.

'They are so much more agreeable to live with,' she answered, 'than the uncouth insensitiveness of the English.'

She was very kind to her visitors, doing her best to make them comfortable; but Cleona felt as if in reality they interrupted Lady Raven's communion with the beauty and history with which she had surrounded herself.

She did, however, entertain in her house many of the Italian nobility, and she made it clear that to amuse her son and his guests she had invited a younger and gayer set than those who usually accepted her hospitality.

Cleona felt her heart sink at the idea that they must be constantly at dinner and luncheon parties, balls and assemblies. She had been dreading this moment ever since Beryl's chatter in the carriage had made it very clear what festivities she expected to be waiting for them in Rome.

Cleona realized only too clearly that with no smart clothes to give her confidence she would cut a very poor figure amongst the elegant and luxurious people who spent their time hurrying from one social gathering to another. Desperate, she turned to Swallow with her troubles.

'I have two pounds ten shillings left, Swallow,' she said. 'What can we buy with that?'

'Very little, Miss,' Swallow said uncompromisingly, 'except that I am told materials are cheap enough in Rome.'

'Perhaps we could purchase some more white muslin?' Cleona questioned timidly, afraid to suggest that Swallow should make it up for her.

'We can get that at any rate,' Swallow replied. 'But I declare, Miss, 'tis a shame that you should not have something more modish. Her ladyship was saying only last night that for all the airs and graces Napoleon Bonaparte is giving himself in Paris, Rome is still one of the smartest capitals in the world.'

'At least I shall not need anything thick or warm,' Cleona said, determined to look on the bright side of the situation.

It was, indeed, very hot in Rome. By the middle of the day even the cobbles in the streets were hot to the feet, and after the midday meal everyone retired for a *siesta* with the shutters closed and the sun-blinds drawn so that the rooms had a cool, green, misty look as if one floated under water.

''Tis my appearance in the evening that worries me the

most,' Cleona confided to Swallow as they set off for the shops after breakfast, leaving Beryl asleep in the villa.

'One gown might be enough in some places, Miss,' Swallow retorted, 'but certainly not in Rome.'

'Yet how can I contrive another?' Cleona asked miserably.

Swallow suddenly clutched her arm.

'Look, Miss,' she said. 'What about us buying a ticket for a lottery? I was told when I was in England that they are worth the expenditure of a shilling or so. A lady's maid was telling me how she won quite a comfortable sum of money on only one ticket. What do you say, Miss, that we chance our good fortune?'

'I should say we would be only wasting what little we have,' Cleona answered; but aware of Swallow's excitement and hating to damp it, she went with her to the small kiosk where a pretty girl, dressed in a gold brocaded petticoat and scarlet stockings, with her hair braided with coloured ribbons and bunches of flowers, was striving to attract the attentions of passers-by.

In her soft Italian Cleona asked the price, and because Swallow was so keen on the gamble she finally bought a ticket for the lady's maid and one for herself. As she parted with her money she thought regretfully of the ribbons that it might buy, but she felt that it was in part a repayment to Swallow for all her kindness.

Later, when they returned to the villa with half a dozen yards of white muslin, Cleona told Beryl of their purchase.

'Oh, Cleona, how exciting!' Beryl exclaimed. 'I pray that you gain a prize. I shall buy some tickets this morning—dozens of them. I have always longed to win a lottery.'

'You will have to make haste,' Cleona answered. 'The girl told us this one was to be drawn tonight. They have been selling the tickets for over a fortnight and this is the last day.'

'We will send a footman to get them right away,' Beryl said, and producing several pounds from her purse ordered the lackey to change it into Italian currency and spend it all on lottery tickets.

'I declare that is a shameful waste of money,' Cleona said reproachfully. 'You could have purchased something of value or given the money to the poor.'

'I will give the poor one-tenth of my winnings,' Beryl retorted. 'Pray do not be prosy, Cleona, it doesn't suit you.'

Cleona laughed at the accusation.

'Not prosy, but frugal, because I have to be.'

Impulsively Beryl put her arms round Cleona and kissed her.

'I am only teasing,' she said. 'You are so sweet, dearest, and I love having you with me.'

'And I love being here,' Cleona said. 'Do let us visit some of the sights. I want to see everything.'

Beryl agreed good-naturedly. She was not really interested in anything except the amusement which came from meeting new people and of being acclaimed a success. Italian Society was at her feet first because she was an English beauty and secondly because everyone wanted to meet the future wife of the Earl of Raven.

To please Cleona they set off in the elegant open carriage which Lady Raven had provided for her guests. They visited first the Colosseum and then drove round some of the more ancient streets of the City. Cleona, who was poring over a guide book, exclaimed as they came to a wonderful fountain made of white marble that they must stop and inspect it.

'There are fountains everywhere!' Beryl exclaimed. 'Why this particular one?'

'This is the Fountain de Trevi,' Cleona explained. 'If you drink the water, throw a coin into the fountain itself and make a wish, you will at some time in your life return to Rome.'

This took Beryl's fancy and she replied at once that she must make a wish.

'Alack! I have so many desires,' she said reflectively. 'I am at pains to know which to choose.'

The two girls dismounted from the carriage and went down the steps which led to the fountain. The water was pouring out of either side of the figure of Neptune, and in the great wide basin one could see through the clear water the shining silver of many coins that had been thrown there.

Cleona leaned over the edge, then speaking above the splash of the water she said to Beryl:

'One can almost believe that in actual fact one's wish will come true.'

'I always believe that mine will!' a voice said, and both Cleona and Beryl turned in surprise to see that Lord Raven had come down the steps towards them.

'You have surprised us, my lord,' Beryl exclaimed.

'I saw the carriage as I was passing down another street,' he explained, 'and followed you.'

'Did you suspect we were away to some clandestine assignation?' Beryl asked provocatively.

'I had an idea that Miss Wickham was intent on sight-seeing,' he replied.

'I am, indeed!' Cleona answered. 'I find Rome fascinating. It is even more beautiful that I expected it to be.'

'And nearly as gay as I hoped,' Beryl said with a little smile.

'We are lunching today with Prince Camillo Borghese,' Lord Raven stated.

'Yes, and I am looking forward to making the acquaintance of His Highness,' Beryl replied. 'He is one of the richest men in Italy and a member of a great Roman house. But do you know, Sylvester, Cleona declares that she will not come. She prefers marble to princes and ruins to palaces.'

'That makes me sound as if I were sadly lacking in civility,' Cleona said quietly. 'It is only, as I said to Lord Raven, that I do not wish to force myself on your friends. They are not interested in me, only in meeting your lordship and Beryl.'

'I think you are being unduly modest, Miss Wickham,' Lord Raven said dryly.

His tone somehow made Cleona feel that once again she had been in the wrong. She did not know why, but he always contrived to force her into being on the defensive. Now she turned away and said:

'We are about to make a wish, my lord. Perhaps you, too, have something left to wish for.'

Although she did not look at him, she felt he must be smiling. She had tried to be dignified and rebukeful and succeeded only in sounding like a rather irritating small girl who wanted to scratch because she could not get her own way.

'My wish is worth at least half a guinea,' Lord Raven said, taking a gold coin from his vest pocket and holding it in his hand.

'Mine is worth more than that,' Beryl said, 'but I shall only use Italian money for fear the gods who watch over the fountain like their payment to be in their own currency.'

Cleona fumbled in the little reticule that she carried on her arm. It contained her handkerchief, her smelling salts, a small round mirror which Beryl had given her, and nothing else. To her dismay she remembered that she had placed what was left of her money after shopping with

Swallow in the drawer of her dressing-table. Lord Raven watched her search.

'Dare I offer to assist you?' he asked with mock humility.

As he spoke he shook a handful of money from his purse into the palm of his hand. There were Italian coins of all denominations, from the smallest, with a hole in the centre, to large gold pieces. Cleona hesitated and he added: .

'You seem, Miss Wickham, to be invariably in the position of refusing to take a coin from me. Perhaps one day you will remember that money is of little consequence and it is another coin which is of far more importance.'

'Another coin?' Cleona queried.

She could not forbear the question, feeling curious of what he meant while uneasily aware that he was trying once again to tease her.

'Yes, indeed!' he replied. 'The Coin of Love! Have you never heard of it?'

'I know not what you mean.'

Cleona felt this was a snare, realized that she had already walked into it and now there was no escape.

'Then I must tell you,' Lord Raven said, 'that the Coin of Love is a kiss.'

Cleona knew then that once again he was taunting her. The colour flew into her cheeks and she turned away from him, refusing his proffered hand with the coins in it.

'My wish would not succeed,' she said stiffly, 'if I used any money but my own. I will come again another day.'

'I shall wish now,' Beryl said.

She had been paying but little heed to the conversation. She raised her arm as she spoke and threw her money far into the fountain. It splashed into the water and the ripples from it widened out towards the far edge of the basin.

'I have changed my mind,' Lord Raven said. 'My wish is worth not half a guinea but double.'

He flicked a golden guinea, as he spoke, high into the air and watched it fall into the froth from one of the fountains.

'Was it such a very momentous wish?' Beryl enquired.

'It is to me,' he replied.

'You are making me curious,' Beryl pouted. 'But I know I must not ask you to tell me what it was, for that would bring misfortune.'

'Our wishes must remain secret,' Lord Raven agreed.

'Are you convinced, Miss Wickham, you will not change your mind? I have a feeling that today the gods are listening to our prayers.'

'I shall make my wish then,' Cleona said, 'and promise that as soon as I can I will repay my debt.'

'So you think to obtain credit,' he said, 'preferring to trust the inhabitants of Olympus rather than my humble self.'

'Yes, my lord!' Cleona replied.

She tried to look at him defiantly as she spoke but somehow her eyes could not meet his. And so, instead, without wishing she walked rather quickly back to the carriage.

Because Beryl was so insistent, Cleona agreed to go to luncheon at the Palazzo Borghese. It was a large luncheon party with as guests the distinguished, the notable and the important.

Cleona sat next to an elderly *Duc* and a General who had long since retired from active service. Neither of them could speak English and she struggled with the conversation in Italian, finding it hard sometimes to follow the trend of their discourse and wishing all the time that she was free to wander amongst the beauties of Rome or even to inspect the Palazzo itself.

It was when the guests were having coffee and liqueurs on the terrace that Cleona was surprised to find her host, Prince Camillo Borghese, standing beside her. He was young, being only twenty-seven, and having an exceedingly handsome face with dark curly hair and a good figure.

'Tell me, *Signorina*, what you think of my country?' he asked.

'It is so beautiful that there are no words with which to describe it,' Cleona answered.

'You are beautiful, too,' he said, 'so that is the sort of compliment I like to hear.'

Cleona was not quite certain what she should answer to this. Eagerly he talked to her about himself and his great estates—eighty of them in all; of his Palazzo in Florence; of his villa outside the gates of Rome which housed the famous Borghese collection; of the fabulous family jewels which, he said, were unsurpassed by any other collection in the world.

Cleona listened, finding him a braggart, but realizing that he had, too, a certain charm and attraction.

'Come with me and see some of my pictures,' he invited and led her away from the chattering crowd along cool galleries where the collection of masterpieces were hung. Cleona wished to inspect every one, but she soon realized that the Prince had taken her away from his other guests because he wished to talk to her alone.

'You are beautiful!' he said again. 'So beautiful that I can hardly believe that you are real.'

His hands went out to touch her as he spoke, but Cleona moved away from him.

'I think, Your Highness, we should return to your guests.'

'There is no need for haste,' he said. 'I want to talk with you. From the moment I saw you I realized that you were the one person with whom I wished to be acquainted. Tell me, *Signorina*, do you believe in love at first sight?'

Cleona shook her head.

'Not really,' she answered. 'I think love is something deeper than that. Something which comes from knowing a person and trusting them, from being certain that they would never fail one whatever the circumstances.'

'Time can prove that for me,' the Prince said. 'But to me love is a thing which suddenly is there, like the sun breaking through the clouds. *Signorina*, I am in love!'

'No! No! You are imagining it,' Cleona protested.

She was not afraid of this young man, only rather amused and intrigued by him.

'How shall I prove it?' he said. 'Must I die for you?'

'That is being nonsensical,' she smiled. 'You are far more likely to forget me.'

'That I swear I could never do,' he retorted. 'I will prove to you my love, not in one way but a thousand. Do you not understand that I am your servant, your slave, your adoring and very humble admirer?'

He took her hand as he spoke and covered it with kisses. Cleona had not expected this declaration and for a moment, at the touch of his lips, she did not move. And then as she stood there, the Prince's lips warm and insistent on the palm of her hand, she heard a sound at the far end of the gallery.

Standing watching them was Lord Raven! She felt her heart give a sudden frightened leap, knew that the blood rose guiltily into her face, then asked herself, almost angrily, what business it was of his.

Slowly he walked towards them and the Prince straightened himself and turned at the sound of his footsteps.

'Your Highness, I have come to collect Miss Wickham,' Lord Raven said. 'Lady Beryl and I feel that it is time we must leave.'

'So soon?' the Prince asked. 'There is so much more I wish to show Miss Wickham.'

'That I can well believe,' Lord Raven replied with a twist of his lips. 'But Miss Wickham must pardon me if I tear her away.'

Cleona said nothing but moved resolutely towards the door. She was conscious as she went that Lord Raven, walking beside her, was angry. Why, she could not imagine. She told herself again it was no business of his whom she allowed to kiss her hand or who made love to her. And yet, despite such brave thoughts, she felt unmistakably and inexplicably guilty.

9

CLEONA was awakened by an unusual noise in her bedroom. The Italian chambermaids who usually called her were soft-footed and gentle-handed with the shutters and blinds which covered the windows. This morning it seemed to her that there was an almost deafening clatter and she opened her eyes to see that it was Swallow who was letting in the sunshine.

'Good morning, Swallow,' she murmured sleepily.

Swallow turned towards the bed.

'Oh, Miss, I had to waken you,' she said. 'I felt I would burst if I did not tell you the news!'

'What news?' Cleona asked, awake now and sitting up so that her hair fell over her shoulders and made a natural ornament to the severity of her plain nightgown.

'You have won a prize, Miss! There, didn't I tell you we would be lucky?'

'A prize?' Cleona asked. 'A prize in what?'

She could not for a moment think what Swallow was talking about.

'In the lottery, of course. Miss! You recall that I persuaded you to purchase a ticket. I had a feeling in my bones that you would be fortunate. In fact, as true as I'm standing here, I said to Ellen when we got back, "You mark my words, one of us will be lucky or I'm a Dutchman!"'

'A prize in the lottery!' Cleona exclaimed as soon as she could make herself heard.

'Yes, indeed! 'Tis not the first prize, to be sure. But Captain Ernshaw says he thinks it will be for quite a considerable sum. He sent George to fetch it right away. I gave him your ticket as I thought you would wish me to do, Miss. Because, if you remember, I put it in my own purse for safe keeping.'

'Of course, I remember now,' Cleona said. 'I really never thought of it again.'

'And, Miss, we are all delighted, I'm sure,' Swallow said. 'As I said to Ellen when I heard the news, "If ever a young lady deserves a bit of good luck it's Miss Wickham." '

'Thank you, Swallow. But it is your good luck, too. You must share the prize with me because if it had not been for you I would never have thought of buying the ticket.'

'That's generous indeed, Miss, but I wouldn't think of taking it,' Swallow replied. 'You're no trouble to do things for—not like some young ladies I have known—and always a kind word for all of us.'

'But naturally you must have your share,' Cleona said. 'Are you really convinced that I have won a prize and it is not a mistake?'

She could hardly believe the news, not even when an hour later Captain Ernshaw presented her with the money which the footman had fetched from the municipal building where the draw had been held.

'How much is it?' Cleona asked when she saw the pile of notes and silver in his hand.

'I have been reckoning it up,' Captain Ernshaw answered, 'and in our currency it amounts to about sixty pounds. It is one of the smaller prizes, of course, but I must congratulate you, Miss Wickham.'

'I can hardly believe I am not dreaming,' Cleona told him. 'I have never won anything before in my life—not even a dip at the village fair—and it is all due to Swallow. I have told her she must accept half of my gainings for herself.'

'I should have thought that was decidedly over-generous,' Captain Ernshaw said dryly. 'Money is always useful, you know, Miss Wickham, and this won't go as far as all that.'

'Indeed, I am well aware of it,' Cleona answered.

She felt that even Captain Ernshaw must be aware of the threadbare state of her wardrobe and her urgent need for the most necessary garments of wearing apparel. But she could not disabuse her mind of the thought that it was only fair that Swallow should have half her prize money, and when she returned to her bedroom she argued the matter until Swallow finally capitulated and agreed to take a third.

' 'Tis a small fortune to me, Miss,' she said. 'I shall put it aside with what I am saving for my old age. I'm not like some, who spend every penny they earn and more. I know I shall grow old and nobody will want me, and then it'll be a safeguard against the Poor House to have a little nest-egg tucked away safe and sound.'

'That is why I want you to take more,' Cleona said.

Swallow shook her head.

'There's not many as would make the offer at all, Miss,' she said. 'And don't think I'm not thanking you for the kind thought. But I know my place. It isn't as if you don't want it yourself, either.'

Cleona smiled.

'Now at least I can have some decent gowns, Swallow, and you can throw away that travelling dress and cape of my mother's. I hope never to see myself in that colour again.'

'Indeed, you are right there, Miss. 'Tis not becoming to you,' Swallow said. 'We can buy some splendid materials in the shops and market place and I have heard of a young woman who can make the most fashionable gowns if she is given a copy. What do you say that we ask her to come here and copy some of her ladyship's? I'm not suggesting you should wear the same colours, but the shape is good and if you knew what her ladyship paid for some of those dresses it'd be a shock to you.'

'Oh, Swallow, that is a wonderful idea!' Cleona exclaimed. 'Do you think her ladyship would mind?'

'I am certain sure she won't,' Swallow replied. 'Why, if she's said to me once she's said to me a dozen times: "Swallow, we must find something smart for Miss Wickham to wear." But she wouldn't hurt your pride by offering to give you anything.'

'She knew I would not accept it,' Cleona said. 'But now I can buy things with my own money. Oh, Swallow, how grand that sounds!'

'Well, her ladyship won't be wakening for another two hours at least,' Swallow smiled. 'What do you say to you and I setting off right away, Miss? It's the early bird—as my old grandfather used to say.'

'Go to the shops now!' Cleona cried. 'Do let us do that! It is a famous suggestion!'

'I'll get my bonnet right away,' Swallow said. 'And I'll

tell George to run round to this young sewing woman I was a-speaking of. The sooner she's here, the sooner you'll have a chance of being the Belle o' the Ball, Miss.'

'I am not so ambitious as that,' Cleona laughed.

At the same time, when she saw the materials which could be obtained for quite a modest outlay, she could not help her imagination picturing herself looking very different from what she had done to date. There was crisp dimity, batiste, lawn and sprigged muslin for the daytime. There was spangled gauze, embroidered tulle and satins for the evening.

Cleona found herself hesitating over a material which looked as if it were hung with tiny dewdrops and another which shimmered like water in the moonlight. In the end Swallow persuaded her to have both. She also bought some plumes in the azure blue of the Italian sky to put in a new chip bonnet which framed her small face as if it were a halo.

The footman who had accompanied them to the shops was laden with parcels when finally Swallow gave an exclamation of horror.

'I must be getting back, Miss. 'Tis after eleven o'clock and her ladyship will be wakening. Goodness knows what she will say when she finds I'm not there, and Ellen's that butter-fingered that one can't trust her to do a thing.'

'I have kept you, Swallow; I am sorry,' Cleona said.

'Now, don't fret yourself, Miss,' Swallow answered. 'But I will put my best foot forward, if you don't mind.'

'You go on ahead,' Cleona said. 'I will pay the bill and follow you as quickly as I can.'

'Henry had best come with me,' Swallow said, looking at the laden footman. 'The sooner those things are unpacked and in the making, the better for all concerned.'

'Yes, indeed!' Cleona agreed, visualizing herself floating down the wide marble stairs of the villa in the shimmering gauze, her hair dressed in a new way with perhaps a silver ribbon binding her curls.

She could not help wondering what Lord Raven would think when he saw her. If he had thought her pretty when he believed her to be a dairymaid, what would he think of her when she was dressed as well as, if not better than, other young women of his acquaintance?

Then resolutely she put the thought from her mind. What did it matter to her? she thought. And yet she could not help a tiny feminine yearning to flaunt herself before him, to make him feel ashamed of ever having thought of her as lowly born and a dairymaid.

The salesman was an unconscionable time with the account and when he came Cleona checked it over carefully, having been already warned by Captain Ernshaw that the Italians thought every Englishman and every Englishwoman was excessively wealthy, and charged them accordingly. There were two mistakes in the addition which Cleona corrected. Then she paid what she owed, savouring the delight of fingering the crisp money and at the same time feeling slightly guilty for having spent so much on herself. Indeed, there was not very much left of her winnings and she knew that if she was to give gratuities at the right scale where they were expected of her, she must spend no more on herself.

It was as she came from the shop into the sunshine that she realized that she was not very far from the Fountain de Trevi. She recognized the twisting, narrow street which ran downhill and the church on the corner which she and Beryl had already visited.

On an impulse she walked towards the fountain. Now at least she had a coin of her own that she could throw into the crystal water and make her wish. What, she wondered, did she want more than anything else in all the world? And before she could answer she remembered Lord Raven speaking of the Coin of Love. He had but done it to taunt her, to force her to remember that first time they had met, when he had set his fingers beneath her chin and turned her face up to his and kissed her, before she was aware what he was about.

As she thought of it she could still recall only too vividly the feel of his mouth on hers, the hard possession of his lips, and the anger she had felt later because she had been too astonished, and perhaps too weak, to repulse him.

She had reached the fountain now; and then, as she stepped from the cool shadow of the narrow street into the brilliant sunshine which flooded the open square in which the fountain was built, a commotion a little ahead of her made her oblivious, for the moment, of the gushing water and the beauty of the marble figures.

A man was beating a small grey donkey. He had obviously lost his temper when the donkey had overthrown a huge load of dried grass, for it lay scattered over the cobbles and two ragged children were attempting to gather it up. The man was using oaths which Cleona recognized as blasphemous even while she did not understand them.

The stick in his hand was thick and he was wielding it with all his strength on the back of the poor animal, which, wincing and sidling from side to side, could not escape because the man held it captive by the bridle.

Cleona hesitated for only a brief second. For just one moment she remembered she was a stranger in a strange country, and then the plight of the wretched donkey drove all else from her mind.

'Stop!' she shouted at the man,, but he paid no heed. And then, as she reached his side and realized he was past hearing her, she put out her hands and, with a strength she had not known she possessed, wrenched the stick from his hands.

She took him by surprise or he would not have relinquished it so easily, but now that she was in possession of the weapon he turned to face her, his rage, in a second, transferred from the animal to the girl who faced him.

He would have spoken, but Cleona had taken advantage of his astonishment at her interference and was already berating him.

'How dare you treat an animal like that?' she said in Italian. 'Have you no mercy, no understanding and no pity for a dumb creature who cannot retaliate?'

'It is my donkey,' the man said angrily, 'and who are you to come interfering between a man and his own possessions?'

He glanced over her shoulder as he spoke and realizing that she was not accompanied either by a coach or servants on foot, his confidence returned to him.

'You give me that stick and mind your own business,' he said, using a vulgar phrase and speaking in a patois that was not easy to understand.

'You will promise me first not to go on beating this wretched animal,' Cleona said.

She was well aware, as she spoke, that a crowd was gathering. People were appearing in doorways and down alleys, coming almost, as it seemed, from the very bowels of the earth to find out what the altercation was about. She felt suddenly afraid, and yet she must stand her ground. The donkey, miserable and ill fed, with its ribs showing against its sides, made her forget any fear she might have had for her own safety.

'This is not the first time you have ill-treated this poor beast,' she said. 'Look at the sores on its back. It is old, tired and hungry.'

'What is that to you?' the man retorted. 'Give me my

stick and be off with you. There are plenty of men who will listen to your kind, but I'm not one of them.'

'At least you will not beat this animal any more,' Cleona half commanded, half begged.

'I will beat it again because you have interfered,' the man roared at her and reached forward as if to take the stick from her hand.

Cleona stepped back, but at the same time, with a sense of rising panic, she realized the position in which she had entangled herself. The crowd around them was six deep by now, listening open-mouthed but making no effort to interfere, to take one side or the other. She could not count on their support, even if this man offered her violence.

'Stand back,' she said as he drew nearer to her. But she realized that despite her every resolution her voice trembled a little.

'And who's to make me do that?' he jeered. 'I can take my stick from you and anything else I want.'

There was a little murmur as he spoke from the crowd. To Cleona it sounded is if it were of approval. And she knew, with a sudden sinking of her heart, that this was a moment of real danger. Then there was the sound of a horse's hoofs clattering on the cobbles and a voice behind her said sternly:

'What is going on here?'

With what was almost a sob of relief she turned her head. Sitting astride a spirited black stallion, Lord Raven looked down at her, the crowd pressing away from him.

'Thank goodness you have come,' Cleona said in English. 'This man here was beating his donkey. See how miserable and ill the poor creature is. I have taken his stick from him and he demands it back.'

Lord Raven swung himself down from the saddle.

'Is it true what this lady says of you?' he asked the Italian in his own language.

The man, who had been so bold and blustering when confronted only by a woman, was now cringing and apologetic.

'I am but a poor man, Milor. I have to earn my living. If the animal is ill-behaved, it costs me money. I but tapped it gently with the stick and the lady accused me of being cruel. It's not true. I love my donkey and it loves me.'

'It doesn't appear to me you have expended much affection on it,' Lord Raven said dryly. 'How much do you want for it?'

'You will buy it, Milor?'

113

'That is my intention.'

'Milor, it is my livelihood. I cannot manage without my little Paolo. He is the joy of my heart; so valuable to me that if Milor is interested in him I must ask a big price to compensate me for what I lose.'

Lord Raven looked at the donkey.

'At the outside the poor animal has no more than three months to live,' he said. 'You have neglected it, treated it badly, and seldom, if ever, given it a proper meal. Three scudi is about what its worth, but I will give you ten. 'Tis more than you deserve, but it will enable you to buy another animal to replace this. But remember to treat it well. A healthy servant is better than a sick one.'

He threw down the coins as he spoke. The man grovelled for them in the dust.

'Gracia, Milor; gracia.'

He was gone in a hurry, thinking that perhaps such a generous offer might be regretted. And now, for the first time, Lord Raven turned and looked at Cleona.

'Allow me to make you a present,' he said with a faint smile on his lips.

'No, indeed!' Cleona answered. 'I can afford to buy him for myself.'

She opened her reticule as she spoke and taking out a note valued at ten scudi pressed it in Lord Raven's hand. He looked at it and then at the other notes that he saw she possessed and raised his eyebrows.

'You have perhaps been fortunate at cards?' he questioned.

'I have not won this by gaming,' Cleona said stiffly, and then she added quickly: 'Oh, but I forgot, it was by gambling. I won a prize in the lottery.'

'Then I must congratulate you. Was it a great fortune?'

Cleona could not help laughing.

'No, indeed! It seemed to me a vast amount of money, but already I have spent a great deal of it. I was in need of so many gowns, but I still have a little, as you can see for yourself, enough to buy a donkey.'

'And yet I think that was not your intention when I arrived.'

Cleona forced herself to swallow her pride.

'I . . . I must thank you for . . . helping me,' she said. 'I am aware it was unwise to interfere, but the man was beating the poor beast unmercifully. There was nothing else I could do.'

'No, I can understand that,' Lord Raven said. 'But I must

remind you that the donkey is mine. If you will not accept him from me as a present, then I must offer him to someone else. He is not for sale.'

'Someone else!' Cleona ejaculated. 'But, who?'

Lord Raven shrugged his shoulders.

'To anyone. Perhaps some of these people standing around here.'

'Oh, no,' Cleona said involuntarily. 'You were right when you said he had but a short time to live. He is very old, I am sure of it, and he has been so harshly treated that I would like him to live his remaining days in comfort and happiness.'

'Then you will accept him as a present?'

'But . . . what can I do with him?'

'I was thinking perhaps my mother would have him in her stables,' Lord Raven said. 'At the same time, I would rather say that the beast was yours. I cannot imagine what my head groom will say if I tell him that this is the latest addition to my own horseflesh.'

'Very well, then,' Cleona said a little reluctantly. 'I accept the donkey as a gift, and . . . thank you, my lord.'

Lord Raven held out the note to her and taking it from him she put it back into her reticule. When she had done so she did not look at him. She had the feeling that he was gloating odiously because he had forced his will upon her. And yet, she asked herself, what else could she have done? At least the donkey was saved.

Too old, tired and miserable to realize that his fate and existence had been changed, the animal stood motionless in the middle of the road, its head dropping forward, its whole body sagging with fatigue and ill health.

'Poor thing!' Cleona said.

'It might be kinder to put it out of its misery,' Lord Raven remarked. 'But we will see if plenty of food and a lot of cosseting can keep it alive.'

Cleona patted the donkey's neck. It was too used to blows to understand caresses, and it winced away from the touch of her hand.

'How are we to get it away from here?' she asked.

Lord Raven looked round the crowd still staring at them curiously, and choosing a boy of about fifteen he beckoned him and told him to lead the donkey slowly behind them. The boy was delighted at the commission which he was assured would bring him a generous reward.

'*Si, si, Signor,*' he said, smiling.

He was barefooted and clad in such ragged garments that

it was impossible to tell what had originally been their shape and colour. Cleona looked at him with compassion.

'They are all so poor,' she said almost beneath her breath. 'If only there was something one could do for them.'

'You are not asking me to purchase a number of small boys, are you?' Lord Raven asked.

'No, you have been kind enough already,' Cleona answered. 'It is just that I never believed such poverty could exist. It is bad enough in England, but here it seems almost worse beside such beauty and within sight of so much wealth.'

'You will learn not to notice such contrasts,' Lord Raven said.

'Why should I do that?' Cleona enquired.

'Because young ladies of fashion think only of themselves and their own comforts,' he replied with an edge on his voice. 'They are not concerned with the lower orders of humanity.'

'In which case, they should be,' Cleona replied severely. 'Oh, I know you think I am very ignorant and stupid because I have been nowhere and seen so little. But I do believe that those who are rich and important and have great influence should do something to alleviate the terrible poverty of those less fortunate than themselves.'

She spoke with an almost passionate intensity, but when she looked up at Lord Raven he was not smiling.

'One day,' he said quietly, 'we will speak further of this. But I hardly think that this is the time or place.'

Cleona glanced round her. She had almost forgotten the crowd, but they were still there, staring at the donkey, Lord Raven's fine horse and themselves. She felt suddenly confused and shy, not only of the Italians in their rags, but of the tall, broad-shouldered man beside her.

'We must go back,' she said in a low voice.

She had moved towards the street down which she had come and Lord Raven, leading his horse, walked beside her. Behind them, moving with slow resignation, came the old donkey led by the barefooted boy and followed by a crowd of children laughing, talking and hoping for more excitement and perhaps the chance of a coin or so.

'What made you come here in the first place?' Lord Raven asked, when they had walked a little way in silence.

'I wanted to wish at the fountain,' Cleona answered, and then blushed because it sounded foolish and rather childish.

'I forgot that you had not yet made your wish,' he said.

'I have wondered every day since we came here first if mine would come true.'

'Do you really believe in such things?' Cleona asked.

'I know by the tone of your voice that you think me singularly insensitive and devoid of imagination,' Lord Raven replied.

'I did not say that,' Cleona answered quickly.

'No, but you thought it,' he retorted. 'In fact I have a very good idea of what you do think of me—a brute, a libertine, a man without scruples and perhaps with little honour. Is that not true?'

'Indeed, it is not!' Cleona protested in a low voice.

'Then perhaps today I have found virtue in your eyes, because I have saved the life of an ill donkey. Does that count for anything?'

'It counts for a lot, my lord, and I am . . . grateful.'

They had walked some way before they spoke again. And then, as they began to ascend the incline which led to the villa, Lord Raven said:

'I wonder if the fountain, or anything else, will finally bring you what your heart most desires?'

'And what is that?' Cleona asked.

'Do you not know?' he enquired.

She shook her head.

'No, I have so much already, but I suppose everyone wants more. And yet those are only little things. I have no ardent desire for anything very big or very important.'

'Are you sure of that?'

Cleona nodded. 'Quite sure.'

'And yet, most young women of your age would want love or a husband. The two are seldom compatible.'

'I would not accept one without the other,' Cleona said quickly, before she had time to think. Only as she said the words did she realize that they were almost an accusation when spoken to someone like Lord Raven who was marrying not for love but for convenience, even as Beryl was marrying him for the same reason.

'Do you really believe you can find both?' he asked.

And though she felt once again he was teasing her or drawing her out, she could not prevent herself from answering him truthfully.

'I am sure of it,' she replied. 'And if I do not, then I shall never marry.'

'I wonder if you will give me the same answer in two or three years' time,' he retorted. 'You are very young.'

They had almost reached the gateway to the villa. Cleona turned her head to look at him.

'I assure you, my lord,' she said, 'that everyone in the world is not as cynical as yourself. I believe that one day I shall find a man whom I can love and who will love me, and that if I am fortunate enough to marry him we shall be happy together, content with ourselves, finding the rest of the world well lost and easily forgotten.'

She thought, even as she spoke, that she was inviting him to taunt or mock at her. It would be so easy to call her oversentimental, to laugh at her ideals and even hold her up to ridicule. But Lord Raven did none of these things. Instead he said gently:

'If that is what you are wishing yourself, then I, too, will wish it for you. I think, Miss Wickham, you deserve such happiness.'

Cleona looked at him in surprise, and then, because there was nothing for her to say, she could only turn her head away and hasten her steps towards the villa.

Lord Raven left her at the door saying that he would give instructions that the donkey should be looked after, and Cleona ran quickly up the steps to find Beryl and tell her the events of the morning.

'So Sylvester came to your rescue!' Beryl exclaimed when she had heard about the lottery, the purchases Cleona had made and the incident over the donkey.

'Yes. And I was exceeding glad to see him,' Cleona admitted. 'I thought for one moment that the man might strike me.'

'How could you have been so foolish as to go alone to that part of the city?' Beryl asked. 'And, furthermore, to interfere with one of the common people? You must be more careful, Cleona. I should have thought that you would have learned your lesson when you were carried away by the bandits.'

'I should have done,' Cleona admitted a little ruefully.

'Well, that is the second time Sylvester has saved you,' Beryl said. 'I wonder what will be the third?'

'Let us pray there will not be one,' Cleona said, laughing. 'I am afraid his lordship finds me a tiresome encumbrance.'

'I wouldn't be surprised,' Beryl answered frankly. 'But then one never knows what Sylvester is thinking. However, don't let us worry about him. Let us talk of your new conquest.'

'My new conquest!' Cleona echoed in surprise. 'What do you mean?'

'Look in the next room,' Beryl suggested.

Cleona did as she was told and found an enormous basket of white orchids and on it a crested card addressed to her. There was no need to read the signature to know who had sent it. Cleona felt herself blushing as she turned to where Beryl was watching her with a mischievous expression on her face.

'It is from the Prince Camillo Borghese,' she said almost apologetically.

'Do you realize what this means?' Beryl asked.

'No, what does it mean?' Cleona enquired.

'That the Prince has fallen in love with you,' Beryl said. 'Oh, Cleona, it is the most wonderful thing that could possibly happen. His family won't be pleased for they visualize him as making a great match. But if he should marry you, think of your position.'

'Beryl, you go far too fast,' Cleona expostulated. 'The Prince has not said he wished to marry me.'

At the same time she could remember all too well his words in the picture gallery, the touch of his lips on her fingers. She had not really thought of him again. She had imagined that his extravagant flattery was just Italian politeness, the effusion of a Latin which meant no more than a rather stilted compliment from an Englishman. And yet she was well aware that for the Prince of a noble House to send flowers to an unmarried girl was, in any language, tantamount to a proposal of marriage.

Beryl clasped her hands together.

'Think, Cleona! Think of how important you would be. He is wealthy beyond the dreams of avarice—and he is handsome, too. Personally I thought him fascinating.'

'Whom are you talking about?' the Dowager Lady Raven asked as she came slowly into the *Salon*, a soft scarf trailing behind her as she walked, a long rope of pearls falling from her neck and diamond bracelets jingling at her wrists.

'Have you seen what Prince Camillo has sent Cleona?' Beryl asked, despite a whispered protest from Cleona who felt embarrassed that Lady Raven should know of the gift.

'That exquisite basket of flowers?' the Dowager questioned. 'Did the Prince send it to both of you or to Cleona alone?'

'Cleona alone!' Beryl answered. 'You are aware what that means, Ma'am!'

'The Prince is very impressionable,' Lady Raven said. 'But I think that he would hardly have dared to send such an ostentatious present to one of my guests unless his intentions were honourable. Have you a partiality for him, child?'

'Indeed, Ma'am, I have not thought of His Highness in such a connection,' Cleona replied, blushing a little.

'Italians are very impetuous,' Lady Raven said. 'In England a man will court someone to whom he is attracted for months, or even years, before he declares himself. In this country men fall in love quickly and seldom keep their feelings to themselves. I expect His Highness will call on us this afternoon.'

'I would not wish to be alone with him,' Cleona said quickly.

'It must be obvious,' Lady Raven said. 'If you were to walk in the garden while we were sitting on the terrace there would be nothing incorrect in that.'

'But, I . . . do not think I . . . want to be . . .' Cleona stammered incoherently.

She felt as if they were all pushing her into something that she had not anticipated or even considered. It was as if she were being carried along with the river, the water moving faster and faster, until just ahead, at present out of sight but within hearing, lay the weir.

'Think of those gems, Ma'am,' Beryl was saying to Lady Raven.

'They are indeed magnificent,' the Dowager replied. 'And I believe the best of them have not been worn for years. The Prince's mother was too small to carry the great tiaras or the corsages.'

'Cleona will be able to wear them all,' Beryl enthused. 'I am told that even the Queen has no emeralds to rival those in the Borghese collection.'

'Please, please,' Cleona interrupted. 'You must not speak as if anything was decided . . . the Prince did say some very flattering things to me yesterday; but as you, Ma'am, have so rightly said, the Latin races are impulsive. I am sure that he meant nothing, any more than he means anything serious by this gift of orchids.'

Beryl laughed.

'Think what you please, Cleona. I am convinced His Highness will offer for you when you next meet. It will be beyond anything splendid! Will you be married here or in England?'

'I will not discuss it!' Cleona said.

She was so incensed that she stamped her foot with rage and her cheeks were flushed with an anger that she could not explain even to herself. Then, as she heard the door open at the far end of the *Salon* and Lord Raven came into the room, she turned to Beryl and said in a low voice:

'Please say nothing of this.'

Beryl looked to see who had entered.

'Oh, 'tis only Sylvester,' she said in a tone that was almost disappointed. 'And why shouldn't I tell him, Cleona? He will have to know sooner or later.'

'Why shouldn't you tell me whatever it is?' Lord Raven asked her. He bent to kiss his mother and then raised Beryl's hand to his lips. 'You are both late this morning, and have therefore missed the adventure in which Miss Wickham and I played a notable part. Have you heard about it?'

'My *Major-domo* informs me that you brought back a donkey,' Lady Raven said. 'What in the name of Heaven, Sylvester, can you want with a donkey?'

'I assure you, Mamma, that it is not mine,' Lord Raven replied. 'It belongs to Miss Wickham.'

'To Miss Wickham!' Lady Raven looked at Cleona in surprise.

Before she could speak, Beryl had hastened to tell the story of Cleona's rescue of the ill-treated beast and how they had brought it back to the villa to die. Lady Raven did not seem very interested in the tale.

'I am afraid there are a large number of ill-treated donkeys in Rome,' she said. 'I hope I shall not be asked to house them all.'

'But surely something could be done?' Cleona asked. 'Could not the brutal owners be punished? It is not possible that a Society could be started to prevent cruelty and unkindness?'

'Miss Wickham is full of ideas!' Lord Raven said.

'Cleona, don't you see?' Beryl exclaimed. 'You will be able to do that when you are married. Everyone will listen to you and follow your lead. If you proclaim against cruelty, it would soon become the fashion. As the Prince's wife you will lead Roman Society.'

'As the wife of whom?' Lord Raven enquired.

Beryl smiled at him.

'Haven't you heard—?' she began, but Cleona interrupted.

'Please do not listen to her, my lord,' she said. 'What she

is about to say is but a fabrication! It is all a hum, existing solely in Beryl's busy brain. There is no truth in it!'

'I may be very obtuse,' Lord Raven said slowly and in his most disagreeable voice, 'but I have not the slightest conception what either of you are talking about.'

'We are talking about Cleona,' Beryl replied. 'No, don't be shy, Cleona It is a triumph and you ought to be proud and pleased—I know I am.'

'Proud of what?' Lord Raven asked. There was something almost ominous in the way he asked the question.

'Of her success!' Beryl exclaimed. 'Of her new conquest.'

'It is not true,' Cleona said again despairingly.

Beryl did not listen to her. Instead, with a gesture of her pretty hand she was pointing towards the huge basket of orchids on the table.

'Look what he sent her,' she said. 'White orchids! If that isn't a declaration I should like to know what is. Besides, it was obvious yesterday that he was infatuated, and by this evening she may have had the chance of accepting him.'

'And who might this fortunate gentleman be?' Lord Raven asked.

'Please, Beryl!' Cleona begged, but Beryl was enjoying her part in unfolding the tale.

'The gentleman in question, Sylvester,' she answered, 'is His Highness Prince Camillo Borghese, the richest and most eligible bachelor in all Rome.'

For a moment there was silence, and then in a tone of utter contempt Lord Raven said:

'That nitwit!'

As he spoke he turned on his heel and walked from the *Salon*.

10

'I DECLARE I will do no more sight-seeing today,' Beryl said, sighing exhaustedly as they same from the shadows of St. Peter's and out into the sunlight.

The fountains were playing and pigeons were fluttering down from the colonnade to search for crumbs dropped by the passers-by, and the brilliant red cassocks of a group of priests passing into the church was rivalled by the uniforms of the soldiers standing outside the Papal apartments.

'It is so wonderful that I cannot bear to tear myself away,' Cleona murmured.

It was difficult, after the glories of St. Peter's, to transport herself back to the ordinary mundane affairs and conversations of everyday life. She had felt herself uplifted almost into a spiritual ecstasy as she stared at the exquisite mosaics. While the gilt and gold reredos, the crystal lights and the red silk hangings, all made a kaleidoscope of such beauty that she was speechless in awe and admiration.

Now, instead, she saw the dancing water from the fountains, the carriages with their painted panels and gold-laced attendants, the ragged beggars clustered on the steps and the sunshine which seemed in its intensity to dazzle and bemuse not only the eyes but the senses.

'No more sight-seeing,' Beryl said firmly, walking towards their carriage, which they could see waiting, the claret and silver of Lady Raven's liveries conspicuous even amidst such a riot of colour.

'I will allow you to be chicken-hearted today,' Cleona smiled. 'But we must come again and again.'

' 'Tis too late to change me, dearest. I prefer people to things,' Beryl pouted.

Cleona had to laugh.

'You cannot describe St. Peter's as a thing,' she protested.

But Beryl was not listening. Her face had lit up with a new animation as a gaily painted phaeton, pulled by a pair of perfectly matched bays, stopped a little in front of them. It was easy to recognize who was driving the horses for there was no mistaking Prince Camillo's handsome face or ignoring the spectacular blue of his coat and the provocative angle of his beaver hat.

'Your admirer must have found out where you were going,' Beryl said to Cleona in a low voice.

'Pray be careful!' Cleona said quickly. 'He might hear you.'

'And why not?' Beryl teased.

The Prince had already sprung down from the phaeton, followed by a friend who had been sitting beside him, and he hurried through the crowds towards Beryl and Cleona. When he reached them he swept off his hat with a bow which might have been theatrical but was also exceedingly graceful.

'Your servant, Ladies!' he said. 'Lady Raven was gracious enough to tell me where you had gone. So Count Rezzonico and I followed, to plead that we may have the honour of escorting you home.'

'We shall be enchanted, Your Highness,' Beryl answered, dropping the Prince a low curtsy, then making another not quite so deep to the Count. He was nearly as handsome as his friend, but his good looks were combined with an intelligence which was unmistakably obvious even while he often said very little.

They had met him on previous occasions at Lady Raven's and at the Palazzo Borghese, and Cleona suspected that Beryl had a distinct partiality for him.

It was obvious now at any rate with whom she intended to converse, as dismissing their own carriage they climbed into the Prince's phaeton. Without anything being said Beryl took her place at the back with the Count beside her, while there was nothing left for Cleona to do but climb into the seat next to the driver.

A groom, splendidly dressed, who had held the horses while they were talking, let them go and managed, with a dexterity which was almost phenomenal, to spring up behind as the Prince drove off at a tremendous pace.

There was no doubt he could drive well. At the same time, Cleona found herself catching her breath again and again lest they should run over a child or lock the wheels of some passing vehicle.

'Does Your Highness always drive as fast as this?' she asked a little breathlessly.

Instantly he reined in the bays.

'You would rather we travelled more sedately?' he asked.

'Speed is of little significance when the road is clear,' Cleona answered. 'But in these crowded streets I am afraid that we might hurt or injure someone.'

'Do not fret about such trivialities,' the Prince replied. 'There are far too many people in Rome. Dash it! The streets are alive with the poverty-stricken and homeless. Maybe they would be happier if they were relieved of their sufferings.'

'Surely, Your Highness, there must be better and more humane ways of helping them?' Cleona suggested.

The Prince shrugged his shoulders and was obviously bored with the serious turn the conversation had taken.

'Do not waste your sympathy on such paltry creatures,'

he exclaimed impatiently. 'Give it to me, for I am in dire need of it.'

'But why?' Cleona enquired.

'Because I am ill,' he answered. 'I cannot sleep, I cannot eat. I have seen the most eminent physician in Rome, but he informs me that nothing can be done to cure my malady.'

'But why? What does he diagnose as Your Highness's complaint?' Cleona asked.

The Prince turned to look at her, the expression in his dark eyes exceedingly eloquent.

'I am in love,' he said. 'So in love that at times I fear for my sanity.'

Cleona had been too inexperienced to expect the obvious explanation. Now she flushed and looked away from him.

'If that is indeed the truth, then I am sorry . . . for you,' she faltered.

'It is the truth, I swear it,' he answered. 'Do you desire to know the name of the lady who has captured my heart, my mind and, indeed, my very soul?'

Cleona wished uneasily that she was not in the position when she must listen to such a confession, and yet there was nothing she could do. The Prince was talking with a passionate intensity, but Beryl and the Count seated behind them seemed to be almost out of earshot and, at any rate, were too engrossed in their own conversation to be likely to overhear anything that was said.

'My God, but you are lovely!' the Prince exclaimed. 'So lovely that I think you have bewitched me! Do you know what our old *Major-domo*, who has been with my family for over fifty years, said after you had left the *Palazzo*?'

'No, what did he say?' Cleona asked, feeling that to talk of the *Major-domo* was less embarrassing than to have the Prince speaking of her beauty and his emotions.

'He said,' the Prince replied, 'that you were an *"Inglese oppure un Angelo"*—an Englishwoman like an angel. How apt that was, for, indeed, it is hard to believe you are anything but divine.'

'Please, Your Highness . . . you should not . . . must not talk to me in such . . . a manner,' Cleona stammered.

'Why not?'

Cleona made a little gesture with her hands.

'Because I do not understand it and know not what to say in reply. In England we are not used to compliments.'

'Then it is true that all Englishmen are stiff as ramrods and converse of nothing except their horses and their dogs!

We in Italy understand how to make a woman happy. To us she is not only the most beautiful thing that was ever created, but also the most interesting.'

'It is very flattering to be told such inaccuracies,' Cleona said. 'At the same time one cannot help knowing that Englishmen are more faithful than the men of Your Highness's country.'

'I swear to you that I shall be faithful until I die,' the Prince said persistently.

Blushing, Cleona turned her head away, the brim of her bonnet hiding her face.

'I want to talk to you,' the Prince went on. 'Somewhere where we can be alone together, where I can tell you of my feeling, of the love which consumes me like a burning fire. I love—God! how I love you!'

'No! No!' Cleona replied. 'I beg you not to speak of such things. I do not know Your Highness. We have only just met.'

'I knew what I felt about you the very first moment that I saw you,' the Prince cried excitedly. 'I expected the luncheon at my Palace to be just another function such as takes place almost every day. And then, when you came into the room behind Lady Beryl, I felt as if my very heart stopped beating. Here was the woman—the glorious, beautiful, exquisite woman—for whom I had been looking all my life.'

'Please do not say any more,' Cleona begged.

'But I must,' he insisted. 'I want to tell you what I felt and what I feel now. I love you I cannot say it too often and you must listen to me.'

'No, indeed, I must not,' Cleona answered. 'It is all too soon to speak of such tremendous matters.'

'Then how long must I wait?'

'I do not know. Indeed, I cannot tell you,' Cleona answered. 'We have but the merest acquaintance with each other.'

'On my part I know all that is necessary for me to know about you,' the Prince replied. 'I know that you are beautiful, entrancing, bewitching; that at the mere thought of you my pulses beat, my breath quickens and I long to touch you—as I have never longed for anything before in the whole of my life.'

There was so much emotion in his voice that, alarmed, Cleona looked over her shoulder. Behind her Beryl and the Count were deep in an intimate and apparently absorbing conversation; their faces were close together and the Count was holding one of Beryl's gloved hands in his.

'Look, we are nearing the villa,' the Prince said. 'When can I see you again—and alone?'

'Your Highness is well aware that it is impossible for us to be alone together,' Cleona answered. 'Lady Raven would not approve.'

'Why should she know?' the Prince asked. 'If I wait for you in a closed carriage outside the gates of the villa, will you come for a drive with me?'

'No! Of course not,' Cleona answered.

'Then will you meet me in the garden after everyone else has gone to bed?'

'No, I cannot do that either,' Cleona said.

'Then when can I see you?'

There was no mistaking the urgency of his desire. But they had reached the door of the villa and almost before the footman could run out to help her descend Cleona had reached the ground.

'I must thank you, Your Highness, for the drive,' she said formally, without looking at the Prince, and then turned to hurry into the villa.

She did not see the expression on the Prince's face as he watched her go; and even had she done so she would not have understood that her shyness and her desire to escape him had fanned the fire of his passion into a blaze.

Prince Camillo Borghese was not in the habit of being repulsed by the women he pursued. They were usually all too eager to fall into his arms, all too willing to listen to his expressions of love. Cleona's reserve and instinctive evasion of his advances was something new, tantalizing and peculiarly exciting. Then, with a start, he realized that Beryl was holding out her hand to him and saying farewell.

'I have a notion that we shall be seeing Your Highness again soon,' she said with an impudent twinkle in her eye.

'I am always at your ladyship's command and service,' he answered.

'And at Cleona's, too?' she questioned, laughing.

'Miss Wickham knows that I am her devoted slave,' he replied.

'I hope she is duly appreciative,' Beryl murmured, and then, with a last glance under her eyelashes at the Count, she walked up the steps of the villa, leaving the two gentlemen standing bareheaded behind her.

She moved slowly and with dignity until the door closed behind her. Then, picking up her skirts, she ran upstairs to

Cleona's bedroom. As she had expected, she found Cleona standing at the window overlooking the panorama of gardens, olive trees, spires, domes and roofs which lay beneath them.

'Tell me, my dearest love, what did he say to you?' Beryl asked.

'You should not have put me into the shaming position of having to listen to him,' Cleona answered. 'It was exceeding embarrassing.'

'He is crazed about you, I can see that,' Beryl cried. 'You were clever not to fall into his arms too easily. At the same time, you must not drive him too far.'

'I do not think I really like him,' Cleona said slowly. 'Underneath that charming manner he is hard and callous.'

Beryl gave a little cry.

'Was there ever such a girl for picking faults!' she exclaimed. 'What do you expect—perfection in a man who is as rich as Croesus and as handsome as Apollo?'

'I wonder if such things really count?' Cleona asked.

'Lud, if they do not, what does?' Beryl enquired. 'Heavens, my dearest, I declare you quite frighten me when you talk in such a way. But I know 'tis only pretence. When the Prince offers—you will accept him. So now let us talk about me.'

There was something in her tone which made Cleona turn round quickly.

'What about you?' she enquired.

'I crave your help,' Beryl answered. 'The Count has invited me to visit the Carnival with him tonight.'

'The Carnival in the streets!' Cleona enquired. 'But you know what Lady Raven said this very morning about——'

'Yes, of course I recall her ladyship's words,' Beryl interrupted. 'She said it was vulgar and noisy and that people of sensibility closed their doors and windows and sat at home when the Carnival was taking place. Fiddle! The Dowager is old and I am young, and the Count says it is all incredibly gay, so I intend to go with him.'

'Beryl, you dare not!' Cleona exclaimed. 'Think how insistent her ladyship was that we could not go out tonight—and Lord Raven agreed with her.'

'Sylvester is only a spoil-sport,' Beryl said. 'If he wished to take part himself, he would go, you can be sure of it! He is merely bored with the Carnival so he agreed with his Mamma. A fig for his fusty ways. I am going, no one shall prevent me!'

'But how?' Cleona asked.

128

'I have it all planned,' Beryl replied. 'If only Lady Raven retired to bed earlier, it would be easier. She likes to sit reading, and if I wait until she is fatigued I shall miss hours of fun. No, I have to be cunning and you, dearest, will have to proffer me your help.'

'You know I will do anything you ask,' Cleona smiled. 'At the same time I think it is a crazy notion. If you are discovered, her ladyship will be incensed with you and Lord Raven will be furious.'

'Oh, to the gallows with your glooms!' Beryl exclaimed. 'Do not let us worry about the future. Let us live in the present! I will explain to you what I desire of you.'

Cleona realized that it was no use trying to divert Beryl from the course on which she had set her mind. And somehow, despite her worst forebodings, she could not help becoming a little excited and responsive to the gaiety and the thrill in Beryl's voice and the dancing light in her eyes.

'Last time we stayed in, dearest,' Beryl began, 'do you remember how you and her ladyship sat in the *Salon* while I walked through the open windows and sat at the far end of the garden? I must have been there for over an hour before her ladyship closed her book and went up to bed, and when I came in from the garden a little later you were alone working at your embroidery.'

'Yes, I remember all that,' Cleona said.

'Well, that is exactly what I plan will happen tonight,' Beryl went on. 'But you will be sitting in my place at the end of the garden while Lady Raven fondly believes it is me.'

'Where am I supposed to be?' Cleona asked.

'You are going to have a headache and go to bed immediately after dinner,' Beryl replied. 'I could do that myself, but her ladyship might be suspicious. I wish now I had not made such a fuss about going to the Carnival. If I had not argued with the Dowager and with Sylvester—if I had not brought up the subject at all—I could have retired to bed and slipped out as soon as the coast was clear. Now, if I have a headache it will be suspect. In fact there was a very ominous look in his lordship's eyes as he said, "I think my mother has made it very clear that she does not wish any of her household to attend these rowdy junketings!"'

Beryl mimicked Lord Raven's voice so cleverly that Cleona could not help laughing.

'Perhaps he is right and they really are very rough.

Supposing you get hurt in the crowds?' she said apprehensively.

'The Count will look after me,' Beryl said confidently. 'We shall be masked and nobody will know who we are. Oh, dearest, think what a thrill it will be! Do not try to dissuade me, Cleona, because I have set my heart on going.'

'So I can see,' Cleona said ruefully. 'But I think your scheme is a mad one.'

'No, it is perfectly feasible,' Beryl said. 'As you know, Lady Raven never interferes with us except in a matter like this. If I say that I wish to be alone, she would not dream of interrupting my solitude. It is the sort of thing she does herself, so she understands the urge of the soul for self-communion—or whatever nonsense such people call it.

'To continue—all you have to do is to slip behind the ilex trees at the end of the terrace and take from me my red silk wrap which I shall be wearing round my shoulders. Just put it over your head and then sit on the seat with your back to the house. No-one will suspect that I am not sitting there. When I return, we will slip into the house together.'

'It all sounds very easy,' Cleona said with a sigh. 'But what . . . what of Lord Raven?'

'You heard his lordship say this morning that he was dining with the Duc de Ferassi. Later, if it suits him, he will go to the Carnival. All men are hypocrites and Sylvester is no exception. He agrees with his mother that it is not suitable for us, and yet he is perfectly prepared to sample the delights of it himself.'

'But he is a man,' Cleona protested.

'Yes, yes, I know; and we are women and therefore have no partialities and are of no consequence. Well, I am going to have all the fun I can get before I grow too old to enjoy it,' Beryl said. 'Think of my future—shut up in Raven Royal as if I were a prisoner.'

'Oh, Beryl, that is not fair,' Cleona said. 'You will have a wonderful position as his lordship's wife.'

'Only if I fight for everything I want,' Beryl answered. 'He talks now of spending only a short time of the year in London. He wants to concentrate on improving his estate. As I told him, I shall die of the boredom of it.'

Cleona said nothing. In some obscure way it always hurt her when she heard Beryl disparaging Raven Royal. She could not understand how anyone could prefer the tawdry amusements of London to the beauty and peace of Raven Royal.

But she had learned of old that it was impossible to argue with Beryl. Spoiled by having the world at her feet, Beryl invariably had her own way whatever the opposition to her wishes, and Cleona knew now that, crazy though the scheme for tonight might be, she, like so many other people before her, would do as Beryl desired.

It was, however, with a sinking heart and a feeling of acute unhappiness because she must tell a lie, that when dinner was over she asked Lady Raven's permission to retire.

'I think the sun has given me a slight indisposition,' she said in a low voice.

'I am not surprised,' Lady Raven answered. 'It has been very hot today. Go to bed, child, and get your beauty sleep.'

Cleona curtsied and then, when her hostess kissed her gently on the cheek, felt as if she must sink into the floor as Beryl winked at her behind Lady Raven's back. With burning cheeks she said good night and went from the *Salon*.

Slipping out of the villa by a side door, she reached the terrace by a way that was not discernible from the windows and waited behind the ilex trees. She hadn't been there more than a few minutes before Beryl came sauntering along the terrace, her long wide wrap of red silk trailing over her shoulders and rustling behind her on the flagstones. She stood for a moment as if in contemplation of the view and then, in a second, was at Cleona's side.

'You will not be disturbed,' she said. 'Her ladyship quite understands my desire to be alone. She says she felt like that herself when she was young and in love.'

Beryl made a little grimace of sheer naughtiness and slipping her wrap round Cleona's shoulders kissed her on the cheek and then ran down the stone steps which led to yet another terrace and below that to the road.

Draping the wrap carefully so that it hid her fair hair, Cleona moved back on to the terrace where a stone seat, carved and ornamented, was set in the semi-circle of the balustrade. From it one could look over the city which lay below, breath-taking now as one by one the lights gleamed out and the stars shimmered above the sable sky.

Below on the road Cleona heard the sound of horses' hoofs driving away. The Count must have been waiting for Beryl, she thought with a little flutter of her pulses and a sudden dryness of her mouth as she realized that she must play her part as it had been allotted to her.

Accordingly she settled herself on the stone seat on which a number of soft cushions had been placed, for it was a favourite view-spot for all the visitors to Lady Raven's villa. As she sat there, Cleona felt as if eyes were boring into her back, seeing through the inadequate disguise of a silk wrap, detecting the lie by which she had feigned an illness.

Then she told herself this was but nerves. Lady Raven would be content to believe what she had been told. She would read, as was her wont, and then retire to her own bedchamber. There was no reason at all why she should question the silent figure in the garden.

After a while, when there was nothing to break the silence but the chirp of the crickets and the soft movement of the leaves stirring in the night breeze, Cleona felt her agitation subside and the beauty of the night begin to take a hold on her.

The fire-flies were hovering over the garden. There was the fragrance of orange-blossom, of tuberoses and carnations. It seemed almost intoxicating, seeping into Cleona's senses until she felt herself longing for the romance which was irresistibly a part of this enchanted night.

She found herself wanting to be loved by someone she could love in return. A man to whom she could surrender herself and her heart. She felt her breath quicken at the thought. Would she ever find him?

Resolutely she tried to put the question from her. She must think of the wonders of Rome and forget the frailties and the yearnings of men and women. How much she had seen already! How much she had learned!

She was reliving all that she had beheld in St. Peter's when suddenly behind her she heard a footstep on the terrace. One moment she was so deep in her own thoughts that she did not realize the danger. And then, the next moment, with a startling leap of her heart the full implication of what it meant swept over her in a kind of terror.

The footsteps were drawing nearer. Perhaps it was a servant, she thought, coming out with a message. By now it was very dark and instinctively with trembling fingers she pulled the wrap closer round her so that very little of her face could be seen and it enveloped her almost like a shroud.

Nearer and nearer the footsteps came, and now Cleona was praying that they would go away and leave her in peace. Wildly she wondered if Beryl could be near, and then realized that at the most not more than an hour had passed since Beryl had driven away.

Someone had stopped beside her and then a voice spoke and Cleona felt that she must faint at the sound of it.

'My mother told me that you wanted to be alone,' Lord Raven said. 'But I felt that such a wish would not exclude the man to whom you are betrothed.'

As he spoke he sat down on the bench beside Cleona, and she held her breath as if she felt that even that might betray her. She was paralysed with fear, unable to decide what she must do, unable even to think.

'How pleasant it is here,' Lord Raven said in a deep voice. 'And how pleasant to find you alone, my dear. It is not often that we are together like this—our lives are too gay, too full.'

Cleona thought wildly that she must speak; she must tell him who she was. And then, even as she searched for words, conscious that it was almost impossible to speak and that the throbbing of her heart seemed to drum the very thoughts from her mind, Lord Raven made a movement.

He put his arms around her and drew her close to him. And before she could cry out, before she could move to repulse his encircling arm, his other hand had tilted her head back against his shoulder and his lips were on hers.

She felt his mouth, hard, warm and possessive, as she had felt it once before. For one moment she was still out of sheer astonishment and terror; then, as she tried to struggle, his hold on her tightened, his lips grew more insistent. Her hands went out to push him from her. She tried to wrench herself free of his mouth and his arms, and realized, with something akin to terror, that she was his prisoner.

It was too dark to see him. She could only feel him, strong, virile and so large that it seemed to her, in contrast, she was utterly helpless, tiny and ineffectual. She had never realized, she thought, that a kiss could hold a woman utterly captive. Perhaps it was his strength, perhaps, in some degree, her own fear. She felt as if he utterly possessed her, taking her very will from her and conquering her mind until she was just a creature who must obey him.

Closer and closer he held her, and still she struggled, her hands fluttering like ghosts in the darkness, her lips quivering ineffectually beneath his. Then, as suddenly as he had taken her, she was free. But instead of being able to fight him she could only tremble ineffectually in his arms and her voice, when at last it came from between her lips, was hardly more than a whisper.

'Please . . . please . . . I am . . . I am . . . not . . . Beryl.'

'So I perceive.'

His voice was dry and yet there was some other emotion in it, too—one that she did not recognize.

'I . . . I was here . . .' She started to speak, to stammer, and then something in his attitude, something perhaps which she sensed rather than saw, made her stiffen herself and say accusingly: 'You knew! You knew before you touched me!'

'Yes, I knew—or rather, shall I say, I suspected.'

There was no apology in his voice, only something which might have been a note of triumph.

'How could you? How . . . how . . . dare you?'

'If you dare to pretend to be the woman to whom I am betrothed, you must take the consequences.' There was no doubting the severity in his voice now.

It was then, at that moment, the moon came from behind the clouds which had veiled it all evening. By its light Cleona could see his face all too clearly—the dark, deepset eyes, the straight, uncompromising eyebrows and the full lips with the cynical smile at the corners of them—lips that had touched and held hers for the second time.

With a gesture that was almost piteous she pulled at the wrap which had fallen from her bare shoulders, as if, too late, she would protect her inviolability.

'You had no . . . right to . . . kiss me,' she said in a voice that she meant to sound strong and angry but which, in fact, was soft and weak.

'You place yourself in the sort of position when such an action seems inevitable,' Lord Raven replied, and now there was no mistaking the smile on his lips.

'You are . . . cruel!'

She did not know why, but suddenly Cleona felt curiously near to tears. She knew she ought to be angry, she ought to hate him because he had insulted her, and yet the words that she wanted to say were lost because she felt suddenly so small and helpless, so alone and defenseless.

'Why are you here—masquerading?' His voice was grave, but for once he was not sneering or taunting her.

'Beryl had a notion to go to the Carnival,' she answered. 'She is young, she wanted the . . . the gaiety and the . . . fun.'

'Beryl has always wanted that,' he answered. 'And you? Did you not desire to accompany her?'

Cleona shook her head.

'No, I am afraid of crowds. And besides, nobody invited me.'

'I cannot believe that is truth. What about the Prince?'

'His Highness did not ask me,' Cleona said. 'And I should not have gone if he had.'

'You love him?'

She was so surprised at the question, she felt that for a moment she could not have heard it aright. She glanced at him. She was still so near to him because, although he had taken his arms away from her, she was still as close as she had been when they had encircled her. His eyes seemed to bore their way into her very innermost thoughts, and because she knew that he was looking for something beneath the surface she did not turn away, but faced him proudly.

'No, I do not love him,' she answered.

'But you will marry him just the same?'

She shook her head.

'I shall never marry where I do not love.'

'You are convinced of that?'

'Absolutely!'

'I wonder if you are speaking the truth?' Lord Raven appeared to be speaking more to himself than to her.

Because there seemed nothing for her to say, she did not answer but only sat close against him, feeling still that strange, unaccountable weakness which made her want to cry. Suddenly she could bear it no more.

'May I go, my lord?' she asked.

Even as she said the words she remembered that Beryl had not yet returned. Was it her duty to stay? As if he sensed her conflcting feelings, he answered:

'You can go if you wish. I will wait for my betrothed!'

She fancied there was something stern in his voice.

'Please do not be angry with Beryl,' she pleaded. 'She would not have been discovered if you had not come home so unaccountably early.'

'The *Duc* was unfortunately indisposed,' Lord Raven said, 'and so his guests dispersed immediately dinner was over. I came back to spend a quiet evening with my mother and her guests. She told me Beryl was sitting out here, but I find you. Would you call this a quiet evening?'

'I . . . would not know.'

He was teasing her again, but somehow it did not arouse

135

her, as it usually did, to indignation. Instead she turned her head away so that her features were silhouetted against the darkness of the trees. After a moment he said:

'Why are you crying?'

'I am . . . not.'

'I think you are.'

Even as he spoke a tear ran unchecked down Cleona's cheek and was followed by another. She searched for her handkerchief and realized she had come without one even as he put a large white square of soft lawn into her hand. She lifted it to her eyes. It smelt of lavender water and tobacco—a masculine combination which reminded her of her father and made her want to cry more than ever. She was suddenly so terribly alone, so defenseless, so lost, without anyone to whom she could turn and of whom she could seek advice.

'You haven't answered my question,' Lord Raven said. 'Why are you crying?'

'I do not . . . know.'

The tears were checked, but there was a little sob on her breath.

'If I am in any way responsible, will you grant me pardon?'

His voice was kinder than she had ever heard it and in some inexpressible manner it made everything harder to bear than before.

'I . . . no . . . I do not know.' She rose to her feet with a wild desire to escape. 'Please may I . . . go? Oh . . . please?'

She did not wait for his answer but ran across the terrace, the tears blinding her so that the light from the *Salon* was only a golden haze ahead of her. Only as she reached the windows and stepped into the room did she remember that she should have gone into the house by a side door. Then with a sense of relief she saw there was no-one there—the Dowager had retired for the night.

Instinctively she turned back from whence she had come. She could see Lord Raven sitting where she had left him on the stone bench in the curve of the balustrade. He was not looking after her; his back was turned and he was looking out over the lighted city.

And then as she watched him she saw him bend forward and pick up something from the stones at his feet. She guessed it was the handkerchief he had lent her—the handkerchief which was wet with her tears.

11

CLEONA awoke with the feeling that something was wrong. At first she did not know whether it was in her dreams or in reality. Then the events of the night before and the memory that she had sobbed herself to sleep came flooding back into her consciousness and her heart was heavy and an unusual cloud of depression lay over her spirits.

What had Lord Raven thought as she ran away from him with the tears coursing down her cheeks? How could she have been so foolish? Why had she not railed at him for what he had done? To him it might seem a just punishment for her deceit in pretending to be Beryl. But surely, she thought as almost instinctively she raised her fingers to her lips, the punishment had exceeded the crime?

She felt herself blushing as she remembered how long his mouth had possessed hers, how helpless she had been beneath his lips and within the encirclement of his arms. And now, with a sense of panic, she wondered if she could ever face him again. How could she meet those dark, penetrating eyes, know that his mouth was curling in a sarcastic, taunting smile, and remember that she had been closer to him than to any other man in the whole of her life?

It was, indeed, the second time he had kissed her. But how different this last kiss was from the first!

The door opened behind Cleona and she started at the sound, looking, as she turned in the sunlight, like a frightened nymph. But it was only Beryl who came into the room, her dark hair falling over her shoulders, dressed in a muslin wrapper which revealed rather than concealed the curves of her young body.

'I thought you might be awake, dearest,' she said, 'and I am consumed with longing to tell you what happened last night.'

Cleona clasped her hands together.

'Can you ever forgive me?' she asked. 'But I beg of you to believe it was not my fault. Was he very angry?'

'Who? Sylvester?' Beryl asked. 'He read me a lecture, of course. But what do I care? As a matter of fact I was, in a way, thankful that you had not waited up for me.

For imagine, I did not return until after four in the morning!'

'What could you have been doing?' Cleona exclaimed.

'That is what I wish to relate,' Beryl answered. 'Oh, dearest, it was the wildest fun. I enjoyed myself more than I have ever enjoyed anything before. It was worth a sermon from Sylvester, I can tell you that.'

'But his lordship must have been furious,' Cleona said.

'As mad as fire,' Beryl smiled. 'But it doesn't signify. As I told him, 'twas his own fault for casting such a damper on something I particularly desired to do.'

'What did he say to that?' Cleona asked.

'I really did not listen to his prosing,' Beryl answered airily.

Cleona had the impression that she was deliberately making light of what must have been an unpleasant moment; and feeling that it was not her concern what happened between Beryl and the man she was to marry, she said tactfully:

'Tell me of your adventures.'

There was no doubt that Beryl was only too eager to relate the events of the evening.

'It was so gay!' she exclaimed. 'I cannot imagine anything like it happening in dull old London. The streets were full of musicians and everyone was wearing a disguise. There were clowns, gypsies, men on stilts, and others with huge heads made of plaster. There were brigands, pirates and every kind of gallant who might have stepped from the pages of a story book. And the women were entrancing! All were masked and all were wearing the loveliest costumes.'

'Did you look very conspicuous?' Cleona asked.

'No, of course not. We were not so bird-witted as to go into that crowd undisguised. The Count had brought me a domino of blue satin spangled with stars, and with it was a little *tricorn* hat and a lace mask, which made me look like some lady from Venice. He was dressed as a *toreador*— and a very handsome one he made, I can assure you!'

'And where did you go?' Cleona asked.

'We wandered through the streets and then we visited inns and restaurants. There was dancing and singing at all of them. Perfect strangers invited us to take a glass of wine with them and I danced with one man who I swear was the Duc de Ferrara, and another who I discovered was a baker's assistant—and, incidentally, he was by far the better dancer of the two!'

'Were you not frightened?' Cleona asked.

'Of what?' Beryl replied. 'Of being free and untrammelled by convention for an evening?'

'Not exactly that,' Cleona answered. 'But of talking with strange men and letting them think that perhaps they could take liberties with you.'

'You forget the Count was with me,' Beryl said with a smile. 'He looked after me most carefully and with a great show of jealousy.'

'Is he in love with you?'

'He is crazy about me,' Beryl said. She stretched her hands suddenly above her head in a sensuous gesture of a woman who knows her own attractions and glories in them. 'Is there anything,' she asked softly, 'more exciting than being loved and in being made love to by a man who is driven almost to madness by his desires?'

'Lord Raven returned early,' Cleona said. 'Did he tell you?'

'I gathered that had occurred,' Beryl replied. 'But to tell the truth, I had anticipated that some catastrophe was bound to happen as I was so late. I am sorry, dearest, that you should have been involved, but when I found what fun the Carnival was I could not tear myself away. In fact I thought I might as well be hanged for a sheep as for a lamb.'

Beryl laughed as she spoke and somehow it was impossible for Cleona either to rebuke her or even to resent her naughtiness. Indeed, her gaiety was infectious and Cleona found her own oppression vanishing as Beryl continued to recount incidents which had happened the previous night.

'Oh, it was fun, fun, fun!' she said finally. 'And coming home I vowed to myself that never again would I allow myself to be bullied into the boring restrictions of what older people—and his lordship—call conventional behaviour.'

'If you behaved like that very often and were discovered, your reputation would suffer and then you would be ostracized by the best Society,' Cleona warned her.

'A fig for the best Society!' Beryl said. 'Why should men have all the fun in life? They can go where they wish and talk to whom they please, but we poor females must sit cooped up in the prison they call home, awaiting their return.'

She stretched herself again and then threw herself on the bed, padding the pillows comfortably behind her shoulders.

'I let the Count kiss me good night,' she said a little dreamily.

'Beryl, you could not have allowed such a thing!' Cleona exclaimed.

'I did. He is a very experienced lover. In fact, I declare I have almost lost my heart to him.'

'But . . . but . . . do you often allow men to . . . kiss you?' Cleona asked in a low voice.

Beryl looked at her and laughed.

'If they attract me! Does that shock you? You are so innocent and unsophisticated, Cleona. One day you will wake up and find what the world is really like.'

'Do you really like . . . being kissed?' Cleona stammered.

'Yes, really!' Beryl replied mockingly. 'Why not try letting the Prince kiss you and see what you feel about it?'

Cleona gave a little shudder. Somehow the idea revolted her. She had not thought of such a thing before, but now the memory of the Prince's sensuous mouth pressed against her hand returned to her all too vividly.

'I would not permit His Highness to touch me,' she said stiffly.

'Wait until you are married,' Beryl said warningly.

Cleona would have answered then that she had no intention of marrying the Prince, but the door opened and Swallow came in with their morning chocolate on a tray.

'I guessed this is where I should find you, milady,' she said to Beryl. 'And I am wondering what your ladyship was doing with one of your newest gowns last night. There's inches of dust and dirt around the hem and a tear in the skirt you could put your hand through.'

Beryl laughed.

'You see,' she said to Cleona, 'it is impossible to hide the evidence of one's crimes.'

'What were you up to, milady?' Swallow asked.

'Don't breathe a word in this household,' Beryl replied. 'But I went to the Carnival.'

'I'm surprised at your ladyship, I am indeed!' Swallow said, without much conviction.

'And I will wager you were there yourself,' Beryl said accusingly.

'I merely stepped out for a few minutes,' Swallow replied. 'It was at the invitation of his lordship's valet, and we were not the only ones who went from this house.'

'Did you not think it was amusing, Swallow?' Beryl asked.

'Indeed I did not, milady,' Swallow answered as she

tidied up the room. 'Too much license and far too much horseplay for my liking. These foreigners are that unrestrained it's not respectable!'

She gave a sniff of disdain as she carried Cleona's clothes from the room, and Beryl and Cleona both dissolved in laughter.

'The English point of view,' Beryl ejaculated when she could speak. 'How droll Swallow is about such things, and yet I swear when she gets the opportunity she is a tremendous flirt.'

'Surely not!' Cleona exclaimed.

'Indeed, so I am told,' Beryl answered. 'But all women are at heart. You will learn, Cleona, when the time comes.'

'I hope not,' Cleona said.

'Why do you say that?' Beryl asked curiously.

'You will think I am stupid and perhaps rather pretentious,' Cleona replied. 'But I do not want to flirt, I want to fall in love with one man; to have him love me. I want to be married and to live in the country and have children. I do not want to be gay or fashionable.'

'What a strange girl you are!' Beryl said. 'And you are so lovely that you could, if you wanted, easily be the toast of St. James's.'

'I should be terrified if I was,' Cleona smiled.

'When I am married to Sylvester you must come and stay with me in London,' Beryl said. 'It would be fun to make you a tremendous success whether you liked it or not. You are much prettier than half the vain beauties of the *beau monde* and you would not interfere with my conquests because we are so different in type. Men who admire brunettes would not admire you.'

'No, of course not,' Cleona agreed. She did not know why, but the fact seemed a curiously depressing one.

'I must go back to my room,' Beryl said. 'I have a *masseuse* coming in a few minutes. You have not forgotten the Ball tonight?'

'The Ball?' Cleona asked.

'Yes, of course. It is part of the Carnival, only our Ball will be very different from the fun and freedom of last night. Only the very best and most important people will be present. Oh dear, I shall miss my baker's assistant! He danced so much better than the *élite!*'

With this parting remark Beryl went from the room, leaving Cleona still standing at the window. How long she stood there she did not know before the door opened and Ellen came in carrying a silver salver.

'His lordship asked me to give you this, Miss, when you woke,' she said.

Cleona looked at the salver in surprise. On it was a note sealed with a wafer. Beside it was one white rose. A very ordinary unexotic rose such as might have been found in any English garden. For a moment she only stared, and then she picked it up and held it to her nose. It had a sweet, familiar fragrance and Cleona thought she was back at the Manor, moving across the ill-kept lawns or idling down by the stream where the rose bushes had grown wild and the honeysuckle rioted over a tumbledown arbour.

Then she remembered that Ellen was waiting and quickly took the note from the salver.

'Thank you, Ellen.'

She waited until she was alone before she broke the wafer. There were only a few words on the sheet of writing-paper—*I hope you forgive me. R.*

She read and re-read them before she understood. They were an apology for what had happened last night. She held the rose to her face again and realized that she was no longer afraid of meeting him. This was his act of reparation for having kissed her cruelly and with the intent to hurt her. This was the holding out of his hand in friendship, and perhaps, too, in sympathy and understanding of the tears that she had not been able to control.

She read the note again, then folded it and hid it away in the back of one of her drawers. But the rose she laid carefully on the dressing-table, intending, when she dressed, to fasten it in the front of her bodice. When he saw it there, he would understand without words that she accepted and reciprocated his gesture.

For the first time she felt that her hatred of Lord Raven no longer lay in her breast like a weapon of which its owner must always be conscious. She had hated him for so long and so violently that it was hard now to believe that such a simple gesture as a note and a flower could really change her feelings so swiftly and so effectively.

And yet she wondered if in the last few days her anger against him had not been evaporating minute by minute. She had never been able to forget how glad she had been to see him when he rescued her from the bandits. Nor, indeed, that ugly moment when the man who had been ill-treating the donkey had seemed about to offer her violence. Each time Lord Raven had saved her from consequences which seemed, in her imagination, to be even worse than the reality. It was little wonder that her hatred had been blunted. And yet the memory of his kisses was always there to ignite the fire of her imagination.

How dared he? She asked the question again, but feebly, knowing in her heart it was just a re-echo of what had gone before and no spontaneous outburst of feeling.

It was, however, one thing to consider Lord Raven dispassionately behind the closed doors of her bedroom, but a very different thing to come face to face with him in reality. Cleona, wearing one of her new dresses of white batiste with a blue sash and a chip straw bonnet trimmed with feathers of the same colour, came down into the *Salon* expecting to find both Lady Raven and Beryl awaiting her, only to discover Lord Raven alone, seated at the open window, a newspaper in his hand.

He rose at her approach and she suddenly found herself tongue-tied, her self-assurance gone. She was only conscious of his great height, the squareness of his shoulders in a steel blue coat which reminded her of an overcast English sky. His cravat was immaculate and his Hessian boots owed their polish, she knew, to a judicious mixture of champagne and blacking.

'May I wish you good morning'?

His voice was grave, but she felt there was a twinkle in his eye. She wished, then, as she had never wished for anything before, that she was not wearing at her breast the white rose he had sent her. She felt it was deliberately coquettish—a gesture, perhaps, that he might misconstrue or which might make it appear as if she condoned rather than deprecated his action in kissing her.

'Good morning, my lord!' Her voice was hardly above a murmur.

Lord Raven set the paper down with a slow deliberateness and then advanced towards her.

'You are better?' he enquired.

'Yes, and I must thank your lordship. It was ... kind of you to ... enquire.'

'My conscience pricked me after you had retired last night. I told myself I had behaved brutally. You are too young for this sort of thing.'

'What sort of thing?' Cleona enquired, curious despite her shyness.

'Intrigue and subterfuge; the lies in which both men and women indulge when they want their own way.'

Cleona gave a little sigh.

'You are telling me how ignorant I am,' she said. 'Beryl has said the same thing.'

'What did she say?'

The question was surprisingly sharp.

'That I must learn more about the ways of the world,' Cleona answered.

'The ways of the world?'

Cleona made a little gesture.

'I think she meant the ways of high Society,' she answered. 'I am shamefully ignorant, as your lordship well knows. For one thing I do not understand how to . . . to flirt.'

'Do you really imagine that you need to learn such lessons?' Lord Raven asked. To Cleona's surprise there was an unmistakable note of anger in his voice.

'I understand that I shall never be a success without them,' Cleona smiled.

To her astonishment he put both hands on her shoulders and turned her around to face him.

'Listen to me,' he said harshly. 'Do not let such nonsensical notions spoil you. Stay as you are.'

She was so surprised that for a moment she could only stare at him. Then, before she could think of an answer, he had released her and walking across the room had rung the bell by pulling at the silk tasselled cord which hung from the wall.

'You must pardon me if I take my leave of you, Miss Wickham,' he said. 'But I have an appointment to drink sherry with Cardinal the Duke of York.'

Cleona wanted to ask him to tell her about the brother of the famous Bonnie Prince Charlie, but it was obvious that Lord Raven had no intention of indulging in further conversation. He bowed politely and left the room just as a footman opened the door in answer to his summons.

She heard him walk away towards the front door where she presumed his curricle would be waiting. Then she sat down in the seat he had vacated and wondered what he had meant by telling her to stay as she was.

The question perplexed her all through the day and it was only when she was dressed for the Ball that night that she found an explanation in that he, thinking her to be quiet and unsophisticated, thought she was a good companion to Beryl.

'If I, too, were smart, amusing and sophisticated he might have even a greater task in looking after us than he has already,' Cleona thought. It was a not very satisfactory explanation and one which seemed unduly depressing, but at least it served.

'He thinks I am unimportant—a mere adjunct to Beryl—and he does not wish to be troubled with me,' Cleona told herself and felt an almost insane desire to show him she could be very different.

Must she always play insignificant and almost ignoble parts in his estimation? she wondered. First, a dairymaid; then the poverty-stricken travelling companion whose clothes were a disgrace and on whom he wished to expend his charity: then, last night, a child who must be punished for acting a falsehood by being paid out in her own coin.

'Why should he think of me in such a way?' she demanded of her reflection in the mirror.

She thought at that moment that she would be a fool if she did not marry Prince Camillo. She had only to bring him to the point of declaring himself, to accept his offer of marriage and to be transformed, by one simple word, into the most fêted and the most envied young woman in the whole of Rome.

'I will accept him,' Cleona said to herself, 'and then they will know that I am not so unimportant as I appear.'

She felt the depression and a sense of shyness which had held her spellbound all day slip away from her, and a sudden fire run through her veins which caused her to hold her head high and made her eyes dangerously bright.

Perhaps some of it was due to anticipation of what she would look like in her new dress. The seamstresses whom Swallow had brought to the Villa had been working all day and most of the previous night on the gown which now hung in the wardrobe awaiting her.

When Beryl had finished with the hairdresser he came to Cleona's room. She showed him the dress that she was to wear and he swept her fair hair high on her head. It gave her height and at the same time contrived, in some strange manner, to make her look even younger and more appealing than when it was dressed in its usual fashion.

At last Cleona was ready except for her gown. Ellen brought it to her and she slipped it on. It was daring, exquisite and yet very young. Soft, almost transparent gauze fell from the high waist like a cascade from one of the fountains. There were silver ribbons which tied over the shoulder, crossed under Cleona's pointed breasts and fell to the floor at the back in a tiny pretence train. There was a stole, soft and white, to drape over her naked arms and float out on either side of her like sails carrying her over a smooth sea.

For a moment Cleona stared at herself in the mirror and asked the eternal question: 'Can this be I?' And even as she formulated the words she knew the answer. It was herself as she had dreamed she might be. The butterfly had emerged from the chrysalis and now at last she could erase from her mind the recollection of that old, darned and faded cotton dress which had led Lord Raven into mistaking her for a dairymaid as he ordered her to open the gate for himself and his horse.

With an unusual sense of the dramatic she waited deliberately until everyone had gone downstairs for dinner. She heard the guests arrive and then, just before it was time for the meal to be announced, she walked slowly across the hall and in through the great open doors of the *Salon*.

It was not yet dark outside, but the candles were lit in the great crystal chandeliers hanging from the ceiling and in the silver sconces which decorated the walls. In their light Cleona might have been Aphrodite rising from the waves with the salt spray still clinging to her, as she moved across the polished floor to where Lady Raven was holding court.

It was Beryl who saw her first—Beryl, excitingly seductive in a ruby-red gown which made her look, as she said herself, 'like a scarlet witch'. She was fascinating and provocative enough to entice any man. But Cleona was as fair and fresh as the orange blossom on the tree which surrounded the villa and as pure and innocent as the white jasmin which climbed over the balustrade of the terrace. There was, as she appeared, a moment's silence, and then Beryl exclaimed:

'My dearest love, I declare I did not recognize you!'

Cleona heard the surprise in her voice and saw the admiration in the eyes of the men grouped around her. But she was seeking only one face, asking a question of only one pair of dark eyes.

Then across the candle-lit room Lord Raven faced her, but she saw neither astonishment nor admiration in his expression. He was watching her, yet she could learn nothing from his enigmatic indifference. But there was unmistakably a cynical smile at the corners of his mouth.

A sense of disappointment kept Cleona silent until they reached the dining-room. During dinner she answered politely the diplomat on her left and listened to effusive compliments of the nobleman on her right. From him, however, she learned that the Ball was to take place in the *Palazzo* of the Duc de Bossigna.

Cleona could not help but feel warmed and flattered by his compliments. And yet, when she reached the Ball, she felt it would have been hard for anyone to be outstanding in such a distinguished gathering. The jewels of the ladies surpassed anything that she could ever have imagined. Each one seemed to blaze like a constellation. Even the seams of their gowns were studded with diamonds.

The gentlemen, too, were not easily outshone. Brilliant, colourful uniforms, evening clothes covered with decorations and jewelled handles to their swords made them almost as spectacular as the women. With a sense of relief Cleona found herself looking again and again at the quiet sobriety of Lord Raven's well-cut satin coat.

He was following the fashion set by Beau Brummell in dispensing with all fripperies, jewellery and unnecessary ornamentation. A lesser man might have seemed insignificant, she thought, but with his great height and broad shoulders it was impossible to ignore him.

She danced with several gentlemen in the party; and then, as she rested after a somewhat arduous waltz, she found Prince Camillo beside her. He raised her hand to his lips.

'I have been looking for you all the evening.'

'We have not been here long, Your Highness," she replied.

'May I have this dance?'

She was about to answer him when she found Lord Raven beside them.

'Miss Wickham is already promised to me, Sire.'

Cleona looked up in surprise. It was the first time he had approached her or asked her for the favour of a dance, and suddenly she was annoyed that he should presume to interfere between herself and the Prince. If this was his idea of wishing her to stay as she was, then it was only a trap to prevent her from enjoying herself with other men. And undoubtedly it was a presumption on his part which she was not prepared to tolerate. She drew herself up a little stiffly.

'I think your lordship is mistaken,' she said. 'I was not aware that you had invited me to dance with you.'

'Then I am asking you now,' he replied gravely.

Cleona smiled with what she hoped was the sophisticated, poised smile of a woman of the world.

'How gratifying, but I am afraid your lordship is too

late. His Highness has already honoured me with an invitation.'

She held out her hand to the Prince as she spoke. There was a glint of triumph in his eyes as he said:

'Better luck next time, Raven!' Then he drew her skilfully into the throng of dancers.

The Prince danced well and Cleona found herself suddenly elated at the idea of scoring over Lord Raven, of paying him back just a little for treating her as if she were a child and of no consequence. She wondered now, as she moved over the floor as if she had wings on her feet, how she could have been so stupid as to have cried in his presence last night or to have been afraid this morning of meeting him again. Perhaps this was what was meant by flirting, playing off one man against another. If that was true, then she was flirting and enjoying it for the first time in her life.

'You are wonderful, exquisite; I adore you!'

She heard the Prince's words as if they came from a long way away. It was hard to concentrate on what he was saying when she had so much to think about.

'You are different tonight—and yet even lovelier! You look like one of the statues in my villa outside the walls of the city. Sometimes you are as cold and aloof to those who adore you as they are, but tonight I believe that I can make you come alive.'

Cleona found herself dimpling at him.

'Your Highness says such charming things that I feel as if I am taking part in a play.'

'A play is a pretence,' the Prince protested. 'What I am saying is real and true. I love you!'

His voice rose a little with passion and the intensity with which he was speaking. Cleona looked alarmed.

'Ssh . . . Your Highness,' she admonished. 'People will overhear you.'

'You are right,' he said. 'What I have to say must be said alone.'

'No, I did not mean that,' Cleona protested, but already he had drawn her to the edge of the floor, and although she tried to protest he drew her out of the great ballroom and through some crowded ante-rooms to where an open window led into the garden.

'I do not wish to go outside,' Cleona said hastily, but the words died on her lips, for the garden was a scene of enchantment.

She had never seen anything like it before. There were fairylights outlining all the paths and displayed amongst the shrubs. There were Chinese lanterns hanging from the branches of the trees. At least a dozen fountains were cunningly lit so that the water in every colour of the rainbow flew flashing to the sky and then descended, iridescent and glittering, into the shining basin below.

It was all so lovely that Cleona for a moment could hardly believe that the stars in the sky above and the moon rising up above the ilex trees were not as artificial as the lights in the garden. Everywhere there was the fragrance of flowers—a fragrance almost intoxicating, it was so pungent and alluring.

'Come, there is something I want to show you,' Prince Camillo said.

'We must not go far,' Cleona said nervously.

'Are you afraid of me or of a reprimand from your watchdog—milord Raven?' the Prince asked.

He could not have said anything more likely to incite Cleona to defiance.

'His lordship does not command me,' she replied half angrily.

'Then why fret about the conventionalities?' he asked. 'I will take care of you. Come, I want to show you the Temple of Love.'

He pointed, as he spoke, to where just ahead of them stood a little Grecian temple, also cleverly lit so that the white marble of its pillars glowed like a jewel against the darkness of the sky.

'How lovely!' Cleona exclaimed.

'As lovely as you,' the Prince whispered.

She felt his hand drawing her forward. Her instinct told her she should resist, but her brain reminded her that to do so was to behave as Lord Raven commanded.

'In the Temple of Love,' the Prince told her, 'there is a statue which is considered lucky by all those who ask a favour of it. I have a favour to ask—both of the statue and of you.'

For one moment Cleona hesitated and the Prince, sensing her indecision, redoubled his entreaties.

'Please do not refuse me,' he pleaded. 'It is such a little thing to ask of you, and yet who would be so unwise as to turn aside from the Temple of Love? Is not love the greatest, strongest and most irresistible force in all our lives?'

He was so handsome, so young and so obviously sincere

that it would have been churlish to repulse him. Cleona made no further resistance, but let him lead her along the path to where the Temple gleamed, white and inviolate beneath the stars.

12

'WHAT gown will you wear tonight, my love?' Beryl asked, coming into the bedchamber where Cleona was resting on her bed.

'I had not given it much thought,' Cleona answered, smiling.

Beryl sat down with a flourish which made the carved bedposts shiver.

'What a strange creature you are, dearest!' she remarked. 'You become a success overnight and yet you treat such a monumental occurrence as if it were of supreme indifference to you.'

'You exaggerate,' Cleona answered with a smile.

'No, I swear it to be the truth,' Beryl replied. 'Everyone at the Ball last night was exclaiming at the beauty of your countenance and enquiring as to your identity. I think I must have revealed who you are to a hundred admiring gentlemen.'

'Fine feathers make fine birds,' Cleona answered. 'Nobody noticed me when I wore my shabby garments.'

'Why should they?' Beryl enquired. 'People are judged by their outward appearance. As I have said often enough, a heart of gold is usually hardly worth the labour of digging for it!'

Cleona laughed.

'You are not to be cynical, Beryl. And if we are talking about someone being a success, what about you? I saw the Count looking utterly downcast yester evening when you hardly so much as cast a glance in his direction.'

' 'Twas good for him,' Beryl dimpled. 'But I won't be sidetracked, my love, into talking about myself just because you wish to be secretive. I will not blab of your affairs, and I am not bacon-brained. I know as well as you why the party tonight is being given.'

'In truth, I have no comprehension of what you are

saying,' Cleona cried in bewilderment. 'Lady Raven announced at luncheon that we were to dine at the Villa Borghese. That is all I know.'

'Fiddle!' Beryl exclaimed rudely. 'You cannot be such a simpleton as to see nothing significant in the fact that her ladyship was awoken almost at dawn by a note beseeching us to honour the Villa Borghese with our presence. Why should a dinner party be given in such a hurry unless it is this very evening that the Prince has decided to declare himself?'

Cleona said nothing. She was, indeed, at a loss what to say. Always reserved, having had few friends in her life in whom she could confide, she could not now bring herself to talk freely, even to Beryl, of what had occurred the previous evening. She felt it would be betraying the Prince to tell anyone, even her closest friend, of what had taken place in the Temple of Love.

She saw now that it had been a mistake to go there with him. And yet she was honest enough to admit to herself that although she had guessed that when they were alone he might seize the opportunity to offer for her hand, she had not been entirely certain in herself what would be her reply. It would have been untrue to say that she was not a little tempted by the position he could offer her.

It would also have been impossible and unnatural for any young woman not to be flattered by the attentions of so charming and attractive a personage; and Cleona, who had known so few men in her sheltered life, could not help but be a little thrilled by the Prince's obvious admiration and the almost intoxicating words with which he declared his adoration for her.

The Temple of Love, built in the Grecian fashion, contained only a comfortable couch covered with cushions and a statue of Venus being caressed by several little cupids. But from it one could look back over the garden with its twinkling lights to the huge edifice that was the *Palazzo* and hear the music floating softly through the darkness as if on enchanted wings.

For a moment Cleona had been engrossed in the vista, and then, realizing that the Prince was strangely silent, she turned to look at him. Two lanterns hanging from the ceiling of the Temple revealed the passion in his deep-set eyes as he watched her, his very body seeming tense as if with an effort at self-control.

'We must return to the ballroom, Your Highness!' Cleona said a little nervously.

'Not yet!' he answered. 'I wish to talk to you.'

'Perhaps we shall be . . . missed,' Cleona hesitated.

'Why must you play with me?' he asked hotly. 'Why must you stand there looking as cold and unapproachable as the statue behind you? You know that I love you and yet you show me less kindness than you give to the lowest servant in your employ.'

'That is not true,' Cleona protested.

'It is true,' he answered wildly. 'I love you! Let me tell you how much and how deeply.' As he spoke, he took her hand in his. 'I want you to marry me. I have never before said that to any woman, but I know that I cannot contemplate life without you. Be my wife and I will make you happy, I swear it.' He bent his head as he spoke and covered her hand with his kisses.

Cleona wondered for the moment if she had heard him aright. Was it really true that she, insignificant and unwanted, who had been brought abroad by the charity of a friend, had received an offer of marriage from the richest and most eligible bachelor in the whole of Rome, a member of the most powerful family in Italy?

She was fascinated, as it were, at the picture of herself receiving so much homage and was, for the moment, almost divorced from what was actually happening. So that the Prince, mistaking her silence for consent or believing, perhaps, that no woman, however elusive, would refuse such an offer, drew her into his arms.

It was only then, as his lips brushed her cheek seeking her mouth, that Cleona awoke to the reality of the situation and struggled against him.

'No! No!' she said quickly. 'Please, Your Highness, do not . . . touch me.'

It was too late. His lips, hot, greedy and insistent with passion, fastened themselves on hers. For a moment she could not move, and then with a violence that took the Prince by surprise she struggled free. Her hands pushed him from her and she sped to the far corner of the Temple, standing there in what seemed to him an adorable confusion.

'You must not . . . kiss . . . me,' she stammered.

'Why not?' he enquired, smiling, a look of triumph in his eyes.

Her breath was coming quickly between her lips as if with fright, but there was a dignity in her voice as she replied:

'I am honoured by Your Highness's offer . . . of marriage, but I have not yet given you . . . my answer.'

'Do not play with me,' he said, going towards her. 'Cannot you see that you have already driven me to madness by my need of you? I am like a man who is dying of thirst and yet you forbid me the touch of your lips which would save my life. I adore you! I worship you! Give me your answer quickly.'

'I am sorry . . . Your Highness,' Cleona said. 'I am very sensible of your condescension . . . but it is . . . no.'

'No!' There was no mistaking the surprise in the sharpness of the Prince's ejaculation.

'I cannot . . . marry you.'

'But, why?'

'Because I do not love Your Highness. Oh, I see that it was wrong of me to let you say so much . . . to come here alone . . . with you. But I was not sure . . . I thought that perhaps . . .' Her voice trailed away as the Prince drew nearer and stood looking at her.

'You are very young,' he said softly. 'Perhaps I have frightened you. It is hard for a man to hold himself in check when a woman is so lovely, so sweet as you. But I will teach you to love me, my little English statue. In my arms you shall learn what love means.'

'No . . . indeed. I am . . . sorry, but . . . it is impossible!'

'The English are so cold,' the Prince continued. 'They are also exceedingly slow. It takes them a long time to get to know anyone, to acknowledge a friend—let alone a lover. I must give you more time, my beloved.'

Cleona twisted her fingers together.

'Please believe me, Sire, that it will be . . . useless,' she whispered.

He seemed not to have heard her.

'I will go on asking you,' he said. 'I will see you every day. I will make love to you from the moment the sun rises until the moon sets. I will melt that little frozen heart of yours. I will make you come to life so that you will no longer be a cold statue but a living, pulsating woman—wanting me as I want you.'

Cleona gave a little shiver.

'We must go back to the ballroom, Your Highness. Please take me back!'

There was something so urgent in the appeal that the Prince checked the wild, impetuous words which rose to his lips.

'It shall be as you wish,' he said gallantly. 'Because I love you, I desire to serve you.'

He kissed her fingers again and then, opening her hand, pressed her lips hungrily against the soft palm before encircling her small wrist with kisses.

'We must . . . go!'

She slipped away from him, moving so quickly down the path which led to the more crowded parts of the garden that there was nothing he could do but follow her.

The band was playing, couples were moving gracefully over the polished floor of the great ballroom. They might never have been away. And yet, as Cleona accepted an invitation to dance from a young Naval Attaché and looked back over her shoulder to see the Prince watching her from the doorway, she knew that something significant and fundamental had happened.

Unmistakably and irrevocably she knew that she could never marry Prince Camillo Borghese. It was one thing to say that she would never marry a man she did not love, and quite another to know, in actual fact, that she would not and could not marry a man who loved her and who had offered her his hand and heart.

She was aware now that she had hoped, secretly, that she would be able to love the Prince and that if, indeed, he did offer for her she would wish to accept the honour and the dignity of bearing his name. But now it was impossible. She had known, as his lips had touched first the cheek and then her mouth, that he could never mean anything more in her life than someone of whom she would think kindly.

She had, indeed, felt almost a horror of him when he kissed her. She had known in that split second that she would never love him, could never give herself into his keeping—however important or however distinguished he might be. Position, rank and wealth did not enter into it. It was merely a matter that he was a man and she was a woman, and she could never belong to him.

She had been bemused and nearly carried away by Beryl's talk of what she had to gain by becoming the Princess Camillo Borghese, but she knew now that position was not of the least consequence beside the fact that she could never, even if it meant starving in the gutter, consent to become the wife of the Prince.

Cleona danced with first one partner and then another. She talked, she laughed, she appeared, outwardly, her ordinary normal self. And yet, when she reached home she knew she had changed.

'What do I want?' she asked of her heart when she was alone in the darkness of her bedroom. 'Why can I not love the Prince? Why does the mere thought of being possessed by him fill me with horror?'

She did not know the answer to her own questions, but they had remained with her all night, and now it was with a sense of foreboding that she realized she must see the Prince again this evening. There was nothing she could do to prevent it. She was all too well aware that if she told Beryl, or even Lady Raven, that she had refused an offer of marriage from His Highness, they would look at her in consternation and suspect her of being deranged.

They would not be able to conceive any possible reason why she should refuse to marry a Prince of the Blood Royal, and in consequence Cleona could think of no good reason why she should not accompany them tonight to the Villa Borghese.

'You must look your most alluring, my love,' Beryl was saying. 'I will send my hairdresser to you and he must contrive some new and original coiffure. Now, let me inspect your gowns.' She rose from the bed and pulled open the door of the wardrobe.

'Delicious! Delectable! Of a surety this is what you must wear,' she cried, bringing out a dress that had come that very morning from the skilful hands of the seamstress.

'If that pleases you,' Cleona murmured, and wondered why her lips would not tell the truth and say that she would prefer to stay at home.

All the same she had to admit, when she was ready and taking a last look at herself in the mirror before she descended to the *Salon*, that Beryl's choice had been unerringly the right one. The gown was of white tulle sprigged with tiny blue flowers not unlike forget-me-nots. There was a blue sash to accentuate the high waist, and the *décolletage* was very low, revealing the whiteness of her neck as the tiny puff sleeves slipped from her shoulders.

The hairdresser had exclaimed in delight when he saw the dress and sent Ellen hurrying with instructions to the gardeners. When she returned she carried a wreath of flowers which seemed the very replica of those which embroidered the dress. Arranged in Cleona's hair, it made her the very impersonation of Spring—she might have been Persephone coming from the dark bowels of the earth to bring hope and sunshine to less enlightened mortals.

Beryl approved of her appearancce with a cry of sheer delight when she joined the others downstairs.

'I feel in my bones that this is going to be a momentous evening, dearest,' she said with meaning, and Cleona wished that she could reveal that nothing could be said tonight which had not been said already.

'Why momentous?' Lord Raven asked sharply.

'You must not ask questions, Sylvester,' Beryl replied mysteriously. 'Perhaps we shall be able to tell you tomorrow.'

'Tell me what?' he enquired.

Cleona had not looked at Lord Raven when she came into the *Salon*. She would not seek his approval of her new gown. Last night she had felt defiant. Tonight, for some reason she could not define to herself, she was merely shy and apprehensive.

Now at last she glanced towards him and thought that whoever else looked distinguished his lordship would easily eclipse them. He made all the Roman nobility seem not only small, but gaudy and ostentatious. The diamond buckles which held his breeches at the knee and the plain silver ones on his shoes were his only ornamentation.

'Would you kindly inform me what you are all talking about?' Lord Raven asked. There was an unrepressed note of irritation in his voice which made her mother say hastily:

'I think it is time that we left for the party. You sound cross, Sylvester, and that is not the right way to start the evening.'

'I detest a conversation which appears to have no meaning,' he said testily.

Beryl laughed.

'You must allow us poor, frail females to have our little secrets,' she said. 'Or how else could we remain the mysterious sex?' She crossed the room, slipped her arm into his and smiled up at him beguilingly. 'This is Cleona's secret and so I will not tease you any more.'

Cleona fancied that Lord Raven's eyes rested on her as if he would penetrate her thoughts and find the truth. Proudly she told herself it was no business of his, and turning her head away she followed Lady Raven to where the coach was waiting for them.

The Villa Borghese, outside the walls of Rome, was more beautiful than Cleona had expected. It was small after the great Palazzo Borghese, but its rooms were rich with the wealth of centuries. Cleona longed to look at the pictures, statues and exquisite hangings which met her eye at every turn, but she found it impossible to think of anything but the Prince, who seemed determined by his behaviour to make her conspicuous.

There were forty guests assembled in the *Salon*, all of them from the noble families of Rome, all of them distinguished and important. And yet their host persisted in talking only to Cleona. She tried to divert his attention, but he would have none of it.

'I think the Duchesse wishes to speak to Your Highness,' she said desperately as he stood at her side staring at her with burning eyes.

'I would rather talk to you.'

'There is another lady beside her who is beckoning to you. Look, you must go.'

'Only if you come with me.'

He was being very difficult, Cleona thought, and it was with a sigh of relief that she heard dinner announced and knew that for the moment, at any rate, he was, by convention and tradition, separated from her. He must take the head of the table with a Princess on his right and a Duchess on his left, while she, an unmarried girl of no consequence, was far away from him with two comparatively unimportant men on either side of her.

The dinner was outstanding among the many luxurious, extravagant repasts at which Cleona had partaken since she came to Rome. Rare and delicate dishes succeeded one another in a vast profusion, all served on gold plate and proffered by flunkeys dressed in such an elaborate gold-laced livery that the eye was almost dazzled by them.

There was music from an orchestra hidden behind a great bank of exotic flowers. There was a fountain which played perfume instead of water, and for all the lady guests there were presents hidden in bouquets of flowers which were presented to them by a tiny negro boy dressed in jewel-embroidered robes and wearing a turban held by fabulous emeralds.

It was all fantastic, extravagant and ostentatious, and when dinner was over they withdrew to another *Salon* where every game of chance lay ready for their delectation. A turn of the card and a fortune changed hands. It was fascinating, Cleona thought, and yet she was glad that she herself was not required to be a participator.

She was watching a table of faro when one of the flunkeys came to her side.

'Someone has called, *Signorina,* who wishes the privilege of speaking with you,' he said deferentially.

'Called to see me?' Cleona asked in surprise.

'*Si, Signorina,* it is urgent.'

Cleona wondered who it could possibly be. Was it someone with a message from England, or was there something wrong at the villa? In which case why did they not ask to speak with Lady Raven? She glanced towards her hostess, wondering if she should say something to her, and saw that she was engaged in a game of whist.

' 'Tis of import, *Signorina,*' the flunkey said again.

'Very well, I will come,' Cleona said, deciding to find out first what was the matter before disturbing Lady Raven.

The man led her from the room down a long passage. At the end of it she climbed a beautifully carved stairway to the first floor, and again there was a long passage hung with fine pictures and carpeted so that Cleona's feet, in her blue satin slippers, made no sound as she followed the footman.

They reached a door. The lackey flung it open with a flourish and Cleona entered. The room was lined with books and there were deep, soft couches covered with coloured cushions. There was a writing-table in the window and bowls of flowers on tables which held a profusion of beautiful and valuable ornaments—but otherwise the room was empty.

Then, as Cleona looked around her, she heard the door behind her shut. She turned; the flunkey had vanished; but standing in the room, smiling at her, was the Prince. He looked at her for a long moment before he locked the door and put the key in his pocket.

'I do not understand, Your Highness,' Cleona said. 'I was told that someone wanted to see me urgently.'

'That is true. I want to see you—and very urgently.'

'Then it was . . . a trick,' she faltered.

'A justifiable one.'

'You know full well I cannot stay here with Your Highness,' Cleona said angrily. 'Unlock the door at once. I must return to Lady Raven. Already she may have missed me.'

'You must stay here until you have heard what I have to say to you,' the Prince replied.

There was something so determined in his voice that Cleona felt suddenly afraid. But there was no sign of it as she held her head high and her eyes met his.

'What is it Your Highness desires to tell me?' she enquired.

'Will you not sit down?'

'I would rather stand.'

'Very well, if you prefer it.'

The Prince walked across the room and seated himself on one of the wide, deep couches. Then he smiled disarmingly.

'Come and sit beside me, little Cleona,' he pleaded. 'What I have to tell you cannot be shouted across the room.'

She hesitated and decided it would be unwise to antagonize him. She was well aware that to stay alone with any man, let alone the Prince, in a locked room was dangerous, and yet it seemed to her she had no alternative. Slowly she moved towards him and seated herself on the couch, but as far away from him as was possible.

'So cold, so distrustful!' he protested. 'Have you forgotten that I want you to marry me?'

'This is not the right way to make me trust Your Highness,' Cleona answered. 'You brought me here by a cheat which was unworthy of you. I beg you to take me back to your other guests as soon as possible.'

'Then listen to what I have to say,' he said. 'Today I had a summons from Paris. Napoleon Bonaparte demands my presence there.' He paused dramatically.

'And are you going?' Cleona asked, wondering why the invitation should perturb him so greatly.

'You do not understand,' he answered impatiently. 'If Bonaparte desires my presence, there is some reason for it. And because I wondered what he could want of me, I went this morning, as soon as I had the invitation, to see the most famous soothsayer in the whole of Rome.'

'A soothsayer!' Cleona exclaimed. 'Do you believe in such things?'

'But, of course,' the Prince answered impatiently. 'Everyone consults Zilukha. She is famous, and, what is more— her prophesies invariably come true.'

'What did she say?' Cleona asked.

'She told me,' the Prince replied, 'that I had reached the cross-roads in my life. Two ways lay open to me. One was the way of my heart, the other led northwards.'

'It sounds the usual chatter of fortune tellers and gypsies,' Cleona said scornfully.

'Wait!' he commanded. 'There is more. If I took the way of my heart, Zilukha said I should find happiness. If the other, I should experience great unhappiness and eventually shame and humiliation. "There are two women in your life," she went on. "One is fair, the other is dark. It is the dark one of whom you must beware."'

The Prince paused and Cleona looked at him enquiringly.

'I still do not understand,' she said.

'To me it is very clear,' the Prince answered. 'You are the fair woman—the way of my heart. When the soothsayer spoke of my journey northward, I knew that she referred to my invitation to Paris. I knew, too, what Bonaparte wanted of me. He intends to marry me to one of his sisters.'

'But how can Your Highness credit such an idea?' Cleona asked.

'I am not a fool,' the Prince answered. 'Have you not heard that as First Consul of France Napoleon is marrying off all his family and making provision for them as best he may? I have learnt, too, that his youngest sister, Pauline, is likely to become a widow. She married young General Leclerc, who was sent to Santo Domingo in order to re-establish slavery there. But the campaign has been disastrous.

'Rumour says that yellow fever has swept the French forces and that twenty-five thousand soldiers are already dead from it. My informant—a man who had just returned from there—told me that when he left Leclerc was dying. By now he may be dead and Pauline on her way back to France. I may be mistaken, and yet instinct tells me that Napoleon is looking for a rich brother-in-law.'

'This is sheer speculation, Sire,' Cleona suggested.

'Zilukha spoke with the eyes of a seer,' the Prince replied. 'Because I believe in her; because, too, I am frightened of my own future, you must marry me—now and at once. That is the way of my heart, the way that will bring me happiness.'

'You cannot be serious!' Cleona exclaimed.

'Indeed I am,' he answered. 'So serious that I have brought you here to tell you what I intend to do. When we go downstairs, I shall announce to my guests the news of our forthcoming marriage.'

Cleona rose to her feet. She was very pale, but her voice was quite steady as she said:

'If you do, I shall deny it. I gave Your Highness my decision last night, and must repeat it again—I am sorry, but I cannot marry you.'

'I was afraid you would say that,' the Prince said. 'I

know that I should wait, that I should give you time to think about it—time to learn to love me. But time is the one thing I cannot afford. If you will not come to me of your free will, I must take you by force.'

'I cannot comprehend your meaning, Sire!' Cleona said, but her hands were trembling as she raised them, as if to protect her breast.

'You need not be afraid of me like that,' he said gently as if he guessed her fears. 'I will not hurt you, for I love you too much. If you wish it, I will go down on my knees at this moment and kiss the very ground on which you stand. But because I must make up your mind for you, because I intend you to be my wife, I shall keep you here until you promise to marry me.'

'And if I still refuse?'

The Prince smiled.

'Can you not understand what will happen?' he asked. 'In an hour's time, perhaps sooner, my guests will realize that we are both missing. Italians are not slow like the English; they jump to conclusions very quickly. At first there will be whispers, a look, perhaps a gesture of amusement. And then, in a little while, they will be talking a little louder. They will ask each other where the Prince can be and what can be keeping him in the company of the charming and beautiful English girl with whom he talked so intently with before dinner.

'Time will pass and the jokes will get broader until the ladies present will take action. They will consider that they have been insulted. Such things do not happen at respectable dinner parties. They will call for their carriages and they will leave, expressing both disgust and anger at the ill manners of their host. They will say many things, but they will know, in their hearts, that they are quite prepared to forgive me. I am a man. It is the woman whom they will not forgive.'

'What do you mean?' Cleona asked, hardly above a whisper.

'I mean,' the Prince answered, 'that from tonight you will cease to exist. If anyone speaks of you, they will not have heard of you; you will not be invited to any parties, to any functions at which Society is present. And if they call on Lady Raven, they will make it very clear that you must not be present.'

Cleona stared at him with wide eyes.

'How can you conceive of doing such a cruel thing when you say that you . . . love me?'

'You have a motto in your country,' he replied, 'which says "All is fair in love and war". This is love and I want you for my wife.'

'I will not allow you to blackmail me in such a way,' Cleona cried.

She tried to run to the door, fruitless though she knew it to be. But as she turned, the Prince with a laugh held out his arms and caught her.

'Why do you fight against me?' he asked, and now his voice was raw and deep with passion. 'You are so lovely, so enchanting. I love you, and we shall be very happy together.'

Cleona gave a little cry, but his lips were on hers. And then, even as she struggled from the hard possession of his mouth, the handle of the door was turned violently.

The Prince raised his head, but as Cleona drew in her breath ready to scream he placed his hand quickly over her mouth. The handle turned again before there was a sudden shuddering impact against the door as if someone thrust a broad shoulder strongly against the frail wood.

Still holding Cleona with one arm, the other hand hard across her lips, the Prince stared almost fascinated. There was another crash and now the door, ornamented by exquisite mediaeval carvings, gave way before the overwhelming force behind it. The lock splintered and broke, the door flew open and Lord Raven walked into the room.

For a moment neither the Prince nor Cleona could move, and as they stared, their eyes wide with astonishment, Lord Raven solemnly bent his head and flicked the dust from his coatsleeve. Then slowly and with astonishing poise he moved forward languidly, still intent on discovering some real or imaginary dust upon the unruffled surface of his sleeve.

'I am afraid, Your Highness,' he said in a bored voice which had suddenly assumed the fashionable drawl of St. James's, 'that the hot weather has induced your doors to stick. I have the same trouble at home in a damp winter. Let me give you the tip. Beeswax is what you need, my dear fellow!'

Quickly the Prince released Cleona; quickly he turned to face the drawling Englishman. He was so livid with rage that his face had assumed an almost unnatural pallor, and his hands were clenched together as he took a step forward.

'You come here . . .' he began accusingly.

'Yes, Sire, I have come here,' Lord Raven drawled, 'to tell you that most regretfully we must leave your so delightful party. My Mother is a trifle fatigued and she requests Miss Wickham to accompany her home.'

At last it seemed to Cleona that the paralysis which had held her spellbound since Lord Raven's entrance released her limbs so that she could run forward and reach his side. She was trembling all over as she stretched out towards him and clasped his arm, holding on to him with clinging fingers as a drowning man might grasp at a straw.

'Thank God you have come,' she murmured.

He looked down at her and his face was quite expressionless.

'Do not perturb yourself unduly,' he said. ' 'Tis not serious. But my Mother is not as young as she was and we must take every care of her.'

The Prince had drawn himself up and almost instinctively his right hand had gone to his side as if to seize a sword, which fortunately was not there.

'My lord,' he thundered, 'I demand——'

' 'Tis most kind of Your Highness to demand the carriages,' Lord Raven interrupted. ' 'Twas just what I was going to ask you to do. It seems uncivil to hurry away so early, but I know that you, as a leading member of Roman Society, would not wish anything to happen to a British subject who was your guest. International incidents cause so much trouble and so much—gossip.'

There was no mistaking the warning in Lord Raven's voice. For a moment he forgot to drawl and his voice was like a whip. The Prince was silent. He was defeated and he knew it. He could only bite his lips with rage as Lord Raven bowed and without saying anything further drew Cleona, still clinging to his arm, from the room.

She was trembling as they went down the passage which led to the flight of stairs, and she had an almost irresistible instinct to run, to rush away as quickly as she could from the man who was watching them. But Lord Raven's walk was leisurely and because she still clung to him for support she must set her pace by his. Only as they reached the lower passage could she at last compose herself enough to murmur:

'I do not know . . . what you must . . . think of me.'

He looked down at her then and she thought that his face was severe.

'I think,' he replied, 'that you have a touch of Roman fever. It is very prevalent here amongst visitors and to avoid it you must take every care.'

'Please,' she whispered, 'can I . . . explain?'

'My Mother is waiting,' he answered coldly.

They had reached the door of the *Salon* and gently but firmly he disengaged her hand from his arm.

'I have much enjoyed instructing you about the treasures of the villa,' he said.

It was a statement of fact made in a cold voice which somehow struck chill into Cleona's very bones. She knew then that he despised her, that he was condemning her for making a fool of herself, for having become embroiled in dangers from which only by his presence of mind and quickness of intuition had she been rescued.

She wanted to explain, wanted to tell him how, if she had been foolish enough to fall into a trap, it had not been intentional. But somehow she knew that he would not listen, knew, by the sternness of his jaw and the hard line of his mouth, that he condemned her unheard.

His hand went out towards the door. Behind it Cleona could hear the laughter and chatter of many voices. For one second longer she was alone with him, there was one second in which she might try to explain, might seek his forgiveness. But her lips were dry and she could not force her voice from a throat which seemed suddenly contracted.

And then, as Lord Raven turned the handle and the door opened, she knew with an almost agonizing clarity that she loved him!

13

CLEONA sat at her window all night staring out over the moonlit city and seeing nothing but the inner tumult of her own heart. She felt as if the knowledge of her love for Lord Raven had not only burst upon her like the conflagration of a great fire but as if it also illuminated her secret so that all who looked on her must know it.

As she re-entered the crowded *Salon* of the Villa Borghese where the guests were still gambling, she was concerned not with what they might be thinking of her absence with the Prince but that they might see in her face her new-found love for the man walking at her side.

And because she loved him she was acutely conscious of

Lord Raven's disapproval. Even the square set of his shoulders and the straightness of his back made her feel how bitterly he censored her, and in despair she felt she would never have the chance of explaining that the Prince's intentions had been honourable and that he had wished to marry her.

As she sat alone at her window the whole episode seemed, in retrospect, unreal and theatrical; but she knew now why, in the Temple of Love the night before, she had realized that it was impossible for her to accept the Prince's offer of marriage.

She had thought at the time that her repugnance was merely a distaste for the man himself. She saw now it was something very different—a comparison between him and the man to whom, secretly, her heart had been given for a long time. She had thought that she hated Lord Raven. And yet, looking back over their journey from England, she could see all too clearly how every day, and in fact every hour, had been coloured and enriched by his presence.

It had been a satisfaction in itself to fight with him, because she was acutely conscious of him; to hate him, because she could be thinking of him; to defy him, because in doing so she held his attention. She should have known how much she loved him when he had taken advantage of her masquerading as Beryl to punish and humiliate her.

And yet had it been such a humiliation? Cleona admitted the truth. The touch of his lips had thrilled her! And her tears had been for herself. She had wanted him to seek her out for a very different reason than because he was incensed with her. She had wanted him to seek her lips not as a punishment but because he craved the touch of them.

At the thought Cleona covered her face with her hands and sank down into the depths of her own shame. She was shocked, horrified and disgusted with herself. Still her love would not be denied.

She loved him—the man who was engaged to her greatest friend; the man who looked on her only as a troublesome child who must be rescued from impossible situations, who must be corrected and punished for flouting his authority.

'What am I to do?' Cleona asked the stars.

She longed to run away, to hide herself somewhere where no-one could ever guess of her misery and her yearnings. But there was nowhere she could go!

When they had arrived back that evening from the Villa Borghese, there were letters from England both for Lady Raven and for Beryl. Cleona longed above all else to seek the seclusion of her own bedchamber, but because Lady Raven and Beryl were engrossed in their letters she felt it impolite to interrupt them.

'Oh, pray listen to this!' Beryl exclaimed suddenly, looking up from the letter she was reading. 'Here is some news for you, Cleona.'

'News from England?' Cleona enquired.

'Yes, indeed, in a letter from one of my admirers in London,' Beryl answered. 'You would not know him, but he is a most amusing gossip and is always first to hear any rumour that may be circulating in the *beau monde*. He says: "*Prinny is back at Carlton House and very Engaged, I understand, with Lady Jersey. There is much Talk of his posting so Hastily to Woodstock. He has tried to keep it a Secret, but of course Everyone knows that he was turned down in Favour of Vigor. His Lordship's Betrothal to the fair Eloise has been Announced and a great deal of Money has changed Hands in consequence. The Betting was six to four against her bringing him up to Scratch, so you can imagine that many of our young Blades are badly dicked.*" '

Beryl threw the letter towards Cleona with a little gesture.

'Your Mamma has actually brought it off!' she exclaimed. 'Are you pleased?'

'Yes—very pleased,' Cleona answered. 'It is what Mamma wanted and I pray that she will be happy.'

She tried to speak enthusiastically, but she knew that this meant that, as far as she was concerned, even her home had gone. The new Lady Vigor would not wish to spend money on keeping up the house where she had lived with her first husband and which she had always disliked.

Cleona felt her eyes fill with tears. Because she was ashamed of them, feeling that Beryl and Lady Raven would think her selfish in not being more delighted at the news of her mother's betrothal, she hastily excused herself and went upstairs to her own bedchamber.

There she sat, hour after hour, trying to find some solution to her own problems, trying to sort out her own thoughts and feelings.

Many hours later, as she stared out into the darkness the sky lightened, the stars began to fade, the first pale finger of dawn crept up over the distant hills. Cleona felt not only tired from her long vigil, but utterly miserable.

She felt she must do something, take some action, if only to clear her head of the throbbing questions to which she could find no answer to still her heart from its frenzied beating for a man who could never be hers.

She was still wearing the diaphanous white and blue ball-gown in which she had dined at the Villa Borghese, and now for the first time she realized that she was cold. She shivered as the dawn wind stirred the flowered creeper blooming luxuriantly over the walls of the villa and the trees in the garden below.

Cleona rose and going to her wardrobe took out a soft cashmere shawl which Beryl had lent her to wear over her evening gowns. She wrapped it round her shoulders and slipping from her room went slowly down the stairs, moving silently through the sleeping house, her footsteps so light that she felt as if she were a ghost.

She let herself out of the house through a side door. There was no-one to see her cross the terrace and move down the steps into the flower-filled loveliness of the formal garden. Already the birds were stirring in the bushes, blossoms were opening their petals and there was an air of expectancy, as if the whole earth anticipated the glory of the sun that had not yet risen.

But to Cleona there was only the darkness of her own thoughts. She walked on and on until she came to the wall which surrounded the garden. There was a gate in it which opened on to the lower road. It was through this gate that Beryl had slipped out on the night of the Carnival to enjoy herself with Count Rezzonico while she had taken her place on the terrace—with such vital consequences!

Cleona had a sudden impulse to pass through the gate, to go down into the city, to wander through the empty streets, to look when no one was about at the ruined beauty of the Forum and the splendour of the Coliseum.

She was just about to discover if the gate would open or if it was locked when she heard a carriage coming along the road. She waited, and when after a moment she saw the wavering gleam of its candle-lanterns she quickly drew back into the shadow of some fuschia bushes. She had hardly done so when the carriage drew up outside the gate. Someone was getting out, and almost instantly, long before she saw him clearly, Cleona knew who it was.

The carriage was hired and Lord Raven paid the driver; then, as the man wished him good night in Italian, he drew a key from his pocket and unlocked the gate leading into the garden. Cleona held her breath as the gate swung inwards and he came within a few steps of her. He was still wearing the satin breeches and elegantly cut coat with which he had graced the Prince's dinner party. There was a dark cape over his arm and he carried his hat in his hand.

He locked the gate and then, as he turned, the moonlight was full on his face. He looked stern and preoccupied with his thoughts and there seemed something purposeful about his walk as he moved quickly up the flagged path which led towards the house.

Cleona watched him go. Her heart was beating and her hands were cold as she clenched them together. For a moment she could only watch until he was out of sight; then the full realization of what she had seen made her long to cry aloud her misery. She could only imagine one reason which could have kept Lord Raven out so late.

Cleona sank down on the grass beside the fuschia bush and covered her face with her hands. There was not only the thought of Beryl to torture her but the thought of another woman as well—an unknown woman who had kept Lord Raven by her side till dawn had broken.

What was she like? Cleona wondered. Was she dark or fair? Had she blue eyes or grey? Was she tall or short?

The poison shaft of jealousy seemed to stab right into her very heart; and then, as she sat there in an unhappiness too poignant for tears, she knew, with a despair born of her love, that even this made no difference to her feelings for Lord Raven. Whatever he might do, however much he shocked and antagonized her, she still loved him more than life itself!

Lord Raven let himself into the house through a French window which he had left unlatched. It was still very early in the morning, but the sun was rising and he knew it would not be long before the housemaids came downstairs to start their cleaning. Nevertheless, he seemed in no hurry as he moved through the shuttered and curtained *Salon*.

The air was heavy with the fragrance of flowers and there was the usual air of untidiness which always exists in a room before it has been cleaned and straightened. There were crumpled cushions, empty wine glasses, a disarranged rug and on the table, lying open, Beryl's letters from England.

Lord Raven hesitated for a moment and then, ignoring the closely inscribed sheets of writing-paper, picked up an envelope. He examined it closely and nodded his head as if what he saw confirmed his suspicions. The letter had been opened and sealed down again before Beryl received it. He threw the envelope down on the table and slowly walked upstairs to his bedchamber.

He had a great deal to think about as he closed the door of his room and went at once to his writing-table. The candles had guttered low, and blowing them out he crossed the floor to fling wide the shutters and let in the pale, almost iridescent morning light.

For a moment he took a deep breath and then, returning to his writing-table, unlocked a drawer with a key which he carried on his fob. Inside, amongst various other papers, was one which contained the cypher which Canning had asked him to use when communicating any information of great urgency. He read it carefully and set it down in front of him.

There was a quill at his right hand, writing paper in a leather holder and ink in an ornate gold and marble inkstand. But Lord Raven did not write. With his chin resting on his hands he sat thinking of what he had learned.

He had, in fact, spent the night with a woman, but not for the reason that Cleona suspected. Not only she but anyone else in Rome would have thought the same thing had they seen Lord Raven come from a *Piazza* which was well known, not to say notorious. Its owner, Elandi Dimagili, was the most famous courtesan in the whole of Italy.

As beautiful as any of the beautiful women who had made a success of her profession in the past, Elandi had not only looks but brains. She was rich; she owned one of the most fabulous *Piazzas* in Rome; she had furniture, jewellery and pictures worth a tremendous fortune. But she had one passion which transcended all else—a love for her country.

She had hated the French when they came swaggering destructively into Italy, and she hated Napoleon Bonaparte because she believed that sooner or later he would attempt to destroy the country she loved.

It was quite by chance that Lord Raven had learned that Elandi believed that only England could save Europe from the stranglehold of the tyrant. He had been half afraid that the stories of her patriotism had been exaggerated, but when he talked with her he found them to be indisputably true.

He had then made a momentous decision and taken a

grave risk in letting her know that he was interested in finding out what Bonaparte's plans were for the future both of Italy and of the rest of the Continent. Elandi had only to whisper to one person that the English Lord who had come to Italy ostensibly in search of amusement had deeper and more political interests and his usefulness would be over from that very moment.

The majority of Italians were terrified of Bonaparte. They knew how weak and helpless their country was; they knew only too well from past experience the force and power of the tyrant to whom they must surrender because there was no other alternative.

There was nothing strange in Lord Raven's being a visitor at Elandi's house. No man who visited Rome and called himself a man would forbear to pay his respects to the most beautiful and spectacular woman of her generation. What was strange was that often, after everyone else had left, he and Elandi would sit talking in lowered voices, usually until the dawn broke.

Lord Raven was openly congratulated on having received Elandi's favours. No-one would have believed him had he replied that he had never ventured further than to kiss the tips of her soft fingers.

That evening, when he was dressing for the Prince's dinner party, a note, scented with the perfume of tuberoses, was brought to him in his bedchamber. It had been delivered by a carriage drawn by four milk-white horses and driven by a black negro wearing a crimson uniform plentifully embellished with gold braid.

The Italian servants at the villa had received the note with what almost amounted to reverence. They had the utmost respect for any man who was smiled on by Elandi, to whom they offered the same tokens of esteem and the same adoration as their ancestors had accorded to the Virgins in the Temple of Vesta.

Lord Raven read the note and then, holding it to the flame of one of the candles on his dressing-table, watched it burn away to ashes. He had said nothing, but his valet had immediately laid out on a chair the dark cape which he habitually used on his nocturnal visits to the city.

When he arrived at Elandi's *Piazza* some time after midnight, it was to find a party in full swing. The men present all bore noble, aristocratic names and they were, indeed, representative not only of Roman Society but of many other countries of which they were the chosen representatives.

There were other women present, but they were of little consequence. It was Elandi who held the stage, who was the centre of all eyes. Wearing a gown so diaphanous that the Grecian proportions of her exquisite body were clearly visible, she was adorned round her neck and at her wrists with emeralds worth a king's ransom, but on her head there was a simple wreath of tuberoses.

She welcomed Lord Raven with a witty remark and a touch of her hand. He toasted her in wine which had mellowed in some great Cardinal's cellars and drank it in a jewelled goblet which had graced the table of the Borgias. There was music and conversation which would have delighted a connoisseur in the art and wisdom of living.

And then, gradually as it grew later, the company began to thin out. It was, however, three o'clock before Elandi and Lord Raven were alone. The last guest to go had clapped him on the back.

'Damme, Raven, you're a devilish lucky chap,' he said. 'You came, you saw and you conquered, eh?'

Lord Raven bowed.

'Your Excellency flatters me.'

'If I thought I could outstay you, I should do so,' was the reply.

As the door closed behind the Ambassador, Lord Raven looked at Elandi. She was looking inexpressibly alluring. Her eyes were a little shadowed with tiredness, but her mouth was red and inviting and her skin white as a magnolia in contrast to the green of her emeralds.

She threw herself down on a long, low couch covered with a tiger skin. There was an inexpressible grace in every movement she made. Lord Raven's eyes were on hers; he merely stood and waited.

'I have found out what you desired to know,' she said at length in her low, musical voice which was a little husky with weariness.

'You are sure it is correct?'

'Quite sure. It came from a source which is indisputable.' She glanced over her shoulder as if afraid. 'He arrived last night from Paris. He had been with Bonaparte up to the last moment before he left.'

Lord Raven drew up an armchair so that he was close beside the couch.

'What news did he bring?' he asked.

'Bonaparte intends to make himself Emperor!'

Lord Raven raised his eyebrows.

'A fabrication!'

'It is the truth! And the nation will accept him. Can you doubt it?'

'No! But I can hardly credit it.'

'One can credit anything with Bonaparte,' Elandi interrupted. 'And there is more.'

'Relate to me all you know.'

'He plans to invade England from Boulogne. One hundred and fifty thousand men are to be encamped there and already flat-bottomed boats are being specially constructed for their transport.'

Lord Raven was silent for a moment.

'He will not succeed. The Channel is an almost impregnable defence.'

'But he will try. England must be prepared.'

'Yes, we must be prepared.'

They sat and talked until one by one the candles in the sconces flickered and went out. Finally, Lord Raven rose and walking across the room drew back the heavy brocade curtains.

'It will soon be dawn,' he said. 'I must go.'

'Yes, my friend,' Elandi answered softly. 'You must go. And now we must say good-bye.'

He turned at that and went back to the couch. She was lying relaxed against the silk cushions and she looked little more than a child. There was something childlike, too, and a little wistful in the smile she gave him. He went down on one knee beside her.

'How can I thank you for what you have done?'

'I have done it for Italy,' she answered. 'And perhaps, in a small degree, for you, too.'

He lifted her hand to his lips.

'You know I am grateful, and England will be grateful too. We are in your debt, Elandi.'

'Will you remember me?' she asked. 'We may never meet again—but will you remember me?'

'I shall never forget you,' he answered, looking deep into her eyes.

She made a little sound that was curiously like a sob, and then in a voice that was hardly above a whisper she said:

'If you must go, go quickly. I have always detested saying good-bye. This time it is harder than usual.'

Lord Raven hesitated for a moment and then he bent his head and kissed her. It was a kiss without passion; a kiss of gratitude and reverence and perhaps, too, one of regret.

It left Elandi deathly pale. She said nothing as he released her and only her hands quivered as he stood towering above her, his eyes on her face.

'I shall never forget,' he said quietly again, and then he went from the room. . . .

Lord Raven picked up his pen and started to write, but even as he formed the first word he changed his mind. It was too dangerous. There were men who could read any cypher, however complicated, however obscure. There were those to whom even the Diplomatic Bag was not sacrosanct.

He threw down his pen and walked to the window. The sun was rising; everything was tinged with gold. The birds were singing in the garden below, the butterflies were fluttering, crimson and orange, white and blue, amongst the flowers. But as he regarded so much beauty Lord Raven was scowling.

Cleona had slipped back to her room unseen and unperceived about twenty minutes after Lord Raven had passed her in the garden below. She had passed through so many emotions that evening that now she felt numb and past any feelings whatsoever. Utter fatigue had swept away everything but a longing for sleep. She slipped off her clothes and no sooner had her eyes closed on the pillow than she fell asleep.

She slept dreamlessly and deeply and awoke to find the sunshine streaming into her room and Beryl seated on the window-ledge.

'I thought you were never going to awake, my dearest love,' she said. 'You must have been very tired last night.'

'I was—exhausted,' Cleona answered truthfully.

'I have so much to discuss with you,' Beryl continued. 'What we shall wear tonight for the Masked Ball. Whom we shall invite to luncheon tomorrow—because you remember that Lady Raven said we could have a party.'

Cleona forced herself to concentrate on what Beryl was saying. She felt bemused and a little stupid, and yet the memory of all that she had felt and experienced last night was flooding back to her consciousness.

'There is something else I wanted to talk to you about,' Beryl said. 'But it has gone from my mind. Oh, yes, now I remember it. Look what arrived for you about twenty minutes ago.'

She pointed as she spoke to a huge basket of red roses

which had been placed on a table just inside the door. Attached to the ribbon was a note.

'Do you see what it says?' Beryl begged. 'There is no need to guess from whom it comes.'

Cleona stared distastefully at the beautiful present. She had a curious reluctance even to touch the note which she could see was penned in the Prince's handwriting, but because Beryl was watching her she forced herself to get out of bed and take it from the basket of flowers.

'His Highness is certainly very attentive,' Beryl said. 'Did he say anything of any import last night?'

Cleona did not answer. She was reading what the Prince had written.

Forgive me! My only excuse is that I love you, even though you do not love me. I am leaving for Paris today, so we will not meet again. Good-bye.

Camillo.

Cleona read it through, then folded it over. Beryl watched her with bright eyes.

'What does he say?' she asked at last, unable to restrain her curiosity.

'The Prince is leaving for Paris,' Cleona answered. 'He told me yesterday that Bonaparte had commanded his presence there. He believes that the First Consul wishes him to marry one of his sisters.'

Beryl's face was all consternation.

'Oh, Cleona, and I was so certain that he would offer for you. Dearest, are you distressed?'

Cleona could not help smiling.

'No, not in the very slightest,' she answered. 'I did not care for His Highness in that way.'

'But he made it so obvious that he was taken with you,' Beryl cried. 'I thought he was serious.'

'Do not think on it again,' Cleona begged.

'The sly wretch!' Beryl exclaimed. 'I am almost convinced that he has insulted you! I believe that Sylvester should call him out. I shall speak to his lordship about it.'

'No! No! Please do nothing of the sort,' Cleona cried. 'The Prince has not insulted me and even to speak jokingly of a duel would be in the worst possible taste.'

'All the same, I think he has behaved very shabbily,' Beryl said. 'He has made everyone talk about you and speculate as to his intentions, and now he lopes off to

Paris just because Bonaparte has whistled to him as though he were a dog. If you ask me, that is just what he is—a dog to come to heel at the command of his master!'

'Beryl, you must not say such things!' Cleona pleaded. 'And I promise you that I was not in the least degree enamoured with His Highness.'

'But you would have married him if he had asked you,' Beryl said positively. 'Oh, Cleona, I did so wish you to be rich and powerful.'

'I shall never marry anyone,' Cleona replied.

'Dearest, what a ridiculous statement!' Beryl exclaimed. 'Of course you will. You are so pretty and so sweet, you are sure to find yourself a distinguished and important husband.'

'I do not want one,' Cleona protested. 'When we return to England, I shall find myself a position.'

'A position!' Beryl exclaimed. 'I shall be out of all patience with you in a moment! Besides, what could you do? The only employment for a lady is to be a governess, and who wants to teach somebody else's squalling brats?'

Cleona gave a little sigh.

'It seems wrong, somehow, that women should be so restricted,' she said quietly. 'But I am sure I shall find something—perhaps as companion to an elderly lady.'

'If you are set on being a companion, you had best be one to me,' Beryl smiled. 'Do not think that because I am married I shall not need you, Cleona. I shall always want you with me.'

'No!' Cleona answered. 'No! No!'

She turned away as she spoke, leaving Beryl staring at her open-mouthed. But before she could say more the door opened and Swallow came in.

'His lordship wishes particularly to speak to your ladyship,' she announced.

'What can he want at this hour?' Beryl enquired.

'May I come in?' Lord Raven's voice came from behind Swallow.

Beryl looked at Cleona who was standing at the far end of the room. She had slipped on her white wrapper over her nightgown, her fair hair fell over her shoulders, and her face, as she looked towards the door, was very pale. As if he could not wait for permission, Lord Raven came in through the door.

'I am sorry to inconvenience you,' he said. 'But what I have to say is of the utmost import. We leave for England today.'

'Today!' Beryl cried. 'But why? How can we? What has happened?'

'Nothing that I need explain,' Lord Raven replied. 'I must only ask you to trust me and believe that this decision has not been made unnecessarily.' He paused for a moment and looked at Swallow, who, realizing she was intruding, went from the room, closing the door behind her.

'What is this broil, Sylvester?' Beryl enquired.

'I have information which necessitates my return,' Lord Raven answered. 'If you must know what it is, my uncle, who has brought me up since I was a boy, is ill.'

Beryl laughed.

'That is just fustian and we all know it. It may be a good excuse for the servants and your fat-witted friends, but you might have a little dependence on Cleona and me!'

'If I tell you the truth, will you keep it to yourselves?' Lord Raven answered, looking first at Beryl and then at Cleona, who had not moved or spoken since he came into the room.

'Yes, yes, of course,' Beryl answered impatiently. 'You can rely on us to be as silent as the grave. Can he not, Cleona?'

Cleona did not answer, but as if he took her acquiescence for granted Lord Raven said:

'The reason we must leave can be told in one word—Bonaparte. It will in a brief while not be safe for us to remain in Italy, nor on the Continent for that matter. We are returning home by sea.'

'By sea!' Beryl gave a little cry.

'Yes, in a man-o'-war. I have already sent Captain Ernshaw ahead to arrange matters.'

'Sylvester, you are always delighting me with your original notions. I should like nothing better than a voyage in a sail-of-the-line. I have a *penchant* for sailors.'

'We leave for Naples this afternoon. I have told your maid to start packing.'

'And your Mother?' Beryl enquired. 'Is she accompanying us?'

'My Mother has refused to leave Italy. I have argued with her, I have pleaded, but she will not return to the fogs and cold of England. I think she is safe enough here because she has Italian blood in her and whatever happens the Italians will treat her as one of themselves.'

'So it is a war you fear,' Beryl remarked. 'I always did hear that it was an uneasy peace.'

'Yes, war!' Lord Raven answered briefly, and his manner made it clear that he would say no more.

There was a knock on the door.

'Come in,' Lord Raven said, speaking with the air of authority as if he were in his own bedchamber rather than Cleona's.

Swallow entered and crossed the room to Beryl's side.

'There is someone to see your ladyship,' she said a little breathlessly. As she spoke she held out a silver salver on which lay a card. Beryl took it in her hand and there was no mistaking the sudden tenseness in her attitude or the strangeness of expression which transformed her face.

'I will come immediately,' she said, in so low a voice that it was almost inaudible.

She rose to her feet and without excuse and without looking either at Lord Raven or Cleona went from the room. Swallow followed her. There was silence and then Lord Raven, looking at Cleona, said:

'I hope you are in good health this morning.'

'Yes . . . thank you.'

She had dropped her head and he could hardly hear her reply, but it seemed to satisfy him.

'I must go and see about the arrangements for our departure,' he said. 'We must leave as soon as the heat of the day is past.'

He waited for her comment. Cleona did not speak and after a moment he turned and went from the room.

14

'I SHALL never see him again!' Cleona said the words out loud and heard the despair in them whisper round the room.

A little earlier she had wanted to run away to hide herself. But now she knew the mere thought of not being able to see Lord Raven, of parting from him when they reached England, was an agony even worse than anything she had anticipated before.

She could see their journey all too vividly. The long days in the coach, then the weeks aboard the man-o'-war, when Beryl and Lord Raven would be together and she would feel the odd man out. Then England and good-bye!

She did not know where she would go on her return or what would happen. The future was veiled in mist not unlike tears.

With an effort she forced herself to think of her packing. As she dressed a footman brought in her trunks and set them down in the room. He was followed by Ellen, who was looking flustered and on edge.

'Miss Swallow says I am to help her first, Miss,' she said. 'I must do as she wishes, and then I will come to you.'

'Do not worry about me, Ellen,' Cleona answered. 'I will pack for myself.'

'Oh, you mustn't do that, Miss!' Ellen exclaimed, shocked at the idea of anyone in Cleona's position doing anything for herself. 'I will be along later, I promise you that. It is only, what with Miss Swallow a-nagging at me to come here and do this and not that, I don't know if I'm on my head or my heels.'

Cleona had to smile. She was well aware that Swallow easily got upset when anything untoward happened. And Ellen was very much of the same temperament, so that they bickered at each other like a couple of fishwives.

'Then pray do not worry about me, Ellen,' she said again, soothingly. But she spoke to the air, for Ellen had already whisked from the room and only the trunks stood open waiting for Cleona to start filling them.

She had much more to pack than when she had come to Rome. There were new gowns, ribbons and bonnets, and half-a-dozen things that Beryl had lent her and then said she must keep.

She was trying to fold her gauze dress so that it would not be crushed when Beryl came into the room. It must have been over an hour since she had hurried away because Swallow had told her there was someone downstairs waiting to see her. And now, as Cleona, kneeling beside her trunk, looked up at her, it seemed as if a very different person stood in Beryl's shoes.

She was dressed in her travelling cape and wore her most becoming hat trimmed with crimson feathers, but there was a radiance about her face that had not been there before. And there was a tender light in her eyes which made her seem softer, sweeter and infinitely more beautiful.

'Cleona, I have got something to relate to you.' She

spoke in a low voice and yet there was a thrill behind every word.

'What is it?' Cleona asked, rising to her feet.

Beryl looked at her for a moment and then drew a deep breath.

'Oh, my dearest love, I am so happy,' she said.

'Why? What has happened?' Cleona asked, bewildered.

'Ian is here—and he is free!' Beryl spoke the words as if they came from Heaven itself, yet for a moment Cleona did not understand.

'Free?' she questioned.

'Yes, free! His wife died three weeks ago. As he was in France, he did not receive the news for some time. Then, as soon as he heard of her demise, he hurried here posthaste to me.'

'Do you still love him?' Cleona asked.

'Still?' Beryl echoed. 'I have always loved him. I have never loved anyone else. Oh, Cleona, isn't it beyond everything fortunate? Could anything be more wonderful than that Ian can offer for me?'

'So you intend to . . . marry him?' Cleona said slowly.

'Tomorrow!' Beryl answered. 'We are leaving this instant for Milan. Ian has made arrangements for us to be married there and then we are travelling to Spain for our honeymoon.'

'But, Beryl, how can you do this?' Cleona asked.

'We can and we will,' Beryl replied a little defiantly. 'Oh, I know people will be scandalized. They are going to say that Ian should have waited at least a year before taking another wife; that he should wear the willow for a woman he never cared about and who has been raving mad for these past five years. This is what will be expected of him—and he is just not going to conform to it. We are going to be married at once! We are going to be together, now and for always.'

'But . . . Beryl, what will your father and . . . and Lord Raven say?'

Beryl smiled mischievously and two dimples appeared in her cheeks.

'They will say a lot,' she answered. 'But I shall not be there to hear them. Can you not understand, dearest, that I am running away for the second time?'

Cleona sat down on the bed and stared up at her friend.

'You cannot do it, Beryl! Everyone will be horrified!'

'What do I care if they are? I do not care a fig for any of them,' Beryl said, snapping her fingers. 'I love Ian and he loves me. He will look after me, Cleona, and I shall not get into trouble ever again once I am married to him. I shall do what he tells me, make no mistake about that. I adore being mastered and it is on his orders that we are leaving now. He has got everything planned, so I am going with him now—this minute!'

'Have you told Lady Raven?' Cleona asked.

'No, nor Sylvester either,' Beryl replied. 'I am too much of a coward! That can be your job.'

'Mine?' Cleona went pale.

'Yes, dearest, yours,' Beryl answered. 'They cannot be angry with you, for it is none of your doing. And why should I listen to their protests, arguments and reproaches? Whatever they say will have no effect because I would marry Ian—if the whole world stood in my way. I love him. No-one can conceive how much I love him.'

'But . . . but what will Lord Raven say?'

'I have not the slightest curiosity as to what he will say!'

Cleona was silent for a moment and then she said:

'I cannot contemplate speaking to his lordship on this matter, Beryl!'

Beryl ran forward to put her arms round her.

'But you will do it,' she said. 'Because I ask it of you. You have always been my one true friend, dearest, and now I trust you to help me with the most important thing that has ever happened to me in the whole of my life. You will, won't you?'

Cleona could not resist the pleading in her voice.

'I suppose so,' she said a little ruefully.

Beryl kissed her with the triumphant air of one who intended to achieve her object and has achieved it.

'I knew you would not fail me, my love. And now I must go. Ian is waiting below and I am taking Swallow. You do not mind that, do you? Ellen will attend to you on the journey home.'

Cleona laughed.

'It would not signify if I did mind,' she said. 'Oh, Beryl! I do hope you will be happy.'

'I know I shall be,' Beryl answered, suddenly solemn. 'I will be a good wife to Ian. I am making no mistake this time, I promise you that.'

Cleona was silent for a moment and then she asked:

'And Lord Raven? Do you think he loves you?'

Beryl answered quickly.

'Yes, of course he does—as much as Sylvester is capable of loving anyone. He is a strange man, as you have seen for yourself. I believe that he loves me in his own way—or at least I have no reason to think otherwise.'

'You are sure of it?' Cleona enquired.

There was something in her tone which made Beryl look at her intently.

'What are you hinting at, dearest?' she enquired. 'Have you been listening to the gossips? Have you heard that Sylvester has been seen night after night at the house of Elandi Dimagili, the most famous of all the Italian courtesans?'

Cleona turned to look at her with startled eyes.

'Do you know of such things?' she enquired.

'But of course I know about them,' Beryl said with a little shrug of her shoulders. 'There are always people ready to tell me where Sylvester has been and what he has been doing. If you have heard him returning at dawn, I can assure you his movements are no secret to me and I have had no desire to curb his amusements.'

'Did you not care?' Cleona asked.

Again Beryl shrugged her pretty shoulders.

'Why should I?' she asked. 'Men will be men, dearest, as you will learn when you have been about London as long as I have. If Sylvester wished to divert himself, I had no desire to prevent him. But I cannot help feeling that this sudden urgency of his to return home, this secret information that he has received about the possibility of war, may have been conveyed to him by the lady we have just mentioned, or one of her kind.'

Cleona walked to the window and stood looking down into the garden.

'I heard his lordship come in last night,' she said in a low voice. 'I wondered where he had been.'

'So that is why you are enquiring if he still loves me,' Beryl smiled. 'What a simple goose you are. Of course he does. A betrothed is one thing, a droxie a very different pair of shoes. And that is why you must break the news of my departure to him as gently and as kindly as possible. He will not be best pleased that I have played him false for a second time and that now at last Father's fifteen thousand acres of good Oxfordshire soil are lost to him for ever.'

Cleona turned towards her suddenly.

'Please, Beryl, do not make me do this.'

'You have already promised,' Beryl said inexorably. 'And now, dearest, I must go.' She kissed her on either cheek and said: 'We shall be together as soon as I return to England. Ian and I will not hurry our journey for he has property in Spain and I intend my honeymoon to be a lengthy and very wonderful adventure. But the moment I come home I shall want to see you, my dearest love. Until then, *au revoir*.'

She kissed Cleona again, clung her for a moment and then, before the latter could collect her scattered wits, had run from the room.

Cleona stared for a moment at the bedroom door and then went to the window. From there she had just a brief glimpse of the drive as it twisted away from the front door towards the gate on to the road. She stood there watching, hardly daring to breathe, until suddenly there flashed into view a great travelling coach with emblazoned panels and a high pile of trunks. It was drawn by six horses, their silver harness jingling and flashing in the sunlight as they passed by. Beryl had gone!

Cleona put her fingers to her temples as if in an effort to think. She had promised Beryl that she would break the news and now the moment was upon her. She recollected that Lady Raven would still be in bed. Often, after a party, she stayed in her room for at least half a day, sleeping and reading and having no desire for discourse after the exhaustion of a late night. Lord Raven would, in all likelihood, be somewhere in the house or grounds.

Slowly Cleona picked up a leaf-green stole which matched the sash she wore with her white muslin dress and went from the room. Slowly she walked down the long, twisting staircase into the drawing-room. It was empty; the sunshine was coming through the open windows. There was no-one to be seen and the terrace outside was equally without a sight or sign of the man she sought.

It seemed to Cleona as if her feet would hardly carry her across the worn flagstones of the terrace to the balustrade from which she could look over the garden below. It took her an immeasurably long time to reach this point of vantage. The gardens were a blaze of colour. Butterflies were hovering in crowds over the crimson, pink, blue and yellow blossoms in full bloom. There was the exotic perfume of tiger lilies, the chirp of the crickets, the rustling movements of the scuttling lizards and, high in the trees, the song of the birds.

Slowly, every footstep an effort of determination, Cleona descended the stone steps. She had an idea where she might find Lord Raven. She was not mistaken. In a small, secret herb garden surrounded by clipped hedges, there was a little fountain. Two stone cherubs held aloft a dolphin from whose mouth the water spurted high to fall, iridescent and golden, into a marble basin decorated with flying fish.

On one side of the garden was a wall on which, warm in the sunshine, hung golden and crimson peaches. The sweet perfume of the herbs gave the air a strange, almost exotic fragrance, and the bougainvillaea and shrubs, with their brilliant flowers, were almost dazzling to the eye.

In an alcove over which jasmin grew in thick profusion there was a seat covered with crimson cushions, on which Lord Raven was seated. He held a book in his hands, but he was not reading. He was watching the fountain, his eyes intent on the water as it glittered iridescent against the blue sky tinkling musically, as the hopes of man may rise and fall and rise triumphantly again.

Cleona, moving softly in her heel-less slippers, had almost reached his side before he saw her. And then, as if instinctively rather than actually hearing her, he turned his head. The sunshine made her hair a halo round her little face, her eyes were dark with worry and her lips trembled as she said:

'Can I speak with you, my lord?'

'But, of course.' He got to his feet and bowed. 'I am sorry I did not hear your approach. Have you finished packing?'

'Yes, thank you.'

It was with difficulty that Cleona could say the words. And, as he held a cushion against her back, she sank down on the seat beside him, her hands clasped together in her lap, her head half turned away from him so that her little tip-tilted nose and delicate features were silhouetted against the darkness of the arbour. There was silence as Lord Raven sat down, set aside his book and watched her.

'You wished to speak with me,' he prompted at length.

'Y . . . yes.' Cleona could not help the tremble in her voice.

'I am waiting.'

'It is hard . . . to say . . . what I have to . . . tell you.'

'Hard?' he questioned. 'Surely we are friends—or should I say enemies—enough to be able to speak the truth.'

There was a note in his voice which made her suspect he was laughing at her. The shame that she had felt last night when he had rescued her from the Prince's room welled up in a great confusion once more, to make her wish that the ground would open and swallow her up.

What must he have thought, she wondered for the thousandth time, as he broke down the door to find her in the Prince's arms? Did he believe that she had gone to his private room willingly, of her own accord? Did he think that she had enticed the Prince into believing he had the right to insult her in such a way?

She felt herself trembling, then forced herself to think not of herself but of Lord Raven. If he loved Beryl with the same love which shook and confused her now, she was, indeed, sorry for him. He, too, must know what it was to have an aching heart, a spiritual wound which seemed so much worse a hurt than any physical one could be.

Almost impulsively she turned towards him, only to find his eyes fixed on hers with that penetrating look that she most dreaded, so that the words that she was about to speak seemed to die on her lips.

'I am waiting,' Lord Raven said again. But now his voice was more gentle.

'I am afraid, my lord, that what I have to say will . . . distress you,' Cleona began.

He raised his eyebrows at that.

'Indeed!'

'That is why it is so . . . hard to begin, to find the . . . right words.'

'I can be brave on occasions,' he said, with an almost whimsical smile.

'I know that,' Cleona replied. 'Indeed, I think you are very brave—and perhaps first I ought to thank you for what you did last night.'

With a little sigh she realized that the conversation had once again got back to herself. Somehow it was impossible to prevent it.

'There is no need to thank me,' Lord Raven answered. 'I am only greatly relieved that we managed to avoid what might have been a very unpleasant incident. I was half afraid the Prince would challenge me to a duel, which would have caused a most regrettable scandal.'

'You . . . you were very . . . clever with His Highness . . .' Cleona said. Her voice died away as she realized she had not yet begun the task which Beryl had set her.

'Shall we forget what happened?' Lord Raven asked. 'There is no reason to give it undue importance by talking about it or indeed in remembering it.'

'I wish to forget every second that I . . . spent with the Prince!' Cleona said passionately.

'Then forget it,' Lord Raven said, with what seemed an almost harsh note in his voice.

Again there was silence.

'It was about something else that I had to ... speak with you,' Cleona said with an effort.

'Yes?'

'It is about ... yourself.'

'Something that concerns me?' Lord Raven questioned. 'What can it be?'

'I am afraid you will be ... hurt and ... unhappy,' Cleona said.

'Does it matter if I am?' he enquired. 'You should be glad of it. You have wished me ill often enough.'

Cleona trembled at the raillery in his tone, and her hands fluttered as if in protest, then came to rest again.

'I have been ... incensed with your lordship on occasion,' she said. 'But this is ... something different. And I would not wish you real ... unhappiness.'

'That is generous of you.'

Cleona made a sudden gesture.

'Please,' she pleaded. 'I am trying to tell you ... something.'

'I apologize if I am interrupting your discourse. Will you not come to the point?'

'It is ... it is about ... Beryl.'

'Something that Beryl has asked you to tell me?'

'Yes ... that is it.'

'And why is my betrothed not honouring me with her own confidence?'

Cleona took a deep breath.

'Because she has gone away.'

She dared not look at Lord Raven as she spoke; and then quickly, beause at last she had found herself able to speak, she went on:

'Oh, I beg of you not to be enraged with her. Lord Mountavon arrived to say that he was free and his wife was dead. ... He and Beryl have gone to Milan to be ... married. It must seem wrong and wicked to you, my lord, but, as you must have known, Beryl has always loved him. There has never been anyone else whom she has cared for in the same way. It was wrong of her to deceive you, but ... love is something none of us can ... control.'

There was a little throb in Cleona's voice as she said the last words.

'Who told you love is beyond our control?' Lord Raven enquired.

'If one loves someone enough,' he repeated. '—That is
'I know it. I am sure of it,' Cleona answered. 'And that is why I beg of you to pardon Beryl. If you love her, you will understand what she is feeling.'

'I would have thought more of her if she had spoken with me herself,' Lord Raven said.

'I can understand that point of view,' Cleona agreed. 'But she was afraid that you would be angry, that you would argue with her and try to dissuade her from leaving. She had made up her mind to go with Lord Mountavon and nothing anyone could say would have stopped her. Please try to understand, and forgive her.' Cleona was pleading now as she turned towards him, her eyes raised to his.

'I have forgiven her,' Lord Raven said.

'That is generous of you. I felt perhaps you would understand. If one loves someone enough one wants them to be happy.'

'If one loves someone enough,' he repeated. '—That is the important thing.'

'I am sure of it,' Cleona answered. 'Love, if it is real, must be generous and unselfish.'

'How do you know?' he enquired.

'Because that is what I——' Cleona was suddenly silent. She realized she was about to betray herself, to say that it was what she felt. It was true, she thought a little wildly. She wanted his happiness. She loved him enough so that if, at this very moment, she could have brought Beryl back and given her into his arms, she would have done so. And because she could not bear to see the hurt in his face, she looked away from him at the golden gaiety of the fountain.

'So you know that true love seeks first the happiness of the person beloved,' Lord Raven said in a quiet voice.

'Yes . . .'

'But how you have learned this? I am interested.'

'Please, do not let us talk about me,' Cleona answered. 'It is you who must try and understand what has occurred.'

'But, I do understand very well. You see, Mountavon is a friend of mine. He saw me immediately on his arrival here this morning. He told me what he was about to do, and because I think that he and Beryl are well suited to each other, I gave him my blessing.'

'So you knew!' Cleona turned round accusingly.

'Yes, I knew.'

'And you let me . . . struggle to tell you. That was cruel and unkind.'

The blood had risen into her cheeks at the vehemence of her accusation and her eyes were bright.

'Perhaps I wanted to hear what your feelings were about love.'

'I do not know why you should be interested,' Cleona answered a little defiantly.

'As my guest, and as a charge on me at this moment, I am naturally interested in all you think and all you do.'

There was a moment's silence and then in a very different tone Cleona said hesitatingly:

'I have thought of . . . that! I understand how . . . irksome it must be for you to have to escort . . . me now that Beryl has gone. Perhaps there will be some . . . other way for me to return home. But even if there is not, I promise you I shall be as little . . . nuisance as possible on the journey.'

'That is considerate of you. You were certainly a considerable anxiety on the way here.'

'I have already apologized for . . . that,' Cleona answered. 'It is not . . . kind of you to remind me of incidents which were not ostensibly my own fault.'

'I often think of your face as I climbed into that room where you were imprisoned by the brigands,' Lord Raven reflected. 'On that occasion, and perhaps again last night, you looked pleased to see me.'

'But I was, of course I was,' Cleona replied. 'I prayed that you would come.'

'You prayed for—me?' There was something in his voice which made her hesitate and feel inexplicably shy.

'Yes. Whom else?'

'Of course! Whom else?' he said in a different voice.

Again there was silence and they both sat watching the fountain, until after a minute, Lord Raven said:

'Unless I am mistaken, you have not yet thrown a coin into the Fountain de Trevi.'

'And now it is too late!' Cleona exclaimed with a little catch in her voice. 'Do you think it really means that I shall never see Rome again?'

'Do you wish to return?'

'But naturally I do. The city is more beautiful than I anticipated and . . . and I have been very . . . happy here.'

'Then whether you throw a coin into the Fountain or not, I expect you will come back,' Lord Raven said. 'But there is another coin of which we spoke and which perhaps you have found on this visit.'

Cleona did not answer and after a moment he said softly:

'The Coin of Love!'

Cleona clenched her hands together. This was harder to bear than even she had expected. She found herself longing to turn towards him, to hold out her hands and feel him take them in his, if only for a moment. She wanted to look at his mouth which had possessed her lips and held her captive, she wanted to look into his eyes even though she was afraid of the penetration of his glance. Instead, she schooled herself to sit still, to keep her head averted, to looked down to where her slippers peeped beneath the hem of her gown.

'Have you really learned about love, little Cleona?' he asked at length with a tenderness which astounded her.

'I do not know what your lordship means,' she replied.

'I think you do,' he insisted. 'When you spoke just now there was a warmth and understanding in your voice that had never been there before. Who has taught you?'

'No one . . . 'Tis not . . . true,' she answered a little wildly.

'And yet I think it is,' he said. 'Rome is a place for love, and here in the sunshine it seems almost unnatural to speak of anything else. Shall we talk of love?'

'No! No!' Cleona said almost passionately.

'So vehement?' he questioned. 'But why? Are you afraid?'

'No . . . or course . . . not.'

'Then why run away from something that can be so beautiful and so wonderful? Love, Cleona, as you so rightly said, is something that we cannot help. It comes upon us unawares and suddenly it is there, filling our lives to the exclusion of all else. Does it feel like that to you?'

'Yes,' Cleona whispered. Then added hastily: 'I . . . do not know. Please . . . I must go back to the house.'

She would have risen, but his hand went out to catch hers. At the touch of him she was suddenly very still. The blood drained away from her face and her eyes were dark and frightened as she turned them towards his.

'Why do you pretend, Cleona?' he asked.

'I am not . . . pretending,' she answered.

'No, I do not think you are,' he said. 'And neither am I. Shall I tell you something? I am in love!'

There was a silence in which it seemed as if the whole world was still and then Cleona asked in a voice which hardly seemed to be her own:

'With . . . whom?'

'Need you really ask?' he enquired. 'Does your heart not tell you the answer?'

There was something white and strained in the face she raised to his and in the trembling of her lips.

'What are you . . . saying . . . to me?' she stammered.

He smiled at the very childish fear which lay behind the question.

'I am saying, my darling, that I love you!' he answered. 'I have loved you for a very long time—longer than I dare admit. And now at last I can tell you so.'

The whole world was suddenly too glorious to be endured, and yet she dare not believe it.

'But it . . . it cannot be . . . true,' she said at length, and there was a catch in her voice as if the tears were very near.

'It is true,' he said gently. 'Did you know the truth that night when I carried you to safety with your arms around my neck? Did you know it last night when the sight of you in another man's arms nearly drove me to commit murder in my rage and jealousy?'

'I . . . I thought you were angry with . . . me,' Cleona faltered.

'And I was,' he answered. 'So angry that I longed to take you in my arms and kiss you, as I kissed you that night when you were deceiving me by pretending to be Beryl. You were incensed with me then, but I could not help but find out for myself if your lips were as sweet as they had been the first time I ever touched them.'

Cleona was trembling, and now he reached out his arms and drew her close to him.

'I love you!' he said softly. 'I love you more than I thought it possible to love any woman. Do you believe me?'

Cleona's eyes were on his face as if searching for the truth.

'How did you know that I . . . loved you?' she whispered.

'Perhaps because I wanted you so desperately that my need of you was irresisitible,' he answered. And then, before she could speak again, he put his hand under her chin, tipping her head back gently against his shoulder.

'The Coin of Love—my darling,' he murmured. 'How I have longed to give it to you.'

His lips were very near to hers and yet still he did not kiss her.

'You are so adorable, so sweet. I will make you happy,' he vowed. And then his mouth was on hers and the world and everything in it disappeared into the glory and wonder of a kiss that she could answer not only with her lips but with her whole body.

'I love you! I love you!'

The words seemed to be echoed in the music of the fountain and the song of the birds.

'I love you!' sang Cleona's heart, as a flame within her rose to answer the fire in his kiss.

And now once again he was looking down at her, his eyes penetrating into the very innermost secrets of her soul.

'I love you!' he said again, and softly against his lips she whispered her response:

'I love . . . you. . . .'

Barbara Cartland, the world's most famous romantic novelist, who is also an historian, playwright, lecturer, political speaker, and television personality, has now written over 280 books and sold nearly 150 million books over the world.

She has also had many historical works published and has written four autobiographies, as well as the biographies of her mother and that of her brother, Ronald Cartland, who was the first Member of Parliament to be killed in the last war. This book has a preface by Sir Winston Churchill.

She has recently completed a novel with the help and inspiration of the late Earl Mountbatten of Burma, Uncle of His Royal Highness Prince Philip. This is being sold for the Mountbatten Memorial Trust.

Miss Cartland, in 1978, sang an Album of Love Songs with the Royal Philharmonic Orchestra.

In 1976, by writing twenty-one books, she broke the world record and has continued for the following three years by writing twenty-four, twenty-one, and twenty-three.

She is unique in that she was one and two on the Dalton List of Best Sellers, and one week had four books in the top twenty.

In private life Barbara Cartland, who is a Dame of the Order of St. John of Jerusalem, Chairman of the St. John Council in Hertfordshire and Deputy President of the St. John Ambulance Brigade, has also fought for better conditions and salaries for Midwives and Nurses.

As President of the Royal College of Midwives (Hertfordshire Branch) she has been invested with the first badge of Office ever given in Great Britain, which was subscribed to by the Midwives themselves. She has also championed the cause for old people, had the law altered regarding gypsies, and founded the first Romany Gypsy Camp in the world.

Barbara Cartland is deeply interested in Vitamin Therapy and is President of the British National Association for Health. She has a Health and Happiness Club in England and has just started one in America where she has a selection of her own "Be Lovely" cosmetics, her Album of Love Songs, and many other things of unique and original interest. Her book *The Magic of Honey* has sold throughout the world and is translated into many languages.

She has a magazine, *Barbara Cartland's World of Romance*, now being published in the United States.

BARBARA CARTLAND'S NEW MAGAZINE

SPECIAL OFFER

If you love Barbara Cartland's books, you'll feel the same way about her new magazine. Barbara Cartland's World of Romance is the new monthly that contains an illustrated Cartland novel, the story behind the story, Barbara's personal message to readers, and many other fascinating and colorful features.

You can save $4.73 when you try an Introductory 9-month subscription. On newsstands, 9 issues cost $13.50. But with this coupon, you pay only $8.77!

Less than 98¢ an issue for nine months of the best in romantic fiction.

NO RISK: If you don't like your first copy for any reason, cancel your subscription and keep the first issue FREE. Your money will be refunded in full.

SUBSCRIBE TODAY. Just send your name and address with this coupon and $8.77 to Box BM, c/o Jove Publications, Inc., 200 Madison Avenue, New York, N. Y. 10016. Make check or m.o. payable to *World of Romance*.

SPECIAL DISCOUNT COUPON—WORTH $4.73